THE LAYTON COURT MYSTERY

ANTHONY BERKELEY

THE LANGTAIL PRESS
LONDON

This edition published 2010 by
The Langtail Press

www.langtailpress.com

ISBN 978-1-78002-020-4

to my father

My Dear Father,

I know of nobody who likes a detective story more than you do, with the possible exception of myself. So if I write one and you read it, we ought to be able to amuse ourselves at any rate.

I hope you will notice that I have tried to make the gentleman who eventually solves the mystery behave as nearly as possible as he might be expected to do in real life. That is to say, he is very far removed from a sphinx and he does make a mistake or two occasionally. I have never believed very much in those hawk-eyed, tight-lipped gentry, who pursue their silent and inexorable way straight to the heart of things without ever once overbalancing or turning aside after false goals; and I cannot see why even a detective story should not aim at the creation of a natural atmosphere, just as much as any other work of the lighter fiction.

In the same way I should like you to observe that I have set down quite plainly every scrap of evidence just as it is discovered, so that the reader has precisely the same data at his disposal as has the detective. This seems to me the only fair way of doing things. To hold up till the last chapter some vital piece of evidence (which, by the way, usually renders the solution of the puzzle perfectly simple), and to achieve your surprise by allowing the detective to arrest his man before the evidence on which he is doing so is ever so much as hinted to the reader at all, is, to my mind, most decidedly not playing the game.

With which short homily, I hand the book over to you by way of some very slight return for all that you have done for me.

CONTENTS

chapter one

Eight o'Clock in the Morning

William, the gardener at Layton Court, was a man of melancholy deliberation.

It did not pay, William held, to rush things; especially the important things of life, such as the removal of greenfly from roses. Before action was taken, the matter should be studied, carefully and unhappily, from every possible point of view, particularly the worst.

On this summer's morning William had been gazing despondently at the roses for just over three quarters of an hour. Pretty soon now he would feel himself sufficiently fortified to begin operations on them.

'Do you always count the greenfly before you slaughter them, friend William?' asked a sudden voice behind him.

William, who had been bending forward to peer gloomily into the greenfly-blown intricacies of a *Caroline Testout*, slewed hastily about. He hated being accosted at the best of times, but there was a spontaneous heartiness about this voice which grated intolerably on all his finer feelings. The added fact that the act of slewing hastily about had brought a portion of his person into sharp and painful contact with another rose bush did not tend to make life any more cheerful for William at that moment.

'Weren't a-countin' em,' he observed curtly; and added naughtily under his breath, 'Drat that there Mr Sheringham!'

'Oh! I thought you must be totting up the bag in advance,' remarked the newcomer gravely from behind an enormous pipe. 'What's your record bag of greenfly, William? Runs into thousands of brace, I suppose.

Well, no doubt it's an interesting enough sport for people of quiet tastes. Like stamp collecting. You ever collect stamps, William?'

'Noa,' said William, gazing sombrely at a worm. William was not one of your chatty conversationalists.

'Really?' replied his interlocutor with interest. 'Mad on it myself once. As a boy, of course. Silly game though, really, I agree with you.' He followed the direction of William's eyes. 'Ah, the early morning worm!' he continued brightly. 'And defying all the rules of its calling by refusing to act as provender for the early bird. Highly unprofessional conduct! There's a lesson for all of us in that worm, William, if I could only think what it is. I'll come back and tell you when I've had time to go into the matter properly.'

William grunted moodily. There were many things in this world of which William disapproved; but Mr Roger Sheringham had a class all to himself. The gospel of laughter held no attractions for that stern materialist and executioner of greenfly.

Roger Sheringham remained singularly unperturbed by the sublime heights of William's disapproval. With hands thrust deep into the pockets of a perfectly incredible pair of grey flannel trousers he sauntered off among the rose beds, cheerfully poisoning the fragrant atmosphere with clouds of evil smoke from the peculiarly unsavoury pipe which he wore in the corner of his rather wide mouth. William's eloquent snorts followed him unheeded; Roger had already forgotten William's existence.

There are many who hold that eight o'clock in the morning is the most perfect time of a summer's day. The air, they advance, is by that time only pleasantly warmed through, without being burned to a cinder as it is an hour or two later. And there is still quite enough dew sparkling upon leaf and flower to give the poets plenty to talk about without forcing them to rise at six o'clock for their inspiration. The theory is certainly one well worth examination.

At the moment when this story opens Mr Roger Sheringham was engaged in examining it.

Not that Roger Sheringham was a poet. By no means. But he was the next worst thing to it – an author. And it is part of an author's stock-in-trade to know exactly what a rose garden looks like at eight o'clock on a summer morning – that and everything else in the world besides. Roger Sheringham was refreshing his mental notes on the subject.

While he is doing so let us turn the tables by examining him. We are going to see quite a lot of him in the near future, and first impressions are always important.

Perhaps the first thing we notice about him, even before we have had time to take in his physical characteristics, is an atmosphere of unbounded, exuberant energy; Roger Sheringham is evidently one of those dynamic persons who seem somehow to live two minutes to everybody else's one. Whatever he happens to be doing, he does it as if it were the only thing that he had ever really intended to do in life at all. To see him now, looking over this rose garden, you would think that he is actually learning it by heart, so absorbedly is he gazing at it. At least you would be ready to bet that he could tell you afterwards just how many plants there are in each bed, how many roses on each plant, and how many greenfly on each rose. Whether this habit of observation is natural, or whether it is part of the training of his craft, there can be no doubt that Roger possesses it in a very high degree.

In appearance he is somewhat below the average height, and stockily built; with a round rather than a long face, and two shrewd, twinkling grey eyes. The shapeless trousers and the disreputable old Norfolk jacket he is wearing argue a certain eccentricity and contempt for convention that is just a little too self-conscious to be quite natural without going so far as to degenerate into a pose. The short-stemmed, big-bowled pipe in the corner of his mouth seems a very part of the man himself. Add that his age is over thirty and under forty; that his school had been Winchester and his university Oxford; and that he had (or at any rate professed) the profoundest contempt for his reading public, which was estimated by his publishers at a surprisingly large figure – and you have Roger Sheringham, Esq., at your service.

The sound of footsteps approaching along the broad gravel path, which separated the rose garden from the lawn at the back of the house, roused him from his studious contemplation of early morning phenomena. The next moment a large, broad-shouldered young man, with a pleasing and cheerful face, came into sight round the bend.

3

'Good heavens!' Roger exclaimed, in tones of the liveliest consternation. 'Alec! And an hour and a half before it need be! What's wrong with you this morning, Alec?'

'I might ask the same of you,' grinned the young man. 'It's the first time I've seen you down before ten o'clock since we came here.'

'That only gives us three mornings. Still, a palpable point. By the way, where's our worthy host? I thought it was a distressing habit of his to spend an hour in the garden every morning before breakfast; at least, so he was telling me at great length yesterday afternoon.'

'I don't know,' said Alec indifferently. 'But what brings you here anyway, Roger?'

'Me? Oh, I've been working. Studying the local flora and fauna, the latter ably represented by William. You know, you ought to cultivate William, Alec. You'd have a lot in common, I feel sure.'

They fell into step and strolled among the scattered beds.

'You working at this hour?' Alec remarked. 'I thought you wrote all your tripe between midnight and dawn.'

'You're a young man of singular literary acuteness,' sighed Roger. 'Hardly anybody would dare to call my work tripe. Yet you and I know that it is, don't we? But for goodness' sake don't tell anyone else your opinion. My income depends on my circulation, you know; and if it once got noised about that Alexander Grierson considered – '

Alec landed a punch on the literary thorax. 'Oh, for heaven's sake, shut up!' he grunted. 'Don't you ever stop talking, Roger?'

'Yes,' Roger admitted regretfully. 'When I'm asleep. It's a great trial to me. That's why I so much hate going to bed. But you haven't told me why you're up and about so early?'

'Couldn't sleep,' responded Alec, a trifle sheepishly.

'Ah!' Roger stopped and scrutinised his companion's face closely. 'I shall have to study you, Alec, you know. Awfully sorry if it's going to inconvenience you; but there's my duty to the great British public, and that's plain enough, my interesting young lover. So now perhaps you'll tell me the real reason why you're polluting this excellent garden with your unseemly presence at this unnecessary hour?'

'Oh, stow it, you blighter!' growled the interesting young lover, blushing hotly.

4

Roger regarded him with close attention.

'Notes on the habits of the newly engaged animal, male genus,' he murmured softly. 'One — reverses all its habits and instincts by getting up and seeking fresh air when it might still be frowsting in bed. Two — assaults its closest friends without the least provocation. Three — turns a bright brick-red when asked the simplest question. Four — '

'Will you shut up, or have I got to throw you into a rose bed?' shouted the harassed Alec.

'I'll shut up,' said Roger promptly. 'But only on William's account; please understand that. I feel that William would simply hate to see me land on one of his cherished rose bushes. It would depress him more than ever, and I shrink from contemplating what that might mean. In passing, how is it that you were coming from the direction of the lodge just now and not from the house?'

'You're infernally curious this morning,' Alec smiled. 'If you want to know, I've been down to the village.'

'So early? Alec, there must be something wrong with you, after all. And why on earth have you been down to the village?'

'To — well, if you must have it, to post a letter,' said Alec reluctantly.

'Ah! A letter so important, so remarkably urgent that it couldn't wait for the ordinary collection from the house?' Roger mused with interest. 'Now I wonder if that letter could have been addressed, let us say, to *The Times*? "Marvellous, Holmes! How could you have surmised that?" "You know my methods, Watson. It is only necessary to apply them." Well, Alexander Watson, am I right?'

'You're not,' said Alec shortly. 'It was to my bookmaker.'

'Well, all I can say is that it ought to have been to *The Times*,' retorted Roger indignantly. 'In fact, I don't mind going so far as to add that it's hardly playing the game on your part that it shouldn't have been to *The Times*. Here you go laying a careful train of facts all pointing to the conclusion that this miserable letter of yours was to *The Times*, and then you turn round and announce calmly that it was to your bookmaker. If it comes to that, why write to your bookmaker at all? A telegram is the correct medium for conducting a correspondence with one's bookmaker. Surely you know that?'

'Doesn't it ever hurt you?' Alec sighed wearily. 'Don't you ever put your larynx out of joint or something? I should have thought that – '

'Yes, I should have liked to hear your little medical lecture so much,' Roger interrupted rapidly, with a perfectly grave face. 'Unfortunately a previous engagement of the most pressing urgency robs me of the pleasure. I've just remembered that I've got to go and see a man about – Now what was it about? Oh, yes! I remember. A goat! Well, good-bye, Alec. See you at breakfast, I hope.'

He seized his astonished companion's hand, shook it affectionately, and walked quickly away in the direction of the village. Alec gazed after him with open mouth. In spite of the length of their acquaintance, he had never got quite used to Roger.

A light tread on the grass behind him caused him to turn round, and what he saw supplied the reason for Roger's hurried departure. A quick smile of appreciation flitted across his face. Then he hurried eagerly forward, and all thought of Roger was wiped from his mind. So soon are we forgotten when somebody more important comes along.

The girl who was advancing across the grass was small and slight, with large grey eyes set wide apart, and a mass of fair hair which the slanting rays of the sun behind her turned into a bright golden mist about her head. She was something more than pretty; for mere prettiness always implies a certain insipidity, and there was certainly no trace of that in Barbara Shannon's face. On the contrary, the firm lines of her chin alone, to take only one of her small features, showed a strength of character unusual in a girl of her age; one hardly looks for that sort of thing at feminine nineteen or thereabouts.

Alec caught his breath as he hurried towards her. It was only yesterday that she had promised to marry him, and he had not quite got accustomed to it yet.

'Dearest!' he exclaimed, making as if to take her in his arms (William had long since disappeared in search of weapons with which to rout the greenfly). 'Dearest, how topping of you to guess I should be waiting for you out here!'

Barbara put out a small hand to detain him. Her face was very grave and there were traces of tears about her eyes.

'Alec,' she said in a low voice, 'I've got rather bad news for you. Something very dreadful has happened – something that I can't possibly tell you about, so please don't ask me, dear; it would only make me more unhappy still. But I can't be engaged to you any longer. You must just forget that yesterday ever happened at all. It's out of the question now. Alec I – I can't marry you.'

chapter two

An Interrupted Breakfast

Mr Victor Stanworth, the host of the little party now in progress at Layton Court, was, according to the reports of his friends, who were many and various, a thoroughly excellent sort of person. What his enemies thought about him – that is, provided that he had any – is not recorded. On the face of it, at any rate, however, the existence of the latter may be doubted. Genial old gentlemen of sixty or so, somewhat more than comfortably well off, who keep an excellent cellar and equally excellent cigars and entertain with a large-hearted good humour amounting almost to open-handedness, are not the sort of people to have enemies. And all that Mr Victor Stanworth was; that, and, perhaps, a trifle more.

If he had one noticeable failing – so slight that it could hardly be called a fault – it was perhaps the rather too obvious interest he displayed in the sort of people whose pictures get into the illustrated weeklies. Not that Mr Stanworth was a snob, or anything approaching it; he would as soon exchange a joke with a dustman as a duke, though it is possible that he would prefer a millionaire to either. But he had not attempted to conceal his satisfaction when his younger brother, now dead these ten years or more, had succeeded in marrying (against all expectation and the more than plainly expressed wishes of the lady's family) Lady Cynthia Anglemere, the eldest daughter of the Earl of Grassingham. Indeed, he had gone so far as to express his approval in the eminently satisfactory form of settling a thousand a year on the lady in question for so long as she continued to bear the name of Stanworth. It is noticeable, however, that a condition of the settlement was the provision that she should continue the use of her title also. Gossip, of course, hinted that this interest sprung from the fact that the origins of the Stanworth family were themselves not all that they might be; but whether there was any truth in this or not, it was beyond question that, whatever these origins might be, they were by now so decently interred in such a thick shroud of golden obscurity that nobody had had either the wish or the patience to uncover them.

Mr Stanworth was a bachelor, and it was generally understood that he was a person of some little importance in that mysterious Mecca of finance, the City. Anything further than that was not specified, a closer definition being rightly held to be unnecessary. But the curious could find, if they felt so minded, the name of Mr Stanworth on the board of directors of several small but flourishing and thoroughly respectable little concerns whose various offices were scattered within a half-mile radius of the Mansion House. In any case these did not seem to make any such exorbitant demands on Mr Stanworth's time as to exclude a full participation in the more pleasant occupations of life. Two or three days a week in London in the winter, with sometimes as few as one a fortnight during the summer, appeared to be quite enough not only to preserve his financial reputation among his friends, but also to maintain that large and healthy income which was a source of such innocent pleasure to so many.

It has been said already that Mr Stanworth was in the habit of entertaining both largely and broad-mindedly; and this is no less than the truth. It was his pleasure to gather round him a select little party of entertaining and cheerful persons, usually young ones. And each year he rented a different place in the summer for this purpose; the larger, the older, and possessing the longer string of aristocratic connections, the better. The winter months he passed either abroad or in his comfortable bachelor flat in St James's Street.

This year his choice of a summer residence had fallen upon Layton Court, with its Jacobean gables, its lattice windows, and its oak-panelled rooms. Mr Stanworth was thoroughly satisfied with Layton Court. He had been installed there for rather more than a month, and the little party now in full swing was the second of the summer's series. His sister-in-law, Lady Stanworth, always acted as hostess for him on these occasions.

Neither Roger nor Alec had had any previous acquaintance with their host; and their inclusion in the party had been due to a chain of circumstances. Mrs Shannon, an old friend of Lady Stanworth's, had been asked in the first place; and with her Barbara. Then Mr Stanworth had winked jovially at his sister-in-law and observed that Barbara was getting a deuced pretty girl in these days, and wasn't there any particular person she would be glad to see at Layton Court, eh? Lady Stanworth had given it as her opinion that Barbara might not be displeased to encounter a certain Mr Alexander Grierson about the place; whereupon Mr Stanworth, having ascertained in a series of rapid questions that Mr Alexander Grierson was a young man of considerable worldly possessions (which interested him very much), had played cricket three years running for Oxford (which interested him still more), and was apparently a person of unimpeachable character and morals (which did not interest him at all), had given certain injunctions; with the result that two days later Mr Alexander Grierson received a charming little note, to which he had hastened to reply with gratified alacrity. As to Roger, it had come somehow to Mr Stanworth's ears (as in fact things had a habit of doing) that he was a close friend of Alec's; and there was always room in any house which happened to be occupied by Mr Stanworth for a person of the world-wide reputation and attainments of Roger Sheringham. A second charming little note had followed in the wake of the first.

Roger had been delighted with Mr Stanworth. He was a man after his own heart, this jolly old gentleman, with his interesting habit of pressing half-crown cigars and pre-war whiskey on one at all hours of the day from ten in the morning onwards; his red, genial face, always on the point of bursting into loud, whole-hearted laughter if not actually doing so; his way of poking sly fun at his dignified, aristocratic sister-in-law; and the very faint trace of a remote vulgarity about him that only seemed, in his particular case, to add a more intimate, almost a more genuine note to his dealings with one. Yes, Roger had found old Mr Stanworth a character well worth studying. In the three days since they had first met their acquaintance had developed rapidly into something that was very near to friendship.

And there you have Mr Victor Stanworth, at present of Layton Court, in the county of Hertfordshire. A man, you would say (and as Roger himself was saying in amazed perplexity less than an hour later), without a single care in the world.

But it is already ten minutes since the breakfast gong sounded; and if we wish to see for ourselves what sort of people Mr Stanworth had collected round him, it is quite time that we were making a move towards the dining room.

Alec and Barbara were there already: the former with a puzzled, hurt expression, that hinted plainly enough at the inexplicable disaster which had just overtaken his wooing; the latter so resolutely natural as to be quite unnatural. Roger, strolling in just behind them, had noted their silence and their strained looks, and was prepared to smooth over anything in the way of a tiff with a ceaseless flow of nonsense. Roger was perfectly well aware of the value of nonsense judiciously applied.

'Morning, Barbara,' he said cheerfully. Roger made a point of calling all unmarried ladies below the age of thirty by their Christian names after a day or two's acquaintance; it agreed with his reputation for bohemianism, and it saved trouble. 'Going to be an excellent day, I fancy. Shall I hack some ham for you, or do you feel like a boiled egg? You do? It's a curious feeling, isn't it?'

Barbara smiled faintly. 'Thank you, Mr Sheringham,' she said, lifting the cosies off an array of silver that stood at one end of the table. 'Shall I give you tea or coffee?'

'Coffee, please. Tea with breakfast is like playing Stravinsky on a mouth organ. It doesn't go. Well, what's the programme today? Tennis from eleven to one; from two to four tennis; between five and seven a little tennis; and after dinner talk about tennis. Something like that?'

'Don't you like tennis, Mr Sheringham?' asked Barbara innocently.

'Like it? I love it. One of these days I must get someone to teach me how to play it. What are you doing this morning, for instance, Alec?'

'I'll tell you what I'm not doing,' Alec grinned, 'and that's playing tennis with you.'

'And why not, you ungrateful blighter, after all I've done for you?' demanded Roger indignantly.

'Because when I play that sort of game I play cricket,' Alec retorted. 'Then you have fielders all round to stop the balls. It saves an awful lot of trouble.'

Roger turned to Barbara. 'Do you hear that, Barbara? I appeal to you. My tennis may perhaps be a little strenuous, but - Oh, hullo,

Major. We were just thinking about getting up a four for tennis. Are you game?'

The newcomer, a tall, sallow, taciturn sort of person, bowed slightly to Barbara. 'Good morning, Miss Shannon. Tennis, Sheringham? No, I'm sorry, but I'm much too busy this morning.'

He went to the sideboard, inspected the dishes gravely, and helped himself to some fish. Scarcely had he taken his seat with it than the door opened again and the butler entered.

'Can I speak to you a moment, please, sir?' asked the latter in a low voice.

The Major glanced up. 'Me, Graves? Certainly.' He rose from his seat and followed the other out of the room.

'Poor Major Jefferson!' Barbara observed.

'Yes,' said Roger with feeling. 'I'm glad I haven't got his job. Old Stanworth's an excellent sort of fellow as a host, but I don't think I should care for him as an employer. Eh, Alec?'

'Jefferson seems to have his hands pretty full. It's a pity, because he really plays a dashed good game of tennis. By the way, what would you call him exactly? A private secretary?'

'Sort of, I suppose,' said Roger. 'And everything else as well. A general dogsbody for the old man. Rotten job.'

'Isn't it rather funny to find an army man in a post like that?' Barbara asked, more for the sake of something to say than anything; the atmosphere was still a little strained. 'I thought when you left the army, you had a pension.'

'So you do,' Roger returned. 'But pensions don't amount to much in any case. Besides, I rather fancy that Stanworth likes having a man in the job with a certain social standing attached to him. Oh, yes; I've no doubt that he finds Jefferson uncommonly useful.'

'Surly sort of devil though, isn't he?' observed Alec. 'Can I have another cup of coffee, please, Barbara?'

'Oh, he's all right,' Roger pronounced. 'But I wouldn't like to be out with that butler alone on a dark night.'

'He's the most extraordinary butler I've ever seen,' said Barbara with decision, manipulating the coffee-pot. 'He positively frightens me at times. He looks more like a prize-fighter than a butler. What do you think, Mr Sheringham?'

'As a matter of fact, you're perfectly right, Barbara,' Alec put in. 'He is an old boxer. Jefferson told me. Stanworth took him on for some reason years ago, and he's been with him ever since.'

'I'd like to see a scrap between him and you, Alec,' Roger murmured bloodthirstily. 'There wouldn't be much to choose between you.'

'Thanks,' Alec laughed. 'Not today, I think. He'd simply wipe the floor with me. He could give me nearly a stone, I should say.'

'And you're no chicken. Ah, well, if you ever think better of it, let me know. I'll put up a purse all right.'

'Let's change the subject,' said Barbara, with a little shiver. 'Oh! Good morning, Mrs Plant. Hullo, Mother, dear! Had a good night?'

Mrs Shannon, small and fair like her daughter, was in all other respects as unlike Barbara as could well be imagined. In place of that young lady's characterful little face, Mrs Shannon's features were doll-like and insipid. She was pretty enough, in a negative, plump sort of way; but interest in her began and ended with her appearance. Barbara's attitude towards her was that of patient protectiveness. To see the two together one would think, apart from their ages, that Barbara was the mother and Mrs Shannon the daughter.

'A good night?' she repeated peevishly. 'My dear child, how many times must I tell you that it is quite impossible for me to get any sleep at all in this wretched place? If it isn't the birds, it's the dogs; and if it isn't the dogs, it's – '

'Yes, Mother,' Barbara interrupted soothingly. 'What would you like to eat?'

'Oh, let me,' exclaimed Alec, jumping up. 'And, Mrs Plant, what are you going to have?'

Mrs Plant, a graceful, dark-haired lady of twenty-six or so, with a husband in the Sudanese Civil Service, indicated a preference for ham; Mrs Shannon consented to be soothed with a fried sole. Conversation became general.

Major Jefferson looked in once and glanced round the room in a worried way. 'Nobody's seen Mr Stanworth this morning, have they?'

13

he asked the company in general, and receiving no reply, went out again.

Barbara and Roger engaged in a fierce discussion on the relative merits of tennis and golf, for the latter of which Roger had acquired a half-blue at Oxford. Mrs Shannon explained at some length to Alec over her second sole why she could never eat much breakfast nowadays. Mary Plant came to the aid of Barbara in proving that whereas golf was a game for the elderly and crippled, tennis was the only possible summer occupation for the young and energetic. The room buzzed.

The appearance of Lady Stanworth caused the conversation to stop abruptly. In the ordinary course of events she breakfasted in her own room. A tall, stately woman, with hair just beginning to turn grey, she was never anything but cool and dignified; but this morning her face seemed even more serious than usual. For a moment she stood in the doorway, looking round the room as Major Jefferson had done a few minutes before.

Then, 'Good morning, everybody,' she said slowly. 'Mr Sheringham and Mr Grierson, can I have a word with you for a moment?'

In deep silence Roger and Alec pushed back their chairs and rose. It was obvious that something out of the ordinary had occurred, but nobody quite liked to ask a question. In any case, Lady Stanworth's attitude did not encourage curiosity. She waited till they had reached the door, and motioned for them to precede her. When they had passed through, she shut the door carefully after her.

'What's up, Lady Stanworth?' Roger asked bluntly, as soon as they were alone.

Lady Stanworth bit her lip and hesitated, as if making up her mind. 'Nothing, I hope,' she said, after a little pause. 'But nobody has seen my brother-in-law this morning and his bed has not been slept in, while the library door and windows are locked on the inside. Major Jefferson sent for me and we have talked it over and decided to break the door down. He suggested that it would be as well if you and Mr Grierson were present also, in case – in case a witness outside the household should be required. Will you come with me?'

She led the way in the direction of the library, and the other two followed.

'You've called to him, I suppose?' Alec remarked.

'Yes. Major Jefferson and Graves have both called to him, here and outside the library windows.'

'He's probably fainted or something in the library,' said Roger reassuringly, with a good deal more conviction than he felt. 'Or it may be a stroke. Is his heart at all weak?'

'Not that I've ever heard, Mr Sheringham.'

By the library door Major Jefferson and the butler were waiting; the former impassive as ever, the latter clearly ill at ease.

'Ah, here you are,' said the Major. 'Sorry to bother you like this, but you understand. Now, Grierson, you and Graves and myself are the biggest; if we put our shoulders to the door together I think we can force it open. It's pretty strong, though. You by the handle, Graves; and you next, Grierson. That's right. Now, then, one – two – three – heave!'

At the third attempt there was the sound of tearing woodwork, and the heavy door swung on its hinges. Major Jefferson stepped quickly over the threshold. The others hung back. In a moment he was back again, his sallow face the merest trifle paler.

'What is it?' asked Lady Stanworth anxiously.

'Is Victor there?'

'I don't think you had better go in for the moment, Lady Stanworth,' said Major Jefferson slowly, intercepting her as she stepped forward. 'Mr Stanworth appears to have shot himself.'

chapter three

Mr Sheringham Is Puzzled

Like many of the other rooms at Layton Court, the library had been largely modernised. Dark oak panelling still covered the walls, but the big open fireplace, with its high chimney-piece, had been blocked up and a modern grate inserted. The room was a large one and (assuming that we are standing just inside the hall with our backs to the front door) formed the right-hand corner of the back of the house corresponding with the dining room on the other side. Between these two was a smaller room, of the same breadth as the hall, which was used as a gunroom, storeroom, and general convenience room. The two rooms on either side of the deep hall in the front of the house were the drawing room, on the same side as the library, and the morning room opposite. A narrow passage between the morning room and the dining room led to the servants' quarters.

In the side of the library which faced the lawn at the back of the house had been set a pair of wide French windows, as was also the case in the dining room; while in the other outer wall, looking over the rose garden, was a large modern window of the sash type, with a deep window seat below it set in the thickness of the wall. The only original window still remaining was a small lattice one in the corner on the left of the sash window. The door that led into the room from the hall was in the corner diagonal to the lattice window. The fireplace exactly faced the French windows.

The room was not overcrowded with furniture. An armchair or two stood by the fireplace; and there was a small table, bearing a typewriter, by the wall on the same side as the door. In the angle between the sash window and the fireplace stood a deep, black-covered settee. The most important piece of furniture was a large writing table in the exact centre of the room facing the sash window. The walls were lined with bookshelves.

This was the picture that had flashed across Roger's retentive brain as he stood in the little group outside the library door and listened to Major Jefferson's curt, almost brutal announcement. With instinctive curiosity he wondered where the grim addition to the scene was lying. The next moment the same instinct had caused him to turn and scan the face of his hostess.

Lady Stanworth had not screamed or fainted; she was not that sort of person. Indeed, beyond a slight and involuntary catching of her breath she betrayed little or no emotion.

'Shot himself?' she repeated calmly. 'Are you quite sure?'

'I'm afraid there can be no doubt at all,' Major Jefferson said gravely. 'He must have been dead for some hours.'

'And you think I had better not go in?'

'It's not a pretty sight,' said the Major shortly.

'Very well. But we had better telephone for a doctor in any case, I suppose. I will do that. Victor called in Doctor Matthewson when he had hay fever a few weeks ago, didn't he? I'll send for him.'

'And the police,' said Jefferson. 'They'll have to be notified. I'll do that.'

'I can let them know at the same time,' Lady Stanworth returned, moving across the hall in the direction of the telephone.

Roger and Alec exchanged glances.

'I always said that was a wonderful woman,' whispered the former behind his hand, as they prepared to follow the Major into the library.

'Is there anything I can do, sir?' asked the butler from the doorway.

Major Jefferson glanced at him sharply. 'Yes; you come in, too, Graves. It makes another witness.'

The four men filed in silence into the room. The curtains were still drawn, and the light was dim. With an abrupt movement Jefferson strode across and pulled back the curtains from the French windows. Then he turned and nodded silently towards the big writing table.

In the chair behind this, which was turned a little away from the table, sat, or rather reclined, the body of Mr Stanworth. His right hand, which was dangling by his side almost to the floor, was tightly clenched about a small revolver, the finger still convulsively clasping the trigger. In the centre of his forehead, just at the base of his hair, was a little circular hole, the edges of which looked strangely blackened. His head lolled indolently over the top of the chair-back, and his wide-open eyes were staring glassily at the ceiling.

It was, as Jefferson had said, not a pretty sight.

Roger was the first to break the silence. 'Well, I'm damned!' he said softly. 'What on earth did he want to go and do that for?'

'Why does anyone do it?' asked Jefferson, staring at the still figure as if trying to read its secret. 'Because he has some damned good reason of his own, I suppose.'

Roger shrugged his shoulders a little impatiently. 'No doubt. But old Stanworth of all people! I shouldn't have thought that he'd got a care in the world. Not that I knew him particularly well, of course; but I was only saying to you yesterday, Alec – ' He broke off suddenly. Alec's face had gone a ghastly white, and he was gazing with horrified eyes at the figure in the chair.

'I was forgetting,' Roger muttered in a low voice to Jefferson. 'The boy was too young to be in the war; he's only twenty-four. It's a bit of a shock, one's first corpse. Especially this sort of thing. Phew! There's a smell of death in here. Let's get some of these windows open.'

He turned and threw open the French windows, letting a draught of warm air into the room. 'Locked on the inside all right,' he commented as he did so. 'So are the other two. Here, Alec, come outside for a minute. It's no wonder you're feeling a bit turned up.'

Alec smiled faintly; he had managed to pull himself together and the colour was returning to his cheeks. 'Oh, I'm all right,' he said, a little shakily. 'It was just a bit of a shock at first.'

The breeze had fluttered the papers on the writing table and one fell to the ground. Graves, the butler, stepped forward to pick it up. Before replacing it he glanced idly at something that was written on it.

'Sir!' he exclaimed excitedly. 'Look at this!'

He handed the paper to Major Jefferson, who read it eagerly.

'Anything of interest?' Roger asked curiously.

'Very much so,' Jefferson replied dryly. 'It's a statement. I'll read it to you "To whom it May concern. For reasons that concern only myself, I have decided to kill myself." And his signature at the bottom.' He twisted the piece of paper thoughtfully in his hand. 'But I wish he'd said what his reasons were,' he added in puzzled tones.

'Yes, it's a remarkably reticent document,' Roger agreed. 'But it's plain enough, isn't it? May I have a look at it?'

He took it from the other's outstretched hand and examined it with interest. The paper was slightly creased, and the message itself was type-written. The signature, Victor Stanworth, was bold and firm; but just above it was another attempt, which had only got as far as V-i-c and looked as if it had been written with a pen insufficiently supplied with ink.

'He must have gone about the business with extraordinary delibera-tion,' Roger commented. 'He goes to the trouble of typing this instead of writing it; and when he finds he hadn't dipped his pen deep enough in the ink-pot, calmly signs it again. And just look at that signature! Not a trace of nerves in it, is there?'

He handed the paper back, and the Major looked at it again.

'Stanworth was never much troubled with nerves,' he remarked shortly. 'And the signature's genuine enough. I'd take my oath on that.'

Alec could not help feeling that Jefferson's words had supplied an an-swer to a question which Roger had purposely refrained from asking.

'Well, I don't know much about this sort of thing,' Roger observed, 'but I suppose one thing's certain. The body mustn't be touched before the police come.'

'Even in the case of a suicide?' Jefferson asked doubtfully.

'In any case, surely.'

'I shouldn't have thought it would have mattered in this case,' said Jef-ferson, a little reluctantly. 'Still, perhaps you're right. Not that it matters either way,' he added quickly.

There was a tap on the half-open door.

'I've telephoned to Doctor Matthewson and the police,' came Lady Stanworth's even tones. 'They're sending an inspector over from Elchester at once. And now don't you think we ought to tell the others in the dining room?'

'I think so certainly,' said Roger, who happened to be nearest to the door. 'There's no sense in delaying it. Besides, if we tell them now it will give them time to get over it a little before the police come.'

'Quite so,' said Jefferson. 'And the servants as well. Graves, you'd better go and break the news in the kitchen. Be as tactful as you can.'

'Very good, sir.'

With a last, but quite expressionless glance at his late master, the burly figure turned and walked slowly out of the room.

'I've seen people more cut up at the death of a man they've lived with for twenty years than *that* gentleman,' Roger murmured in Alec's ear, raising his eyebrows significantly.

'And I wish you would be good enough to break the news in the dining room, Major Jefferson,' Lady Stanworth remarked. 'I really hardly feel up to it myself.'

'Of course,' said Jefferson quickly. 'In fact, I think it would be much better if you went up to your room and rested a little before the police get here, Lady Stanworth. This is bound to be a very great strain. I will tell one of the maids to take you up a cup of tea.'

Lady Stanworth looked a trifle surprised, and for a moment it seemed that she was going to object to this course. Evidently, however, she changed her mind if that was the case; for she only said quietly, 'Thank you. Yes, I think that would be best. Please let me know directly the police arrive.'

She made her way, a little wearily, up the broad staircase and disappeared from view.

Jefferson turned to Roger. 'I think as a matter of fact that I should prefer you to tell the ladies, if you would, Sheringham. You'd do it much better than I. I'm not much use at putting unpleasant things in a pleasant way.'

'Certainly I will, if you'd rather. Alec, you'd better stay here with the Major.'

Jefferson hesitated. 'As a matter of fact, Grierson, I was wondering if you would be good enough to run across to the stables and tell Chapman to have the car ready all day today, as it might be wanted any time at a moment's notice. Will you?'

'Of course,' said Alec promptly and hurried off, only too glad of the opportunity for a little action. He had not yet quite got over that first sight of the dead man in the streaming sunshine.

Roger walked slowly across to the dining-room door; but he was not pondering over what he was going to say. He was repeating to himself over and over again, 'Why was Jefferson so infernally anxious to get rid of the four of us in such a hurry? Why? Why? Why?'

With his hand on the very knob of the door a possible answer came to him, in the form of another question.

'Why was Jefferson so reluctant to admit that the body must not be touched before the arrival of the police?'

It was a somewhat distrait Roger who opened the dining-room door, and proceeded to acquaint three astounded ladies with the somewhat surprising fact that their host had just shot himself through the head.

Their reception of his news did not speak very well for Roger's tact-fulness. It may have been that his preoccupation with what was in his mind prevented him from doing justice to himself; but the fact remains that even he was considerably startled by the way in which his hearers behaved, and it took a good deal to startle Roger.

Mrs Shannon, it is true, merely remarked with a not unjustified annoyance that it was really exceedingly awkward as she had made all her arrangements for being here another ten days and now she supposed they would have to leave at once, and where on earth did anyone think they could go to with the house in town shut up and all the servants away? Barbara rose slowly to her feet, with every trace of colour drained out of her face, swayed a little and, sitting down abruptly, stared with unseeing eyes out into the sunlit garden. Mrs Plant incontinently and silently fainted.

But Roger had other things to do than dancing attendance upon fainting and hysterical ladies. Leaving Mrs Plant somewhat unceremoniously to the ministrations of Barbara and her mother, he hurried back to the library, taking care to step lightly. The sight that met his eyes was exactly what he had expected.

Major Jefferson was bending over the dead man, rapidly and methodically searching his pockets.

21

'Hullo,' Roger remarked easily from the doorway. 'Putting him straight a bit?'

The Major started violently. Then he bit his lip and slowly straightened his back.

'Yes,' he said slowly, after the least possible pause. 'Yes. I can't bear to see this constrained attitude he's in.'

'It's beastly,' Roger said sympathetically, advancing unconcernedly into the room and shutting the door behind him. 'I know. But I shouldn't move him if I were you. Not till the police have seen him, at any rate. They're rather particular about that sort of thing, I believe.'

Jefferson shrugged his shoulders, frowning. 'It seems damned nonsense to me,' he said bluntly.

'Look here,' Roger remarked suddenly, 'you mustn't let this thing get on your nerves, you know. Come and take a turn in the garden with me.'

He linked his arm through the other's and, observing his obvious hesitation, drew him towards the open windows. 'Do you all the good in the world,' he persisted.

Jefferson allowed himself to be persuaded.

For some minutes the two strolled up and down the lawn, and Roger took some care to keep the conversation on indifferent topics. But in spite of all his efforts, Jefferson kept looking at his watch, and it was clear that he was counting the minutes before the police might be expected. What Roger, watch how he might, was unable to discover was whether his companion was eager for their arrival or the reverse. The only thing he knew for certain was that this imperturbable man was, for some reason or other, very badly rattled. It might be the simple fact of his employer's unseemly end which had caused this unwonted state of affairs, Roger thought; for certainly Jefferson and old Stanworth had been a very long time together. On the other hand, it might not. And if this was not the reason, what was?

When they had made the circuit of the rose garden three times, Jefferson halted suddenly.

'The police should be here at any minute now,' he said abruptly. 'I'm going to walk down towards the lodge to meet them. I'll call you when we want you.'

Anything more obvious in the way of a congé could hardly be imagined. Roger accepted it with the best grace he could.

'Very well,' he nodded. 'I'll be somewhere out here.'

Jefferson disappeared rapidly down the drive and Roger was left to continue his walk alone. But he had no intention of being bored. There was, he felt, quite a lot of thinking that he would rather like to do; and the chance of a few minutes' solitude was not unwelcome. He paced slowly back to the lawn again, his pipe in full blast, and reeking clouds trailing lazily behind him.

But Roger was not to do his thinking just yet. Scarcely had he reached the lawn when Alec appeared from the direction of the stables, somewhat hot and flushed. He fell into step with Roger and began to explain why he had been so long.

'Couldn't get away from the wretched fellow!' he exclaimed. 'Had to tell him the whole thing from beginning to - Hullo! What's up?'

Roger had halted and was staring in through the library windows. 'I'll swear I left that door shut,' he said in puzzled tones. 'Somebody's opened it. Come on!'

'Where are you going?' Alec asked in surprise.

'To see who's in the library,' returned Roger, already halfway across the lawn. He quickened his pace to a run and hurried in through the French windows, Alec close on his heels.

A woman who was bending over something on the farther side of the room straightened hastily at their approach. It was Mrs Plant, and the object over which she had been bending was a large safe that stood by the wall close to the little typewriting table. Roger had just had time to see that she was feverishly twisting the knob before she had sprung up on hearing their footsteps.

She faced them with heaving bosom and horrified eyes, one hand clutching the folds of her frock, the other clenched at her side. It was obvious that she was frightened almost out of her wits.

'Were you looking for anything?' Roger asked politely, and cursed himself for the banality of the words even as he spoke them.

With a tremendous effort Mrs Plant appeared to pull herself together.

'My jewels,' she muttered jerkily. 'I asked – Mr Stanworth to – to lock them in his safe the other day. I – I was wondering – would the police take them? I thought it might be better if I – '

'That's all right, Mrs Plant,' said Roger soothingly, breaking in upon her painful utterances. 'The police wouldn't take them in any case, I expect; and you can easily identify what is yours. They'll be safe enough, I assure you.'

A little colour was coming slowly back into her cheeks and her breathing was becoming less rapid.

'Thank you so much, Mr Sheringham,' she said more easily. 'It was absurd of me, no doubt, but they're rather valuable, and I had a sudden panic about them. Of course I ought not to have tried to take them myself. I can't think what I can have been doing!' She laughed nervously. 'Really, I'm positively ashamed of myself. You won't give me away for being so foolish, will you?'

There was a note of urgent appeal in the last sentence that belied the lightness of the words.

Roger smiled reassuringly. 'Of course not,' he said promptly. 'Wouldn't dream of it.'

'Oh, thank you so much. I know I can rely on you. And on Mr Grierson, too. Well, I suppose I'd better run away before anyone else catches me here.'

She made her way out of the room, carefully averting her eyes from the chair by the writing table.

Roger turned to Alec and whistled softly. 'Now what did she want to lie like that for?' he asked with raised eyebrows.

'Do you think she was lying?' Alec asked in puzzled tones. 'I should have said that Mrs Plant was as straight as they make 'em.'

Roger shrugged his shoulders in mock despair. 'And so should I! That's what makes it all the more extraordinary. Yet of course she was lying. Like a trooper! And so ridiculously! Her story's bound to be disproved as soon as the safe is opened. She must have said the first thing that came into her head. Alec, my son, there's something damned queer going on here! Mrs Plant isn't the only one who's lying. Come out into the garden and listen to the duplicity of Jefferson.'

chapter four

Major Jefferson Is Reluctant

Inspector Mansfield, of the Elchester police, was a methodical person. He knew exactly what he had to do, and just how to do it. And he had precisely as much imagination as was required for his job, and not a fraction more. Too much imagination can be a very severe handicap to a conscientious policeman, in spite of what the detective stories may say.

As the inspector entered the library with Jefferson from the hall, Roger, who had heard his arrival and was determined to miss no more of this interesting situation than he could possibly help, contrived to present himself at the French windows, the faithful Alec still in tow.

'Good morning, Inspector,' he said cheerfully.

Jefferson frowned slightly; perhaps he was remembering his last words to Roger. 'These are Mr Sheringham and Mr Grierson, Inspector,' he said a little brusquely. 'They were present when we broke the door in.'

The inspector nodded. 'Good morning, gentlemen. Sad business, this. Very.' He glanced rapidly round the room. 'Ah, there's the body. Excuse me, Major.'

He stepped quickly across and bent over the figure in the chair, examining it attentively. Then he dropped on his knees and scrutinised the hand that held the revolver.

'Mustn't touch anything till the doctor's seen him,' he explained briefly, rising to his feet again and dusting the knees of his trousers. 'May I have a look at that document you spoke of, sir?'

'Certainly, Inspector. It's on the table.'

Jefferson showed where the paper was lying, and the inspector picked it up. Roger edged farther into the room. The presence of himself and Alec had not been challenged, and he wished to establish his right to be there. Furthermore, he was uncommonly curious to hear the inspector's views on the somewhat remarkable document he was now studying.

The inspector looked up. 'H'm!' he observed non-committally, laying the paper on the table again. 'To the point, at any rate. Was Mr Stanworth in the habit of using a typewriter instead of pen and ink?'

'Just the point I mentioned, Inspector,' Roger broke in.

'Indeed, sir?' said the inspector politely. He turned to Jefferson. 'Do you happen to know, Major Jefferson?'

'Yes, I think he was,' Jefferson said thoughtfully. 'He certainly always wrote his letters on it. I fancy he used it a good deal.'

'But to sit down and type a thing like that!' Roger exclaimed. 'It seems so unnecessary somehow.'

'And what do you make of it then, Mr Sheringham?' the inspector asked with tolerant interest.

'I should say it showed a cold-blooded deliberation that proves Mr Stanworth to have been a very exceptional man,' Roger replied quickly.

The inspector smiled faintly. 'I see you're more used to considering characters than actions,' he said. 'Now I should have said that a more ordinary explanation might be that Mr Stanworth, having already something else to type on the machine, slipped in a piece of paper and did that at the same time.'

'Oh!' Roger remarked, somewhat nonplussed. 'Yes, I never thought of that.'

'It's extraordinary what simple things one doesn't think of at times,' said the inspector wisely.

'But in that case,' Roger observed thoughtfully, 'wouldn't you expect to find the other thing he had been typing? It can hardly have left the room, can it?'

'That's impossible to say,' said the inspector, with the air of one closing the subject. 'We don't in the least know what Mr Stanworth did last night. He might have gone out and posted a letter or two before he shot himself; and unless anyone happened to see him we could never know whether he did or not. Now I take it, sir,' he added, turning to Major Jefferson, 'that Mr Stanworth was a rather brusque, decisive sort of man?'

Jefferson considered. 'Decisive, certainly. But I don't know whether you would call him brusque exactly. Why?'

'The wording of this statement. It's a bit – well, out of the ordinary, isn't it?'

'It's quite typical,' said Jefferson shortly.

'It is? That's what I'm getting at. Now have you any idea at all as to the reasons he hints at?'

'Not in the least. I'm absolutely in the dark.'

'Ah! Well, perhaps Lady Stanworth will be able to throw some light on that point later.' He strolled over to the door and began to examine the lock.

Roger drew Alec aside. 'You know, this is jolly interesting, this business,' he murmured. 'I've never seen the police at work before. But the story books are all wrong. This man isn't a fool by any means; very far from it. He caught me out properly over that typing; and twice at that. Perfectly obvious points when they're mentioned, of course; and I can't think why they didn't occur to me. That's the trouble with an *idée fixe*; you can't see beyond it, or even round it. Hullo; he's trying the windows now.'

The inspector had crossed the room and was testing the fastenings of the French windows. 'You said all these were fastened when you got in as well as the door, sir?' he remarked to Jefferson.

'Yes. But Mr Sheringham can answer for that better than I. He opened them.'

The inspector flashed a quick glance at Roger. 'And they were all securely fastened?'

'Absolutely,' said Roger with conviction. 'I remember commenting on it at the time.'

'Why did you open them, sir?'

'To let some air into the place. It smelt of death, if you know what I mean.'

The inspector nodded as if the explanation satisfied him, and at the same moment the front door bell rang.

'I expect that's the doctor,' Jefferson remarked, moving towards the door. 'I'll go and see.'

'That man's badly on the jump,' Roger commented to himself. Aloud he took the opportunity of remarking, 'I dare say you'll find some private papers in that safe which may throw some light on the business.' Roger badly wanted to know what was inside that safe. And what wasn't!

'Safe, sir?' said the inspector sharply. 'What safe?'

Roger pointed out where the safe stood. 'I understand that Mr Stanworth always carried it about with him,' he remarked casually. 'That seems to point to the fact of there being something helpful inside, I should say.'

The inspector glanced round. 'You never know with these suicides, sir,' he said in confidential tones. 'Sometimes the reason's plain enough; but often there doesn't seem any reason for it at all. Either they've kept it to themselves, or else they've gone suddenly dotty. "Temporary Insanity" is more often true than you'd say. Melancholia and such-like. The doctor may be able to help us there.'

'And here he comes, if I'm not very much mistaken,' Roger observed, as the sound of approaching voices reached their ears.

The next moment Jefferson reappeared, showing a tall, thin man with a small bag in his hand into the room.

'This is Doctor Matthewson,' he said.

The doctor and the inspector exchanged nods of acquaintance. 'There's the body, Doctor,' remarked the latter, waving his hand towards the chair. 'Nothing very remarkable about the case; but of course you know the coroner will want a detailed report.'

Dr Matthewson nodded again and, setting his bag upon the table, bent over the still figure in the chair and proceeded to make his examination. It did not take him many minutes.

'Been dead about eight hours,' he remarked briefly to the inspector, as he straightened up again. 'Let's see. It's just past ten now, isn't it? I should say he died at somewhere round two o'clock this morning. The revolver must have been within a couple of inches of his forehead when he fired. The bullet may be – ' He felt carefully at the back of the dead man's head, and, whipping a lancet out of his pocket, made an incision in the skull. 'Here it is,' he added, extracting a small object of shining metal from the skin. 'Lodged just under the scalp.'

28

The inspector made a few brief notes in his pocketbook.

'Obviously self-inflicted, of course?' he observed.

The doctor raised the dangling hand and scrutinised the fingers that held the revolver. 'Obviously. The grip is properly adjusted and must have been applied during life.' With an effort he loosened the clasp of the dead fingers and handed the weapon across the table to the inspector.

The latter twirled the chamber thoughtfully before opening it. 'Not fully loaded, but only one chamber fired,' he announced, and made another note.

'Edges of wound blackened and traces of powder on surrounding skin,' supplied the doctor. The inspector extracted the empty shell and fitted the bullet carefully into it, comparing the latter with the bullets of the unfired cartridges.

'Why do you do that?' Roger asked with interest. 'You know the bullet must have been fired from that revolver.'

'It's not my job to *know* anything, sir,' returned the inspector, a little huffily. 'My job is to collect evidence.'

'Oh, I wasn't meaning that you weren't acting perfectly correctly,' Roger said hastily. 'But I've never seen anything of this sort before, and I was wondering why you were taking such pains to collect evidence when the cause of death is so obvious.'

'Well, sir, it isn't my business to determine the cause of death,' the inspector explained, unbending slightly before the other's obvious interest. 'That's the coroner's job. All I have to do is to assemble all the available evidence that I can find, however trivial it may seem. Then I lay it before him, and he directs the jury accordingly. That is the correct procedure.'

Roger retired into the background. 'I said there weren't any flies on this bird,' he muttered to Alec, who had been a silent but none the less interested spectator of the proceedings. 'That's the third time he's wiped the floor with me.'

'By the way, sir,' the inspector was saying to Doctor Matthewson, 'I take it that as Lady Stanworth sent for you, you have been called in here before since they arrived?'

'That's right, Inspector,' nodded the doctor. 'Mr Stanworth called me in himself. He had a slight attack of hay fever.'

'Ah!' remarked the inspector with interest. 'And I suppose you examined him more or less.'

The doctor smiled faintly. He was remembering a somewhat strenuous half hour he had spent with his patient in this very room. 'As a matter of fact, I examined him very thoroughly indeed. At his own request, of course. He said that it was the first time he had seen a doctor for fifteen years, and he'd like to be properly overhauled while he was about it.'

'And how did you find him?' the inspector asked with interest. 'Anything much wrong with him? Heart, or anything like that?'

'See what he's getting at?' Roger whispered to Alec. 'Wants to find out if he was suffering from any incurable disease that might have led to suicide.'

'There was nothing wrong with him at all,' the doctor said with finality. 'He was as sound as the proverbial bell. In fact, for a man of his years he was in a really remarkably healthy condition.'

'Oh!' The inspector was clearly a little disappointed. 'Well, what about this safe, then?'

'The safe?' Major Jefferson repeated in startled tones.

'Yes, sir; I think I should like to have a look at the contents, if you please. They may throw some light on the affair.'

'But – but – ' Major Jefferson hesitated, and it seemed to the interested Roger that his usually impassive face showed traces of real alarm. 'But is that necessary?' he asked more calmly. 'There may be private papers in there of a highly confidential nature. Not that I know anything about it,' he added somewhat hastily; 'but Mr Stanworth was always exceedingly reticent about the contents.'

'All the more reason for us to have a look at them, sir,' returned the inspector dryly. 'As for anything confidential, that will of course go no farther. That is, unless there is some excellent reason to the contrary,' he added darkly.

Still Jefferson hesitated. 'Of course, if you insist,' he said slowly, 'there is no more to be said. Still, it seems highly unnecessary to me, I must say.'

'That, sir, is a matter for me to decide,' replied the inspector shortly. 'Now, can you tell me where the key would be and what the combination is?'

'I believe that Mr Stanworth usually kept his key-ring in his right-hand waistcoat pocket,' Jefferson said tonelessly, as if the subject had ceased to interest him. 'As for the combination, I have not the least idea what it was. I was not in Mr Stanworth's confidence to that extent,' he added with the least possible shade of bitterness in his voice.

The inspector was feeling in the pocket mentioned. 'Well, they're not here now,' he said. With quick, deft movements he searched the other pockets. 'Ah! Here they are. In the one above. He must have slipped them into the wrong pocket by mistake. But you say you don't know the combination? Now I wonder how we can find that.' He weighed the ring of keys thoughtfully in his hand, deliberating.

Roger had strolled round the room with a careless air. If that safe was going to be opened, he wanted a good look at the contents. Now he paused by the fireplace.

'Hullo!' he remarked suddenly. 'Somebody's been burning something here.' He bent and peered into the grate. 'Paper! I shouldn't be surprised if those ashes aren't all that's left of your evidence, Inspector.'

The inspector crossed the room hastily and joined him. 'I daresay you're right, Mr Sheringham,' he said disappointedly. 'I ought to have noticed that myself. Thank you. Still, we must get that safe opened as soon as possible in any case.'

Roger rejoined Alec. 'One to me,' he smiled. 'Now, if he'd been one of the story-book inspectors, he'd have bitten my head off for discovering something that he'd missed. I like this man.'

The inspector put his notebook away. 'Well, Doctor,' he said briskly, 'I don't think there's anything more that you or I can do here, is there?'

'There's nothing more that I can do,' Doctor Matthewson replied. 'I'd like to get away, too, if you can spare me. I'm rather busy today. I'll let you have that report at once.'

'Thanks. No, I shan't want you any more, sir. I'll let you know when the inquest will be. Probably tomorrow.' He turned to Jefferson. 'And now, sir, if you'll let me use the telephone, I'll ring up the coroner and notify him. And after that, if there's another room convenient, I'd like to interview these gentlemen and yourself, and the other members of the household also. We may be able to get a little closer to those reasons that

Mr Stanworth mentions.' He folded up the document in question and tucked it carefully away in his pocket.

'Then you won't be wanting this room any more?' asked Jefferson.

'Not for the present. But I'll send in the constable I brought with me to take charge in the meantime.'

'Oh!'

Roger looked curiously at the last speaker. Then he turned to Alec.

'Now am I getting a bee in my bonnet,' he said in a low voice, as they followed the others out of the room, 'or did Jefferson sound disappointed to you just then?'

'Heaven only knows,' Alec whispered back. 'I can't make out any of them, and you're as bad as anybody else!'

'Wait till I get you alone. I'm going to talk my head off,' Roger promised.

The inspector was giving his instructions to a large burly countryman, disguised as a policeman, who had been waiting patiently in the hall all this time. While Jefferson led the way to the morning room, the latter ambled portentously into the library. It was the first time he had been placed in charge, however temporary, of a case of this importance, and he respected himself tremendously for it.

Arrived on the scene of the tragedy, he frowned heavily about him, gazed severely at the body for a moment and then very solemnly smelled at the ink-pot. He had once read a lurid story in which what had been thought at first to be a case of suicide had turned out eventually to be a murder carried out by means of a poisoned ink-pot; and he was taking no chances.

chapter five

Mr Sheringham Asks a Question

'Now, gentlemen,' said the inspector, when the four of them were seated in the morning room, 'there is a certain amount of routine work for me to do, though it may strike you as unimportant.' He smiled slightly towards Roger.

'Not a bit,' said that gentleman quickly. 'I'm extraordinarily interested in all this. You've no idea how useful it will be if I ever want to write a detective novel.'

'Well, the chief thing I want to know,' the inspector resumed, 'is who was the last person to see the deceased alive. Now when did you see him last, Major Jefferson?'

'About an hour and a half after dinner. Say ten o'clock. He was smoking in the garden with Mr Sheringham, and I wanted to ask him something about the arrangements for today.'

'That's right,' Roger nodded. 'I remember. It was a few minutes past ten. The church clock in the village had just struck.'

'And what did you want to ask him?'

'Oh, nothing very important. Only what time he wanted the car in the morning, if at all. But I usually made a point of seeing him about that time every evening, in case he had any instructions to give me for the following day.'

'I see. And what did he tell you?'

'That he wouldn't be wanting the car this morning at all.'

'And did he seem quite normal? Not agitated or upset in any way? Perfectly ordinary?'

'Perfectly.'

'And had been all day? At dinner, for instance?'

'Certainly. He was in a very good temper at dinner, as a matter of fact.'

'What do you mean by that?' asked the inspector quickly. 'Wasn't he usually in a good temper?'

'Oh, yes. Usually. But like most strong-minded, self-willed men he could be thoroughly unpleasant if he chose.'

'Now in the course of your duties as his secretary, has it come to your notice whether he has had any bad news lately? Either financial or otherwise?'

'No.'

'Would you have known if he had?'

'I doubt it. If it had been financial, he might have told me, as I frequently had to write letters for him regarding his investments and so forth. But otherwise I am quite sure he would not. Mr Stanworth was very reticent indeed about his personal affairs.'

'I see. He was comfortably off, wasn't he?'

'Very. You might call it more than that.'

'Rich, in fact. And how were his investments laid out? Did he, for instance, put most of his money into one concern?'

'You mean, was he in a position to be ruined by the failure of any single business? No, I'm sure he wasn't. His money was spread over a large number of investments; and to my certain knowledge he still has a very large sum indeed in Government stock.'

'Then we can take it as fairly sure that, whatever caused him to take his life, it was nothing to do with money matters?'

'Yes, I'm quite convinced of that.'

'Then we must look elsewhere. Now, had Mr Stanworth any relations besides his sister-in-law?'

'Not to my knowledge, and I've been with him six years. He had a younger brother, of course, Lady Stanworth's husband; but I've never heard of any others.'

'I see. Well, Major Jefferson, am I to take it that you can't throw any light at all on the reasons for Mr Stanworth's suicide? Think carefully, if you please. Suicide is a pretty serious step, and the reasons must be correspondingly serious. The coroner is bound to do his best to bring them to light.'

'I haven't the least idea,' said Jefferson quietly. 'It is the last thing in the world I should have expected from Mr Stanworth.'

The inspector turned to Roger. 'Now, sir, you were in the garden with him last evening at ten. What happened after that?'

'Oh, we didn't stay out very long after that. Not more than twenty minutes, I should say. I had some work to do, and we went in together.'

'What were you talking about in the garden?'

'Roses chiefly. He was very keen on roses and took a lot of interest in the rose garden here.'

'Did he seem cheerful?'

'Very. He always struck me as an exceptionally cheerful person. Genial, in fact.'

'Did anything he said lead you to think that he might be contemplating taking his life? Not at the time, of course; but looking back on it. No casual remark, or anything like that?'

'Good heavens, no! On the contrary, he talked quite a lot about the future. What part of the country he was going to stay in next year, and that sort of thing.'

'I see. Well, what happened when you went in?'

'We met Mrs Plant in the hall, and he stopped to speak to her. I went on to the drawing room to get a book I'd left there. When I came back they were still in the hall talking. I said good night to both of them and went on up to my room. That was the last I saw of him.'

'Thank you. Then you can't help, either?'

'Not in the least, I'm afraid. The whole thing beats me completely.'

The inspector looked at Alec. 'And you, sir? When did you see him last?'

Alec considered. 'I hardly saw him after dinner at all, Inspector. That is, I didn't speak to him; but I caught a glimpse of him once or twice in the garden with Mr Sheringham.'

'You were in the garden, too?'

'Yes.'

'What were you doing?'

Alec blushed. 'Well, I was – That is – '

Roger came to his rescue. 'Mr Grierson and Miss Shannon, whom you have not yet had the pleasure of meeting, became engaged yesterday, Inspector,' he said gravely, but with a side-long wink.

The inspector smiled genially. 'Then I don't think we need enquire what Mr Grierson was doing in the garden last night,' he remarked jovially. 'Or Miss Shannon, for that matter, when I come to question her later. And you can't help us either in any other direction?'

'I'm afraid not, Inspector. I really knew very little of Mr Stanworth in any case. I only met him for the first time when I arrived here three days ago.'

Inspector Mansfield rose to his feet. 'Well, I think that is all I have to ask you, gentlemen. After all, even if we can't find out what his reasons were, the case is clear enough. The door and all the windows locked on the inside; the revolver in his hand, which the doctor says must have been there during life; to say nothing of his own statement. I don't think the coroner will take very long to arrive at his verdict.'

'What about the inquest?' Roger asked. 'Shall we be wanted?'

'You and Mr Grierson will be, and the other person who was present when the door was broken in – the butler, wasn't it? And of course yourself, Major, and Lady Stanworth; and the last person to see him alive. Who else is there in the party? Mrs and Miss Shannon and Mrs Plant? Well, I don't think they will be required, unless they have any further information of importance. Still, the coroner will notify whom he wants to attend.'

'And the inquest will be tomorrow?' Major Jefferson asked.

'Probably. In a case as simple as this there is no point in delay. And now, Major, I wonder if I might have a word with Lady Stanworth down here. And I wish you'd look round and see if you can hit on the code for that safe. I could get it from the makers, of course, if necessary; but I don't want to have to do that unless I must.'

Major Jefferson nodded. 'I'll try,' he said briefly. 'And I'll send one of the maids to tell Lady Stanworth. She's in her room.'

He rang the bell, and Roger and Alec strolled over to the door.

'And you might warn the others in the household not to leave the premises till I have seen them,' they heard the inspector say as they passed through it. 'I shall have to interrogate everyone, of course.'

36

Roger drew Alec into the dining room and thence out into the garden. They reached the middle of the lawn before he spoke.

'Alec,' he said seriously, 'what do you make of it all?'

'Make of what?' asked Alec.

'Make of what?' Roger repeated scornfully. 'Why, the whole blessed business, of course. Alec, you're uncommonly slow in the uptake. Can't you see that Jefferson is hiding something for all he's worth?'

'He did seem a bit reticent, certainly,' Alec agreed cautiously.

'Reticent? Why, if that fellow's telling one tenth of what he knows I should be surprised. And what about Mrs Plant? And why doesn't anybody know the combination of that safe? I tell you, there are wheels within wheels going on here.'

Alec threw caution to the winds. 'It *is* curious,' he admitted recklessly.

Roger was intent on his own thoughts. 'And why was Jefferson searching Mr Stanworth's pockets?' he demanded suddenly. 'Oh, but of course, that's obvious enough.'

'I'm dashed if it is. Why was he?'

'To find the keys of the safe, I suppose. What else could it be? For some reason or other Jefferson is all against having that safe opened. By the police, at any rate. And so is Mrs Plant. Why?'

'I don't know,' said Alec helplessly.

'Nor do I! That's just the annoying part. I hate things I don't understand. Always have done. It's a sort of challenge to get to the bottom of them.'

'Are you going to get to the bottom of this?' Alec smiled.

'If there's a bottom to get to,' said Roger defiantly. 'So don't grin in that infernally sarcastic way. Dash it all, aren't you curious?'

Alec hesitated. 'Yes, I am in a way. But after all, it doesn't seem to be our business, does it?'

'That remains to be seen. What I want to find out is – whose business is it? At present it seems to be everybody's.'

'And are you going to tell the police anything?'

'No; I'm hanged if I am,' said Roger with conviction. 'I don't mind whose business it is; but it isn't theirs. Not yet, anyway,' he added with a touch of grimness.

Alec was plainly startled. 'Good Lord! You don't think it might be eventually, do you?'

'I'm blessed if I know what to think! By the way, reverting to Jefferson, you remember when I found those ashes in the hearth and suggested that they might be the remains of those mysterious private documents Jefferson had been hinting about? Well, did it appear to you that he looked uncommonly relieved for the moment?'

Alec reflected. 'I don't think I was looking at him just then.'

'Well, I was. And I made the suggestion on purpose, to see how he'd take it. I'd take my oath that the idea appealed to him immensely. Now why? And what's he got to do with Mr Stanworth's private papers?'

'But look here, you know,' said Alec slowly, 'if he really was hiding something, as you seem to think, surely he wouldn't go and give the whole show away by telling us straight out like that what sort of thing it is that he's hiding? I mean, if he really is hiding something he'd mention papers to put us off the scent, wouldn't he? Really, I mean, it would be something quite different. What I mean is – '

'It's all right. I'm beginning to get an idea of what you mean,' said Roger kindly. 'But seriously, Alec, that's rather an idea of yours. After all, Jefferson isn't the man to give himself away, is he?'

'No,' said Alec earnestly. 'You see, what I mean is – '

'Hullo!' Roger interrupted rudely. 'There's the inspector going down the drive. And without Jefferson, by all that's lucky! Let's cut after him and ask him if he's brought anything else to the surface.' And without waiting for a reply he set off at a run in the wake of the retreating inspector.

The latter, hearing their footsteps on the gravel, turned round to wait for them.

'Well, sir?' he said with a smile. 'Remembered something else to tell me?'

Roger dropped into a walk. 'No; but I was wondering whether you had anything to tell me. Found anything more out?'

'You're not connected with the press by any chance, Mr Sheringham, are you?' the inspector asked suspiciously.

'Oh, no; it's just natural curiosity,' Roger laughed. 'Not for publication, and all that.'

'I was thinking you might get me into trouble if it came out that I'd been talking more than I ought to, sir. But I haven't found anything more out in any case.'

'Lady Stanworth wasn't any help?'

'Not a bit, sir. She couldn't throw any light on it at all. I didn't keep her long. Or any of the others, either, for that matter. There was nothing more to be got out of them, and I've got to get back and make out my report.'

'Not even found the safe's combination?'

'No,' returned the inspector disappointedly. 'I shall have to ring up the makers and get that. I've taken a note of the number.'

'And who saw him last?'

'Mrs Plant. He stopped her in the hall to ask her if she liked some roses he'd had specially sent up to her room for her, and left her to go into the library. Nobody saw him after that.'

'And is the body still in there?'

'No, sir. We shan't want that any more. The constable I brought with me, Rudgeman, is helping them take it upstairs now.'

The lodge gates appeared in sight, and Roger halted.

'Well, goodbye, Inspector. Shall we see you over here again?'

'Yes, sir. I shall have to come over about that safe. I don't suppose we'll find anything in it, and it's a ten-mile bicycle ride for me in this heat; but there you are!' He laughed ruefully and went on his way.

Roger and Alec turned and began to pace slowly back to the house.

'So Mrs Plant was the last to see him alive, was she?' observed the former thoughtfully. 'That means she'll be staying over for the inquest. The others will be going this afternoon, I suppose. What's the time?'

Alec glanced at the watch on his wrist. 'Just past eleven.'

'And all that's happened in two hours! My hat! Well, come along with me. If the body's been removed, we may find the coast clear with any luck.'

'What are you proposing to do now?' Alec asked with interest.

'Look around that library.'

'Oh? What's the idea?'

For once in his life a curious reluctance seemed to have settled upon Roger. Almost nervously he cleared his throat, and when at last he did speak his voice was unwontedly grave.

'Well,' he said slowly, picking his words with care; 'there's a thing that nobody else seems to have noticed, but it's been striking me more and more forcibly every minute. I tell you candidly it's something rather horrible – a question that I'm honestly rather frightened of finding the answer to.'

'What are you driving at?' asked Alec in perplexity. Roger hesitated again.

'Look here,' he said suddenly, 'if you were going to shoot yourself, how would you go about it? Wouldn't you do it like this?'

He raised his hand and pointed an imaginary revolver at a spot just above the right-hand end of his right eyebrow.

Alec copied his action. 'Well, yes, I might. It seems the natural way to do it.'

'Exactly,' said Roger slowly. 'Then why the devil is that wound in the centre of Stanworth's forehead?'

chapter six

Four People Behave Remarkably

Alec started, and his broad, good-humoured face paled a little.

'Good Lord!' he ejaculated in startled tones. 'What on earth do you mean?'

'Simply what I say,' returned Roger. 'Why did Stanworth go out of his way to shoot himself in such a remarkably difficult manner? Don't you see what I mean? It isn't natural.'

Alec was staring up the drive. 'Isn't it? But he did it all right, didn't he?'

'Oh, of course he did it,' said Roger in a voice that was curiously lacking in conviction. 'But what I can't understand is this. Why, when he could have done it so easily, did he go about it in such a roundabout way? I mean, a revolver isn't such an easy thing to manipulate unhandily; and the attitude he used must have twisted his wrist most uncomfortably. Just try pointing your forefinger in a straight line at the middle of your forehead, and you'll see what I mean.'

He suited his action to his words, and there was no doubt about the constraint of his attitude. Alec looked at him attentively.

'Yes, it does look awkward,' he commented.

'It is. Infernally awkward. And you saw where the doctor took the bullet from. Almost at the very back. That means the revolver must have been nearly in a dead straight line. You try and see how difficult it is. It almost dislocates your elbow.'

Alec copied the action. 'You're quite right,' he said with interest. 'It is uncomfortable.'

'I should call it more than that. It's so unnatural as to be highly improbable. Yet there's the fact.'

'Can't get away from facts, you know,' observed Alec sagely.

'No, but you can explain them. And I'm dashed if I can see the explanation for this one.'

'Well, what's the idea?' Alec asked curiously. 'You're being infernally mysterious.'

'Me? I like that. It isn't I who am being mysterious. It's everything else. Facts and people and everything. Look here, we won't go in for a moment. Let's find a seat somewhere and try and get a grip on things. I'm getting out of my depth, and I don't like it.'

He led the way to where a few garden chairs were scattered beneath a big cedar at one of the corners of the lawn, and threw himself into one of them. Alec followed suit, somewhat more cautiously. Alec was a big person, and he had met garden chairs before.

'Proceed,' he said, fishing for his pipe. 'You interest me strangely.'

Nothing loth, Roger took up his tale.

'Well, then, in the first place let's consider the human side of things. Hasn't it struck you that there are four separate and distinct people here whose conduct during the last few hours has been, to say the least of it, remarkable?'

'No,' said Alec candidly, 'it hasn't. Two have, I know. Who are the other two?'

'Well, the butler is one. He didn't seem particularly cut up over Stanworth's death, did he? Not that you look for a tremendous display of emotion from a great hulking brute like that, true. But you do look for some.'

'He wasn't vastly upset,' Alec admitted.

'And then there is his position in the household. Why should an ex-prize-fighter turn butler? The two professions don't seem to harmonise somehow. And why should Stanworth want to employ an ex-prize-fighting butler for that matter? It's not what you'd expect from him. He always seemed to me particularly meticulous over points of etiquette. I wouldn't have called him a snob exactly; he was too nice and jolly for

42

that. But he did like to be taken for a gentleman. And gentlemen don't employ prize-fighting butlers, do they?'

'I've never heard of it being done before,' Alec conceded cautiously.

'Precisely. My point exactly. Alec, you're positively sparkling this morning.'

'Thanks,' Alec growled, lighting his pipe. 'But apparently not enough so to make out who the fourth of your suspicious people is. Get on with it.'

'After you with that match. Why, didn't it strike you that somebody else took the news of Stanworth's death with remarkable fortitude? And that after it had been broken to her with a bluntness that verged on brutality.'

Alec paused in the act of applying a second match to his refractory pipe. 'By Jove! You mean Lady Stanworth?'

'I do,' said Roger complacently.

'Yes, I did notice that,' Alec remarked, staring over his pipe at his companion. 'But I don't think there was much love lost between those two, was there?'

'You're right. There wasn't. I shouldn't mind going farther than that and saying that she absolutely hated old Stanworth. I noticed it lots of times these last three days, and it puzzled me even then. Now – ' He paused and sucked at his pipe once or twice. 'Now it puzzles me a good deal more,' he concluded softly, almost as if speaking to himself.

'Go on,' Alec prompted interestedly.

'Well, that's four people; two whose behaviour has not been quite what you'd expect under the circumstances, and two who are downright suspicious. Anyhow, you can say four curious people.'

Alec nodded in silence. He was thinking of a fifth person whose conduct early that morning had been something more than curious. With an effort he thrust the thought from him abruptly. At any rate, Roger was going to know nothing about that.

'And now we come to facts, and the Lord knows these are curious enough, too. First of all, we've got the place of the wound and the extreme unlikelihood (as one would have said if one hadn't actually seen it) of anyone committing suicide by shooting himself in that particular way. About that I'm not going to say any more for the moment. But there are plenty of things to talk about without that.'

43

'There would be, with you anywhere about,' Alec murmured irreverently.

'You wait. This is serious. Now according to what they say, people went to bed in pretty decent time, last night, didn't they? Mrs Plant after meeting Stanworth in the hall; Barbara and her mother soon after you came in from the garden; and Jefferson and you after you'd finished playing billiards?'

'That's right,' Alec nodded. 'Eleven thirtyish.'

'Well,' said Roger triumphantly. 'Somebody's lying! I was working in my room till past one, and I heard footsteps in the corridor not once but two or three times between midnight and then – the last time just as I was knocking off! Of course I didn't pay any particular attention to them at the time; but I know I'm not mistaken. So if everyone says that they were in their rooms by eleven-thirty (except Stanworth, who was presumably locked in the library), then I repeat – somebody's lying! Now what do you make of that?'

'Heaven only knows,' said Alec helplessly, puffing vigorously at his pipe. 'What do you?'

'Beyond the bare fact that somebody's lying, nothing – yet! But that's quite enough for the present. Then there's another thing. You remember where those keys were? In the waistcoat pocket above the one in which he usually kept them. The inspector just remarked that he must have put them in the wrong pocket. Now, do you think that's likely?'

'Might be done. I don't see anything wildly improbable in it.'

'Oh, no; not wildly improbable. But improbable enough, for all that. Have you ever done it, for instance?'

'Put a thing in the wrong pocket? Lord, yes; heaps of times.'

'No, you idiot. Not just in any wrong pocket. In the upper pocket of a waistcoat instead of the lower.'

Alec considered. 'I don't know. Haven't I!'

'Probably not. Once again, it's an unnatural mistake. One doesn't use the upper pockets of a waistcoat much. They're not easy to get at. But consider this. When you want to slip a thing into the lower pocket of a waistcoat that's hanging on a chair, it's the easiest thing in the world to put it in the upper pocket by mistake. Done it myself hundreds of times.'

44

Alec whistled softly. 'I see what you're getting at. You mean – '

'Absolutely! A waistcoat worn by somebody else is in the same category as a waistcoat hanging on a chair. If we're to go by probabilities, then the most likely thing is that somebody else put those keys in that pocket. Not Stanworth himself at all.'

'But who on earth do you imagine did it? Jefferson?'

'Jefferson!' Roger repeated scornfully. 'Of course not Jefferson! That's the whole point. Jefferson was looking for those keys; and it's just because they were in the wrong pocket and he didn't know it, that he couldn't find them. That's plain enough.'

'Sorry!' Alec apologised.

'Well, this is all wrong, don't you see? It complicates things still more. Here's a fifth mysterious person to be added to our list of suspicious characters.'

'Then you don't think it was Mrs Plant?' Alec said tentatively.

'I *know* it wasn't Mrs Plant. She was playing about with the knob of the safe; she hadn't got the keys. And in any case, even if she had, there was no possibility of her getting them back again. No, we've got to look elsewhere. Now let's see, when was that library left empty?' He paused for reflection. 'Jefferson was there alone while I was in the dining room (I should like to know why Mrs Plant fainted, by the way; but we've got to wait for that till the safe's opened); but he didn't find the keys. Then we both went into the garden. Then I met you, and we caught Mrs Plant almost immediately afterwards. How long was I with Jefferson? Not more than ten minutes or so. Then the keys must have been disturbed in that ten minutes before Mrs Plant went into the library (there was no opportunity later; you remember we kept the library under inspection after that till the police arrived). Either then, or – ' He hesitated and was silent.

'Yes?' said Alec curiously. 'Or when else?'

'Nothing! – Well, anyhow, there's plenty of food for thought there, isn't there?'

'It does give one something to think about,' Alec agreed, puffing vigorously.

'Oh, and one other thing; possibly of no importance whatever. There was a slight scratch on Stanworth's right wrist.'

'Rose bush!' replied Alec promptly. 'He was always playing about with them, wasn't he?'

'Ye-es,' Roger replied doubtfully. 'That occurred to me, of course. But somehow I don't think it was a scratch from a rose. It was fairly broad, for instance; not a thin, deep line like a rose's scratch. However, that's neither here nor there; probably it's got nothing to do with anything. Well, that's the lot. Now – what do you make of it all?'

'If you want my candid opinion,' said Alec carefully, after a little pause, 'I think that you're making mountains out of molehills. In other words, attaching too much importance to trifles. After all, when you come to think of it there's nothing particularly serious in any of the things you mentioned, is there? And you can't tell; there may be a perfectly innocent explanation even for Jefferson and Mrs Plant.'

Roger smoked thoughtfully for a minute or two.

'There may be, of course,' he said at length; 'in fact, I hope to goodness there is. But as for the rest, I agree with you that they're only molehills in themselves; but don't forget that if you pile sufficient molehills on top of each other you get a mountain. And that's what I can't help thinking is the case here. Separately these little facts are nothing; but collectively they make me wonder rather furiously.'

Alec shrugged his shoulders. 'Curiosity killed the cat,' he remarked pointedly.

'Possibly,' Roger laughed. 'But I'm not a cat, and I thrive on it. Anyway, my mind's made up on one point. I'm going to nose round and just see whether there isn't any more to be found out. I liked old Stanworth, and as long as it seems to me that there's the least possibility of his having been – ' He checked himself abruptly. 'Of all not being quite as it should,' he resumed after a momentary pause. 'Well, I'm going to make it my business to look into it. Now, what I want to ask you is – will you help me?'

Alec regarded his friend silently for a minute or two, his hand cradling the bowl of the pipe he was smoking.

'Yes,' he announced at length; 'on one condition. That whatever you may find out, you won't take any important steps without telling me. You see, I don't know that I consider this absolutely playing the game in a way; and I want – '

46

'You can make yourself easy on that score,' Roger smiled. 'If we go into it, we go in together; and I won't do anything, not only without telling you, but even without your consent. That's only fair.'

'And you'll let me know anything you may find out as you go along?' asked Alec suspiciously. 'Not keep things up your sleeve, like Holmes did to old Watson?'

'Of course not, my dear chap! If it comes to that, I don't suppose I could if I wanted to. I must have somebody to confide in.'

'You'll make a rotten detective, Roger,' Alec grinned. 'You gas too much. The best detectives are thin-lipped, hatchet-faced devils who creep about the place not saying a word to anybody.'

'In the story-books. You bet they don't in real life. I expect they talk their heads off to their seconds-in-command. It's so jolly helpful. Holmes must have missed an awful lot by not letting himself go to Watson. For one thing, the very act of talking helps one to clarify one's own ideas and suggests further ones.'

'Your ideas ought to be pretty clear then,' said Alec rudely.

'And besides,' Roger went on unperturbed, 'I'd bet anything that Watson was jolly useful to Holmes. Those absurd theories of the poor old chap's that Holmes always ridiculed so mercilessly (I wish Watson had been allowed to hit on the truth just once; it would have pleased him so tremendously) – why, I shouldn't be at all surprised if they didn't suggest the right idea to Holmes time and time again; but of course, he would never have acknowledged it. Anyhow, the moral is, you talk away for all you're worth and I'll do the same. And if we don't manage to find something out between us, you can write me down an ass. And yourself, too, Alexander!'

chapter seven

The Vase that Wasn't

'Very well, Sherlock,' said Alec. 'And what's the first move?'

'The library,' Roger replied promptly, and rose to his feet.

Alec followed suit and they turned towards the house.

'What do you expect to find?' asked the latter curiously.

'I'm blessed if I know,' Roger confessed. 'In fact, I can't really say that I actually expect to find anything. I've got hopes, of course, but in no definite direction.'

'Bit vague, isn't it?'

'Thoroughly. That's the interesting part. All we can do is to look around and try and notice anything at all, however slight, that seems to be just out of the ordinary. Ten to one it won't mean anything at all; and even if it does, it's another ten to one that we shan't be able to see it. But as I said, there's always hope.'

'But what are we going to look for? Things connected with the people you mentioned; or just – well, just things?'

'Anything! Anything and everything, and trust to luck. Now step quietly over this bit of gravel. We don't want everyone to know that we're nosing around in here.'

They stepped carefully over the path and entered the library. It was empty, but the door into the hall was slightly ajar. Roger crossed the room and closed it. Then he looked carefully round him.

'Where do we start operations?' Alec asked with interest.

'Well,' Roger said slowly, 'I'm just trying to get a general sort of impression. This is really the first time we've been able to look round in peace, you know.'

'What sort of impression?'

Roger considered. 'It's rather hard to put into words exactly; but I've got a more or less retentive sort of mind. I mean, I can look at a thing or a place and carry the picture in my brain for quite a time. I've trained myself to it. It's jolly useful for storing up ideas for descriptions of scenery and that sort of thing. Photographic, you might call it. Well, it struck me that if there had been any important alteration in this room during the last few hours – if the position of the safe had been altered, for instance, or anything like that – I should probably be able to spot it.'

'And you think that's going to help now?'

'I don't know in the least. But there's no harm in trying, is there?'

He walked to the middle of the room and turned slowly about, letting the picture sink into his brain. When he had made the complete circuit, he sat on the edge of the table and shut his eyes.

Alec watched him interestedly. 'Any luck?' he asked, after a couple of minutes' silence.

Roger opened his eyes. 'No,' he admitted, a little ruefully. It is always disappointing after such carefully staged preparations to find that one's pet trick has failed to work. Roger felt not unlike a conjuror who had not succeeded in producing the rabbit from the top-hat.

'Ah!' observed Alec noncommittally.

'I can't see anything different,' said Roger, almost apologetically.

'Ah!' Alec remarked again. 'Then I suppose that means that nothing is different?' he suggested helpfully.

'I suppose so,' Roger admitted.

'Now are you going to tell me that this is really devilish significant?' Alec grinned. 'Because if you do, I warn you that I shan't believe you. It's exactly what I expected. I told you you were making too much fuss about a lot of trifles.'

'Shut up!' Roger snapped from the edge of the table. 'I'm thinking.'

'Oh, sorry!'

Roger took no notice of his fellow sleuth's unprofessionally derisive grin. He was staring abstractedly at the big carved oak chimney-piece.

'There's only one thing that strikes me,' he observed slowly after a little pause, 'now I come to think of it. Doesn't that chimney-piece look somehow a bit lopsided to you?'

Alec followed the other's gaze. The chimney-piece looked ordinary enough. There were the usual pewter plates and mugs set out upon it, and on one side stood a large blue china vase. For a moment Alec stared at it in silence. Then:

'I'm blessed if I see anything lopsided about it,' he announced. 'How do you mean?'

'I don't know exactly,' Roger replied, still gazing at it curiously. 'All I can say is that in some way it doesn't look quite right to me. Side-heavy, if I may coin a phrase.'

'You may,' said Alec kindly. 'That is, if you'll tell me what it means.'

'Well, unsymmetrical, if you like that better.' He slapped his knee suddenly. 'By Jove! Idiot! I see now. Of course!' He turned a triumphant smile upon the other. 'Fancy not noticing that before?'

'*What?*' shouted Alec in exasperation.

'Why, that vase. Don't you see?'

Alec looked at the vase. It seemed a very ordinary sort of affair.

'What's the matter with it? It looks all right to me.'

'Oh, there's nothing the matter with it,' said Roger airily. 'It is all right.'

Alec approached the table and clenched a large fist, which he proceeded to hold two inches in front of Roger's nose.

'If you don't tell me within thirty seconds what you're talking about, I shall smite you,' he said grimly. '*Hard!*'

'I'll tell you,' said Roger quickly. 'I'm not allowed to be smitten before lunch. Doctor's orders. He's very strict about it, indeed. Oh, yes; about that vase. Well, don't you see? There's only one of it!'

'Is that all?' asked Alec, turning away disgustedly. 'I thought from the fuss you were making that you'd discovered something really exciting.'

'So I have,' returned Roger, unabashed. 'You see, the exciting part is that yesterday, I am prepared to swear, there were two of it.'

'Oh? How do you know that?'

'Because now I come to realise it, I remember an impression of well-balanced orderliness about that chimney-piece. It was a typical man's room chimney-piece. Women are the unsymmetrical sex, you know. The fact of there being only one vase alters its whole appearance.'

'Well?' Alec still did not appear to be very much impressed. 'And what's that got to do with anything?'

'Probably nothing. It's just a fact that since yesterday afternoon the second vase has disappeared; that's all. It may have been broken somehow by Stanworth himself; one of the servants may have knocked it over; Lady Stanworth may have taken it to put some flowers in – anything! But as it's the only new fact that seems to emerge, let's look into it.'

Roger left the table and strolled leisurely over to the fireplace.

'You're wasting your time,' Alec growled, unconvinced. 'What are you going to do? Ask the servants about it?'

'Not yet, at any rate,' Roger replied from the hearthrug. He stood on tip-toe to get a view of the surface of the chimney-piece. 'Here you are!' he exclaimed excitedly. 'What did I tell you? Look at this! The room hasn't been dusted this morning, of course. Here's a ring where the vase stood.'

He dragged a chair across and mounted it to obtain a better view. Alec's inch or two of extra height enabled him to see well enough by standing on the shallow fender. There was very little dust on the chimney-piece, but enough to show a faint though well-defined ring upon the surface. Roger reached across for the other vase and fitted its base over the mark. It coincided exactly.

'That proves it,' Roger remarked with some satisfaction. 'I knew I was right, of course; but it's always pleasant to be able to prove it.' He bent forward and examined the surface closely. 'I wonder what on earth all these other little marks are, though,' he went on thoughtfully. 'I don't seem able to account for them. What do you make of them?'

Dotted about both in the ring and outside it were a number of faint impressions in the shallow dust; some large and broad, others quite small. All were irregular in shape, and their edges merged so imperceptibly into the surrounding dust that it was impossible to say where one began or the other ended. A few inches to the left of the ring, however, the dust had been swept clean away across the whole depth of the surface for a width of nearly a foot.

'I don't know,' Alec confessed. 'They don't convey anything to me, I'm afraid. I should say that somebody's simply put something down here and taken it away again later. I don't see that it's particularly important in any case.'

'Probably it isn't. But it's interesting. I suppose you must be right. I can't see any other explanation, I'm bound to say. But it must have been a very curiously shaped object, to leave those marks. Or could it have been a number of things? And why should the dust have been scraped away like that? Something must have been drawn across the surface; something flat and smooth and fairly heavy.' He meditated for a moment. 'It's funny.'

Alec stepped back from the fender. 'Well, we don't seem to be progressing much, do we?' he remarked. 'Let's try somewhere else, Sherlock.'

He wandered aimlessly over towards the French windows and stood looking out into the garden.

A sharp exclamation from Roger caused him to wheel round suddenly. The latter had descended from his chair, and was now standing on the hearth-rug and looking with interest at something he held in his hand.

'Here!' he said, holding out his palm, in which a small blue object was lying. 'Come and look at this. I stepped on it just now as I got down from the chair. It was on the rug. What do you think of it?' Alec took the object, which proved to be a small piece of broken blue china, and turned it over carefully.

'Why, this is a bit of that other vase!' he said sagely.

'Excellent, Alexander Watson. It is.'

Alec scrutinised the fragment more closely. 'It must have got broken,' he announced profoundly.

'Brilliant! Your deductive powers are in wonderful form this morning, Alec,' Roger smiled. Then his face became more grave. 'But seriously, this is really rather perplexing. You see what must have happened, of course. The vase got broken where it stood. In view of this bit, that's the only possible explanation for those marks on the chimney-piece. They must have been caused by the broken pieces. And that broad patch was made by someone sweeping the pieces off the shelf – the same person, presumably, as picked up the larger bits round that ring.'

He paused and looked at Alec inquiringly.

'Well?' said that worthy.

'Well, don't you see the difficulty? Vases don't suddenly break where they stand. They fall and smash on the ground or something like that. This one calmly fell to pieces in its place, as far as I can see. Dash it all, it isn't natural! – And that's about the third unnatural thing we've had already,' he added in tones of mingled triumph and resentment.

Alec pressed the tobacco carefully down in his pipe and struck a match. 'Aren't you going the long way round again?' he asked slowly. 'Surely there's an obvious explanation. Someone knocked the vase over on its side and it broke on the shelf. I can't see anything wrong with that.'

'I can,' said Roger quickly. 'Two things. In the first place, those vases were far too thick to break like that simply through being knocked over on a wooden surface. In the second, even if it had been, you'd get a smooth, elliptical mark in the dust where it fell; and there isn't one. No, there's only one possible reason for it to break as it did, as far as I can make out.'

'And what's that, Sherlock?'

'That it had been struck by something – and struck so hard and cleanly that it simply smashed where it stood and was not knocked into the hearth. What do you think of that?'

'It seems reasonable enough,' Alec conceded after consideration.

'You're not very enthusiastic, are you? It's so jolly eminently reasonable that it must be right. Now, then, the next question is – who or what hit it like that?'

'I say, do you think this is going to lead anywhere?' Alec asked suddenly. 'Aren't we wasting time over this rotten vase? I don't see what it can have to do with what we're looking for. Not that I have the least idea what that is, in any case,' he added candidly.

'You don't seem to have taken to my vase, Alec. It's a pity, because I'm getting more and more fond of it every minute. Anyhow, I'm going to put in one or two minutes' really hard thinking about it; so if you'd like to wander out into the garden and have a chat with William, don't let me keep you.'

Alec had strolled over to the windows again. For some reason he seemed somewhat anxious to keep the garden under observation as far as possible.

'Oh, I won't interrupt you,' he was beginning carelessly, when at the same moment the reason appeared in sight, walking slowly on to the lawn from the direction of the rose garden. 'Well, as a matter of fact, perhaps I will wander out for a bit,' he emended hurriedly. 'Won't stay away long, in case anything else crops up.' And he made a hasty exit.

Roger, following with his eyes the beeline his newly appointed assistant was taking, smiled slightly and resumed his labours.

Alec did not waste time. There was a question which had been worrying him horribly during the last couple of hours, and he wanted an answer to it, and wanted it quickly.

'Barbara,' he said abruptly, as soon as he came abreast of her, 'you know what you told me this morning. Before breakfast. It hadn't anything to do with what's happened here, had it?'

Barbara blushed painfully. Then as suddenly she paled.

'You mean – about Mr Stanworth's death?' she asked steadily, looking him full in the eyes.

Alec nodded.

'No, it hadn't. That was only a – a horrible coincidence.' She paused. 'Why?' she asked suddenly.

Alec looked supremely uncomfortable. 'Oh, I don't know. You see, you said something about – well, about a horrible thing that had happened. And then half an hour later, when we knew that – I mean, I couldn't help wondering just for the moment whether – ' He floundered into silence.

'It's all right, Alec,' said Barbara gently. 'It was a perfectly reasonable mistake to make. As I said, that was only a dreadful coincidence.'

'And aren't you going to change your mind about what you said this morning?' asked Alec humbly.

Barbara looked at him quickly. 'Why should I?' she returned swiftly. 'I mean – ' She hesitated and corrected herself. 'Why should you think I might?'

'I don't know. You were very upset this morning, and it occurred to me that you might have had bad news and were acting on the spur of the moment; and perhaps when you had thought it over, you might – ' He broke off meaningly.

Barbara seemed strangely ill at ease. She did not reply at once to Alec's unspoken question, but twisted her wisp of a handkerchief between her fingers with nervous gestures that were curiously out of place in this usually uncommonly self-possessed young person.

'Oh, I don't know what to say,' she replied at last, in low, hurried tones. 'I can't tell you anything at present, Alec. I may have acted too much on the spur of the moment. I don't know. Come and see me when we get back from the Mertons' next month. I shall have to think things over.'

'And you won't tell me what the trouble was, dear?'

'No, I can't. Please don't ask me that, Alec. You see, that isn't really my secret. No, I can't possibly tell you!'

'All right. But – but you do love me, don't you?'

Barbara laid her hand on his arm with a swift, caressing movement. 'It wasn't anything to do with that, old boy,' she said softly. 'Come and see me next month. I think – I think I *might* have changed my mind again by then. No, Alec! You mustn't! Anyhow, not here of all places. Perhaps I'll let you once – just a tiny one! – before we go; but not unless you're good. Besides, I've got to run in and pack now. We're catching the two forty-one, and Mother will be waiting for me.'

She gave his hand a sudden squeeze and turned towards the house.

'That was a bit of luck, meeting her out here!' murmured Alec raptly to himself as he watched her go. Wherein he was not altogether correct in his statement of fact; for as the lady had come into the garden for that express purpose, the subsequent meeting might be said to be due rather to good generalship than good luck.

It was therefore a remarkably jubilant Watson who returned blithely to the library to find his Sherlock sitting solemnly in the chair before the big writing table and staring hard at the chimney-piece.

In spite of himself he shivered slightly. 'Ugh, you ghoulish brute!' he exclaimed.

Roger looked at him abstractedly. 'What's up?'

'Well, I can't say that I should like to sit in that particular chair just yet awhile.'

'I'm glad you've come back,' Roger said, rising slowly to his feet. 'I've just had a pretty curious idea, and I'm going to test it. The chances are several million to one against it coming off, but if it *does* – ! Well, I don't know what the devil we're going to do!'

55

He had spoken so seriously that Alec gaped at him in surprise. 'Good Lord, what's up now?' he asked.

'Well, I won't say in so many words,' Roger replied slowly, 'because it's really too fantastic. But it's to do with the breaking of that second vase. You remember I said that in order for it to have smashed like that it must have been struck extraordinarily hard by some mysterious object. It's just occurred to me what that object might possibly have been.'

He walked across to where the chair was still standing in front of the fireplace and stepped up on to it. Then, with a glance towards the chair he had just left, he began to examine the woodwork at the back of the chimney-piece. Alec watched him in silence. Suddenly he bent forward with close attention and prodded a finger at the panel; and Alec noticed that his face had gone very pale.

He turned and descended, a little unsteadily, from the chair. 'My hat, but I was right!' he exclaimed softly, staring at Alec with raised eyebrows. 'That second vase was smashed by a bullet! You'll find its mark just behind that little pillar on the left there.'

chapter eight

Mr Sheringham Becomes Startling

For a moment there was silence between the two. Then:

'Great Scott!' Alec remarked. 'Absolutely certain?'

'Absolutely. It's a bullet mark all right. The bullet isn't there, but it must have just embedded itself in the wood and been dug out with a penknife. You can see the marks of the blade round the hole. Get up and have a look.'

Alec stepped on to the chair and felt the hole in the wood with a large forefinger. 'Couldn't be an old mark, could it?' he asked, examining it curiously. 'Some of this panelling's been pretty well knocked about.'

'No; I thought of that. An old hole would have the edges more or less smoothed down; those are quite jagged and splintery. And where the knife's cut the wood away the surface is quite different to the rest. Not so dark. No; that mark's a recent one, all right.'

Alec got down from the chair. 'What do you make of it?' he asked abruptly.

'I'm not sure,' said Roger slowly. 'It means rather a drastic rearrangement of our ideas, doesn't it? But I'll tell you one highly important fact, and that is that a line from this mark through the middle of the ring in the dust leads straight to the chair in front of the writing table. That seems to me jolly significant. I tell you what. Let's go out on to the lawn and talk it over. We don't want to stay in here too long in any case.'

He carefully replaced the chair on the hearth-rug in its proper position and walked out into the garden. Alec dutifully followed, and they made for the cedar tree once more.

'Go on,' said the latter when they were seated. 'This is going to be interesting.'

Roger frowned abstractedly. He was enjoying himself hugely. With his capacity for throwing himself heart and soul into whatever he happened to be doing at the moment, he was already beginning to assume the profound airs of a great detective. The pose was a perfectly unconscious one; but none the less typical.

'Well, taking as our starting point the fact that the bullet was fired from a line which includes the chair in which Mr Stanworth was sitting,' he began learnedly, 'and assuming, as I think we have every right to do, that it was fired between, let us say, the hours of midnight and two o'clock this morning, the first thing that strikes us is the fact that in all probability it must have been fired by Mr Stanworth himself.'

'We then remember,' said Alec gravely, 'that the inspector particularly mentioned that only one shot had been fired from Mr Stanworth's revolver, and realise at once what idiots we were to have been struck by anything of the kind. In other words, try again!'

'Yes, that is rather a nuisance,' said Roger thoughtfully. 'I was forgetting that.'

'I thought you were,' remarked Alec unkindly.

Roger pondered. 'This is very dark and difficult,' he said at length, dropping the pontifical manner he had assumed. 'As far as I can see it's the only reasonable theory that the second shot was fired by old Stanworth. The only other alternative is that it was fired by somebody else, who happened to be standing in a direct line with Stanworth and the vase and who was using a revolver of the same, or nearly the same, calibre as Stanworth's. That doesn't seem very likely on the face of it, does it?'

'But more so than that it was a shot from Stanworth's revolver which was never fired at all,' Alec commented dryly.

'Well, why did the inspector say that only one shot had been fired from that revolver?' Roger asked. 'Because there was only one empty shell. But mark this. He mentioned at the same time that the revolver wasn't fully loaded. Now, wouldn't it have been possible for Stanworth to have fired that shot and then for some reason or other (Heaven knows what!) to have extracted the shell?'

'It would, I suppose; yes. But in that case wouldn't you expect to find the shell somewhere in the room?'

'Well, it may be there. We haven't looked for it yet. Anyhow, we can't get away from the fact that in all probability Stanworth did fire that other shot. Now why did he fire it?'

'Search me!' said Alec laconically.

'I think we can rule out the idea that he was just taking a pot-shot at the vase out of sheer *joie de vivre*, or that he was trying to shoot himself and was such a bad shot that he hit something in the exact opposite direction.'

'Yes, I think we might rule those out,' said Alec cautiously.

'Well, then, Stanworth was firing with an object. What at? Obviously some other person. So Stanworth was not alone in the library last night, after all! We're getting on, aren't we?'

'A jolly sight too fast,' Alec grumbled. 'You don't even know for anything like certain that the second shot was fired last night at all, and – '

'Oh, yes, I do, friend Alec. The vase was broken last night.'

'Well, in any case, you don't know that Stanworth fired it. And here you are already inventing somebody else for him to shoot at? It's too rapid for me.'

'Alec, you are Scotch, aren't you?'

'Yes, I am. But what's that got to do with it?'

'Oh, nothing; except that your bump of native caution seems to be remarkably well developed. Try and get over it. I'll take the plunges; you follow. Where had we got to? Oh, yes; Stanworth was not alone in the library last night. Now, then, what does that give us?'

'Heaven only knows what it won't give you,' murmured Alec despairingly.

'I know what it's going to give you,' retorted Roger complacently, 'and that's a shock. It's my firm impression that old Stanworth never committed suicide at all last night.'

'What?' Alec gasped. 'What on earth do you mean?'

'That he was murdered!'

59

Alec lowered his pipe and stared with incredulous eyes at his companion.

'My dear old chap,' he said after a little pause, 'have you gone suddenly quite daft?'

'On the contrary,' replied Roger calmly, 'I was never so remarkably sane in my life.'

'But – but how could he possibly have been murdered? The windows all fastened and the door locked on the inside, with the key in the lock as well! And, good Lord, his own statement sitting on the table in front of him! Roger, my dear old chap, you're mad.'

'To say nothing of the fact that his grip on the revolver was – what did the doctor call it? Oh, yes; properly adjusted, and must have been applied during life. Yes, there are certainly difficulties, Alec, I grant you.'

Alec shrugged his shoulders eloquently. 'This affair's gone to your head,' he said shortly. 'Talk about making mountains out of molehills! Good Lord! You're making a whole range of them out of a single worm-cast.'

'Very prettily put, Alec,' Roger commented approvingly. 'Perhaps I am. But my impression is that old Stanworth was murdered. I might be wrong, of course,' he added candidly. 'But I very seldom am.'

'But dash it all, the thing's out of the question! You're going the wrong way round once more. Even if there was a second man in the library last night – which I very much doubt! – you can't get away from the fact that he must have gone before Stanworth locked himself in like that. That being the case, we get back to suicide again. You can't have it both ways, you know. I'm not saying that this mythical person may not have put pressure of some sort on Stanworth (that is, if he ever existed at all) and forced him to commit suicide. But as for murder – ! Why, the idea's too dashed silly for words!' Alec was getting quite heated at this insult to his logic.

Roger was unperturbed. 'Yes,' he said thoughtfully, 'I had an idea it would be a bit of a shock to you. But to tell you the truth I was a bit suspicious about this suicide business almost from the very first. I couldn't get over the place of the wound, you know. And then all the rest of it, windows and door and confession and what not – well, instead of reassuring me, they made me more suspicious still. I couldn't help feeling more and more that it was a case of *Qui s'excuse, s'accuse*. Or to put it in another way, that the whole scene looked like a stage very carefully arranged for the second act after all the debris of the first act had been cleared away. Foolish of me, no doubt, but that's what I felt.'

Alec snorted. 'Foolish! That's putting it mildly.'

'Don't be so harsh with me, Alec,' Roger pleaded. 'I think I'm being rather brilliant.'

'You always were a chap to let things run away with you,' Alec grunted. 'Just because a couple of people act a little queerly and a couple more don't look as mournful as you think they ought, you dash off and rake up a little murder all to yourself. Going to tell the inspector about this wonderful idea of yours?'

'No, I'm not,' said Roger with decision. 'This is my little murder, as you're good enough to call it, and I'm not going to be done out of it. When I've got as far as I can, then I'll think about telling the police or not.'

'Well, thank goodness you're not going to make a fool of yourself to that extent,' said Alec with relief.

'You wait, Alexander,' Roger admonished. 'You may make a mock of me now, if you like – '

'Thanks!' Alec put in gratefully.

' – but if my luck holds, I'm going to make you sit up and take no-tice.'

'Then perhaps you'll begin by explaining how this excellent mur-derer of yours managed to get away from the room and leave everything locked on the inside behind him,' said Alec sarcastically. 'He didn't hap-pen to be a magician in a small way, did he? Then you could let him out through the key-hole, you know.'

Roger shook his head sadly. 'My dear but simple-minded Alexander, I can give you a perfectly reasonable explanation of how that murder might have been committed last night, and yet leave all these doors and windows of yours securely fastened on the inside this morning.'

'Oh, you can, can you?' said Alec derisively. 'Well, let's have it.'

'Certainly. The murderer was still inside when we broke in, concealed somewhere where nobody thought of looking.'

Alec started. 'Good Lord!' he exclaimed. 'Of course we never searched the place. So you think he was really there the whole time?'

'On the contrary,' Roger smiled gently, 'I know he wasn't, for the simple reason that there was no place for him to hide in. But you asked for an explanation, and I gave you one.'

Alec snorted again, but with rather less confidence this time. Roger's glib smoothing away of the impossible had been a little unexpected. He tried a new tack.

'Well, what about motive?' he asked. 'You can't have a murder without motive, you know. What on earth could have been the motive for murdering poor old Stanworth?'

'Robbery!' returned Roger promptly. 'That's one of the things that put me on the idea of murder. That safe's been opened, or I'm a Dutchman. You remember what I said about the keys. I shouldn't be surprised if Stanworth kept a large sum of money and other negotiable valuables in there. That's what the murderer was after. And so you'll see, when the safe is opened this afternoon.'

Alec grunted. It was clear that, if not convinced, he was at any rate impressed. Roger was so specious and so obviously sure himself of being on the right track, that even a greater sceptic than Alec might have been forgiven for beginning to doubt the meaning of apparently plain facts.

'Hullo!' said Roger suddenly. 'Isn't that the lunch bell? We'd better nip in and wash. Not a word of this to anyone, of course.'

They rose and began to saunter towards the house. Suddenly Alec stopped and smote his companion on the shoulder.

'Idiots!' he exclaimed. 'Both of us! We'd forgotten all about the confession. At any rate, you can't get away from that.'

'Ah, yes,' said Roger thoughtfully. 'There's that confession, isn't there? But no; I hadn't forgotten that by any means, Alexander.'

chapter nine

Mr Sheringham Sees Visions

They entered the house by the front door, which always stood open whenever a party was in progress. The unspoken thought was in the minds of both that they preferred not to pass through the library. Alec hurried upstairs at once. Roger, noticing that the butler was in the act of sorting the second post and arranging it upon the hall table, lingered to see if there was a letter for him.

The butler, observing his action, shook his head. 'Nothing for you, sir. Very small post, indeed.' He glanced through the letters he still held in his hand. 'Major Jefferson, Miss Shannon, Mrs Plant. No, sir. Nothing else.'

'Thank you, Graves,' said Roger, and followed in Alec's wake.

Lunch was a silent meal, and the atmosphere was not a little constrained. Nobody liked to mention the subject which was uppermost in the minds of all; and to speak of anything else seemed out of place. What little conversation there was concerned only the questions of packing and trains. Mrs Plant, who appeared a little late for the meal but seemed altogether to have regained her mental poise after her strange behaviour in the morning, was to leave a little after five. This would give her time, she explained, to wait for the safe to be opened so that she could recover her jewels. Roger, pondering furiously over the matter-of-fact air with which she made this statement and trying to reconcile it with the conclusions at which he had already arrived regarding her, was forced to admit himself completely at sea again, in this respect at any rate.

And this was not the only thing that perplexed him. Major Jefferson, who had appeared during the earlier part of the morning subdued to the point of gloominess, now wore an air of quiet satisfaction which Roger found extremely difficult to explain. Assuming that Jefferson had been extremely anxious that the police should not be the first persons to open the safe – and that was the only conclusion which Roger could draw from what had already transpired – what could have occurred in the meantime to have raised his spirits to this extent? Visions of duplicate keys and opportunities in the empty library which he himself ought to have been on hand to prevent, flashed, in rapid succession, across Roger's mind. Yet the only possible time in which he had not been either inside the library or overlooking it were the very few minutes while he was washing his hands upstairs before lunch; and it seemed hardly probable that Jefferson would have had the nerve to utilise them in order to carry out what was in effect a minor burglary, and that with the possibility of being interrupted at any minute. It is true that he had come in very late for lunch (several minutes after Mrs Plant, in fact); but Roger could not think this theory in the least degree probable.

Yet the remarkable fact remained that the two persons who appeared to have been most concerned about the safe and its puzzling contents were now not only not in the least concerned at the prospect of its immediate official opening, but actually quietly jubilant. Or so, at any rate, it seemed to the baffled Roger. Taking it all round, Roger was not sorry that lunch was such a quiet meal. He found that he had quite a lot of thinking to do.

In this respect he was no less busy when lunch was over. Alec disappeared directly after the meal, and as Barbara disappeared at the same time, Roger was glad to find one problem at least that did not seem to be beyond the scope of his deductive powers. He solved it with some satisfaction and, by looking at his watch, was able to arrive at the conclusion that he would have at least half an hour to himself before his fellow-sleuth would be ready for the trail again. Somewhat thankfully he betook himself to the friendly cedar once more, and lit his pipe preparatory to embarking upon the most concentrated spell of hard thinking he had ever faced in his life.

For in spite of the confidence he had shown to Alec, Roger was in reality groping entirely in the dark. The suggestion of murder, which he had advanced with such assurance, had appeared to him at the time not a little far-fetched; and the fact that he had put it forward at all was due as much as anything to the overwhelming desire to startle the stolid Alec out of some of his complacency. Several times Roger had found himself on the verge of becoming really exasperated with Alec that morning. He was not usually so slow in the uptake, almost dull, as he had been in this affair; yet just now, when Roger was secretly not a little pleased with himself, all he had done was to throw cold water upon everything. It was a useful check to his own exuberance, no doubt; but Roger could wish that his audience, limited by necessity to so small a number, had been a somewhat more appreciative one.

His thoughts returned to the question of murder. Was it so far-fetched, after all? He had been faintly suspicious even before his discovery of the broken vase and that mysterious second shot. Now he was very much more so. Only suspicious, it is true; there was no room as yet for conviction. But suspicion was very strong.

He tried to picture the scene that might have taken place in the library. Old Stanworth, sitting at his table with, possibly, the French windows open, suddenly surprised by the entrance of some unexpected visitor. The visitor either demands money or attacks at once. Stanworth whips a revolver out of the drawer at his side and fires, missing the intruder but hitting the vase. And then – what?

Presumably the two would close then and fight it out in silence. But there had been no signs of a struggle when they broke in, nothing but that still figure lying so calmly in his chair. Still, did that matter very much? If the unknown could collect those fragments of vase so carefully in order to conceal any trace of his presence, he could presumably clear away any evidence of a struggle. But before that there was that blank wall to be surmounted – how did the struggle end?

Roger closed his eyes and gave his imagination full rein. He saw Stanworth, the revolver still in his hand, swaying backwards and forwards in the grip of his adversary. He saw the latter (a big powerful man, as he pictured him) clasp Stanworth's wrist to prevent him pointing the revolver at himself. There had been a scratch on the dead man's wrist, now he came to think of it; could this be how he had acquired it? He saw the intruder's other hand dart to his pocket and pull out his own revolver. And then – !

Roger slapped his knee in his excitement. Then, of course, the unknown had simply clapped his revolver to Stanworth's forehead and pulled the trigger!

He leant back in his chair and smoked furiously. Yes, if there had been a murder, that must have been how it was committed. And that accounted for three, at any rate, of the puzzling circumstances – the place of the wound, the fact that only one empty shell had been found in Stanworth's revolver although two shots had been fired that night, and the fact of the dead man's grip upon the revolver being properly adjusted. It was only conjecture, of course, but it seemed remarkably convincing conjecture.

Yet was it not more than counterbalanced by the facts that still remained? That the windows and door could be fastened, as they certainly had been, appeared to argue irresistibly that the midnight visitor had left the library while Mr Stanworth was still alive. The confession, signed with his own hand, pointed equally positively to suicide. Could there be any way of explaining these two things so as to bring them into line with the rest? If not, this brilliant theorising must fall to the ground.

Shelving the problem of the visitor's exit for the time being, Roger began to puzzle over that laconically worded document.

During the next quarter of an hour Roger himself might have presented a problem to an acute observer, had there been one about, which, though not very difficult of solution, was nevertheless not entirely without interest. To smoke furiously, with one's pipe in full blast, betokens no small a degree of mental excitement; to sit like a stone image and allow that same pipe to go out in one's mouth is evidence of still greater prepossession; but what are we to say of a man who, after passing through these successive stages, smokes away equally furiously at a perfectly cold pipe under the obvious impression that it is in as full blast as before? And that is what Roger was doing for fully three minutes before he finally jumped suddenly to his feet and hurried off once again to that happy hunting ground of his, the library.

There Alec found him twenty minutes later, when the car had departed irrevocably for the station. A decidedly more cheerful Alec than that of the morning, one might note in passing; and not looking in the least like

66

a young man who has just parted with his lady for a whole month. It is a reasonable assumption that Alec had not been wasting the last half hour.

'Still at it?' he grinned from the doorway. 'I had a sort of idea I should find you here.'

Roger was a-quiver with excitement. He scrambled up from his knees beside the waste-paper basket, into which he had been peering, and flourished a piece of paper in the other's face.

'I'm on the track!' he exclaimed. 'I'm on the track, Alexander, in spite of your miserable sneers. Nobody around, is there?'

Alec shook his head. 'Well? What have you discovered now?' he asked tolerantly.

Roger gripped his arm and drew him towards the writing table. With an eager finger he stubbed at the blotter.

'See that?' he demanded.

Alec bent and scrutinised the blotter attentively. Just in front of Roger's finger were a number of short lines not more than an inch or so long. The ones at the left-hand end were little more than scratches on the surface, not inked at all; those in the middle bore faint traces of ink; while towards the right end the ink was bold and the lines thick and decided. Beyond these were a few circular blots of ink. Apart from these markings, the sheet of white blotting paper, clearly fresh within the last day or two, had scarcely been used.

'Well?' said Roger triumphantly. 'Make anything of it?'

'Nothing in particular,' Alec confessed, straightening up again. 'I should say that somebody had been cleaning his pen on it.'

'In that case,' Roger returned with complacency, 'it would become my painful duty to inform you that you were completely wrong.'

'Why? I don't see it.'

'Then look again. If he had been cleaning his pen, Alexander Watson, the change from ink to the lack of it would surely be from left to right, wouldn't it? Not from right to left?'

'Would it? He might have moved from right to left.'

'It isn't natural. Besides, look at these little strokes. Nearly all of them have a slight curve in the tail towards the right. That means they must have been made from left to right. Guess again.'

'Oh, well, let's try the reverse,' said Alec, nettled into irony. 'He wasn't cleaning his pen at all; he was dirtying it.'

'Meaning that he had dipped it in the ink and was just trying it out? Nearer. But take another look, especially at this left-hand end. Don't you see where the nib has split in the centre to make these two parallel furrows? Well, just observe not only how far apart those furrows are, but also the fact that, though pretty deep, there isn't a sign of a scratch. Now, then, what does all that tell you? There's only one sort of pen that could have made those marks, and the answer to that tells you what the marks are.'

Alec pondered dutifully. 'A fountain pen! And he was trying to make it write.'

'Wonderful! Alec, I can see you're going to be a tremendous help in this little game.'

'Well, I don't see anything to make such a fuss about, even if they were made by a fountain pen. I mean, it doesn't seem to take us any forrader.'

'Oh, doesn't it?' Roger had an excellent though somewhat irritating sense of the dramatic. He paused impressively.

'Well?' asked Alec impatiently. 'You've got something up your sleeve, I know, and you're aching to get it out. Let's have it. What do these wonderful marks of yours show you?'

'Simply that the confession is a fake,' retorted Roger happily. 'And now let's go out in the garden.'

He turned on his heel and walked rapidly out on to the sun-drenched lawn. One must admit that Roger had his annoying moments.

The justly exasperated Alec trotted after him. 'Talk about Sherlock Holmes!' he growled, as he caught him up. 'You're every bit as maddening yourself. Why can't you tell me all about it straight out if you really have discovered something, instead of beating about the bush like this?'

'But I have told you, Alexander,' said Roger, with an air of bland innocence. 'That confession is a fake.'

'But *why?*'

Roger hooked his arm through that of the other and piloted him in the direction of the rose garden.

'I want to stick around here,' he explained, 'so as to see the inspector when he comes up the drive. I'm not going to miss the opening of that safe for anything.'

'Why do you think that confession's a fake?' repeated Alec doggedly.

'That's better, Alexander,' commented Roger approvingly. 'You seem to be showing a little interest in my discoveries at last. You haven't been at all a good Watson up to now, you know. It's your business to be thrilled to the core whenever I announce a farther step forward. You're a rotten thriller, Alec.'

A slight smile appeared on Alec's face. 'You do all the thrilling needed yourself, I fancy. Besides, old Holmes went a bit slower than you. He didn't jump to conclusions all in a minute, and I doubt if ever he was as darned pleased with himself all the time as you are.'

'Don't be harsh with me, Alec,' Roger murmured.

'I admit you haven't done so badly so far,' Alec pursued candidly; 'though when all's said and done most of it's guesswork. But if I grovelled in front of you, as you seem to want, and kept telling you what a dashed fine fellow you are, you'd probably have arrested Jefferson and Mrs Plant by this time, and had Lady Stanworth committed for contempt of court or something.' He paused and considered. 'In fact, what you want, old son,' he concluded weightily, 'is a brake, not a blessed accelerator.'

'I'm sorry,' Roger said with humility. 'I'll remember in future. But if you won't compliment me, at least let me compliment you. You're a jolly good brake.'

'And after that, Detective Sheringham, perhaps you'll kindly tell me how you deduce that the confession is a fake from the fact that old Stanworth's pen wouldn't write.'

Roger's air changed and his face became serious.

'Yes, this really is rather important. It clinches the fact of murder, which was certainly a shot in the dark of mine before. Here's the thing that gives it away.'

He produced from his pocket the piece of paper which he had waved in Alec's face in the library and, unfolding it carefully, handed it to the other. Alec looked at it attentively. It bore numerous irregular folds, as if it had been considerably crumpled, and in the centre, somewhat smudged, were the words 'Victor St—,' culminating in a large blot. The writing was very thickly marked. The right-hand side of the paper was spattered with a veritable shower of blots. Beyond these there was nothing upon its surface.

'Humph!' observed Alec, handing it back. 'Well, what do you make of it?'

'I think it's pretty simple,' Roger said, folding the paper and stowing it carefully away again. 'Stanworth had just filled his fountain pen, or it wouldn't work or something. You know what one does with a fountain pen that doesn't want to write. Make scratches on the nearest piece of paper, and as soon as the ink begins to flow – '

'Sign one's name!' Alec broke in, with the nearest approach to excitement that he had yet shown.

'Precisely! On the blotting pad are the preliminary scratches to bring the ink down the pen. What happens in nine cases out of ten after that? The ink flows too freely and the pen floods. This bit of paper shows that it happened in this case, too. Stanworth was rather an impatient sort of man, don't you think?'

'Yes, I suppose he was. Fairly.'

'Well, the scene's easy enough to reconstruct. He tries the pen out on the blotting pad. As soon as it begins to write he grabs a sheet from the top of that pile of fellow-sheets on his desk (did you notice them, by the way?) and signs his name. Then the pen floods, and he shakes it violently, crumples up the sheet of paper, throws it into the waste-paper basket and takes another. This time the pen, after losing so much ink in blots, is a little faint at first; so he only gets as far as the C in Victor before starting again, just below the last attempt. Then at last it writes all right, and his signature is completed, with the usual flourish. He picks up the piece of paper, crumples it slightly, but not so violently as before, and throws it also into the waste-paper basket. How's that?'

'That all seems feasible enough. What next?'

'Why, the murderer, setting the room to rights afterwards, thinks he'd better have a look in the basket. The first thing he spots is that piece of paper. 'Aha!' he thinks. 'The very thing I wanted to put a finishing touch to the affair!' Smoothes it carefully out, puts it in the typewriter and types those few words above the signature. What could be simpler?'

By Jove, I wonder! It's jolly ingenious.'

Roger's eyes were sparkling. 'Ingenious? Yes; but in its very simplicity. Oh, that's what happened, sure enough. There's plenty of corroboration, when you come to think of it. The way the whole thing's got into the top half of the sheet of paper, for instance. That isn't natural, really, is it? It ought to be in the middle, with the signature about two thirds down. And why isn't it? Because the signature was in the middle already, and the fellow had to work upwards from that.'

'I believe you must be right,' Alec said slowly.

'Well, don't be so grudging about it. Of course I'm right! As a matter of fact, those scratches on the blotting paper gave me the idea as soon as I saw them. I'd been puzzling after a way of getting round that confession. But when I found that second sheet in the waste-paper basket of course the thing was as plain as a pikestaff. That was a bad blunder of his, by the way; not to look through the rest of the basket's contents.'

'Yes,' Alec agreed seriously. 'And supposing the inspector had found it. It might have given him something to think about, mightn't it?'

'It might and it mightn't. Of course from the inspector's point of view there's been nothing to afford the least question as to the plain fact of suicide; except the absence of motive, of course, and that's really nothing, after all. He hasn't had his suspicions aroused more or less by accident, as it were, like we have.'

'We've had the luck, all right,' Alec remarked, possibly in his role of brake.

'Undoubtedly, but we haven't let it lie about untouched,' Roger said complacently. 'In fact, I think we've done very well indeed up to now,' he added candidly. 'I don't see how we could have done more, do you?'

'No, I'm dashed if I do,' said Alec with decision.

'But there's one thing needed to round it off nicely.'

'Oh? What's that?'

'To find the murderer,' Roger replied calmly.

chapter ten

Mrs Plant Is Apprehensive

'Great Scott!' Alec exclaimed, considerably startled. 'Find the murderer?'

Roger seemed pleased with the impression he had made. 'Naturally. What else? It's the logical sequel to what we've already done, isn't it?'

'Yes, I suppose so,' Alec hesitated, 'if you put it like that. But – Well, we seem to be getting on so jolly fast. I mean, it's rather difficult to realise that a murder's been committed at all. It all seems so impossible, you know.'

'That's simply because it's something foreign to your usual experience of life,' Roger said thoughtfully. 'I admit that it is a bit of a shock at first to face the fact that Stanworth was murdered instead of committing suicide. But that's not because there's anything inherently improbable about murder itself. Murder's a common enough event if it comes to that. But it doesn't generally take place among the circle of one's immediate friends; that's the trouble. Anyhow, there's no getting over it in this case. If ever a man was murdered, Stanworth was. And very cleverly murdered, too. I tell you, Alec, it's no ordinary criminal we're after. It's an extraordinarily cool, brainy, and calculating sort of person indeed.'

'Calculating?' Alec repeated. 'Then do you think it was premeditated?'

'Impossible to say, as yet. But I should certainly imagine so. It looks as if it had been very carefully thought out beforehand, doesn't it?'

'There doesn't seem to have been much left to chance,' Alec agreed.

'And look at the deliberation of the fellow. Fancy stopping to collect those bits of vase and cover up the traces of that second shot like that!

He must have some nerve. Yes, it certainly looks more and more as if it was a prearranged thing. I don't say for last night in particular; that may only have been a favourable opportunity which the chap was quick to seize. But I do think that he'd made up his mind to kill Stanworth some time or other.'

'You think it was somebody Stanworth knew, then?'

'Oh, there's not much doubt about that. And somebody he was vastly afraid of, too, I should imagine. Why else should he keep a revolver so handy, if he wasn't expecting something of the kind? Yes, that's the line we ought to go on – see if we can discover whether there was anybody among his acquaintances of whom Stanworth was thoroughly frightened. If we can only find that out, and the name of the person as well, the odds are ten to one that we shall have solved the mystery of the murderer's identity.'

'That sounds reasonable enough,' said Alec with interest. 'Got any theory of how it was done?'

Roger beamed. 'I believe I can tell you exactly how it was done,' he said, not without pride. 'Listen!'

He recounted at some length the results of his after-lunch meditations and explained the reasons upon which his conclusions had been based. It took the two of them several circuits of the rose garden before the recital was completed, and then Roger turned expectantly to his companion.

'You see?' he concluded eagerly. 'That accounts for everything except the facts of the confession and the murderer's escape from the library. Now I've cleared up the confession, and we've only got one difficulty to get over. What do you think of it?'

'Humph!' observed Alec cautiously. He paused, and it was evident that he was thinking deeply.

'Well?' asked Roger impatiently.

'There's one thing I don't quite see,' Alec said slowly. 'According to you the shot that killed Stanworth was fired from the other man's revolver. Then how is it that the bullet they took out of his head fitted the empty shell in his *own* revolver?'

Roger's face fell. 'Hullo!' he exclaimed. 'That never occurred to me.'

'I thought it couldn't have,' said Alec complacently. 'That rather knocks your theory on the head, doesn't it?'

'It's one to you, Watson, certainly,' Roger smiled a little ruefully.

'Ah!' observed Alec deeply. He was evidently not going to spoil the impression he had just made by any rash remarks. Alec was one of those fortunate people who know just when to stop.

'Still, after all,' Roger said slowly, 'that's only a matter of detail, isn't it? My version of how it happened may be quite wrong. But that doesn't affect the main issue, which is that it *was* done.'

'In other words, the fact of murder is definitely established, you think, although you don't know how it was carried out?' Alec asked thoughtfully.

'Precisely.'

'Humph! And do you still think the motive was robbery?'

'I do. And – By Jove!' Roger stopped suddenly in his stride and turned exultantly to his companion. 'That may account for Mrs Plant, too!'

'What about Mrs Plant?'

'Well, didn't you notice her at lunch? She was as cheerful and unconcerned as anything. Rather a change from the very perturbed person we surprised at the safe this morning, wasn't it? And on the face of it you'd have expected her to be still more worried, with the prospect of the opening of the safe this afternoon and the proving of her little story to us to be false. But was she? Not a bit of it. She looked as if she hadn't a trouble in the world. You must have noticed it.'

'Yes, I did, now you come to mention it. I thought she must be acting.'

'Mrs Plant wasn't acting at lunch any more than she was telling the truth to us this morning,' said Roger with conviction. 'And why wasn't she? Because for some mysterious reason or other she had no need to be. In other words, she knew that when the safe was opened this afternoon, everything would be all right as far as she was concerned.'

'How on earth did she know that?'

'I wish I could tell you. But consider. If the safe had been robbed last night, Mrs Plant's jewels would have disappeared with the other valuables, wouldn't they? That is, assuming that they had ever been there. Well, there's her answer to us. "Oh, yes, my jewels *were* there, and that's why I wanted to get at the safe; but they've been stolen with everything else, and that's why they're not there now." See?'

'Yes, but what I want to know is, how did she find out that the safe had been robbed and her story to us would hold water after all?'

'And that's exactly what I want to know, too, my excellent Alec. If we only knew that, we should have advanced a long way to the solution of the mystery. All that we can say definitely is that, some time between our finding her in the library and lunch time, information must have reached her about what happened to the safe last night. It seems to me that Mrs Plant is going to find herself in a very awkward position rather soon.'

'But why do you think Mrs Plant wanted to open the safe this morning, if there's no truth in her tale?'

'Obviously there must have been something inside that she badly wanted to get hold of. Equally obviously she now either has got hold of it, or knows that it's in safe keeping. And then we get back to Jefferson again. He's been going through exactly the same sequence of emotions as Mrs Plant. What do you make of that?'

'Surely you're not suggesting that Jefferson and Mrs Plant are in league together, are you?'

'What other conclusion is there? They're both anxious to get something out of that safe before the police open it, and they're both palpably worried to death over something. Yet at one o'clock they're both smiling away to themselves as if a tremendous load had been taken off their minds. I'm afraid that they're not only in league with each other, but with a mysterious third person as well. How else can you account for their behaviour?'

'Good Lord! You don't mean that they're acting with – with the murderer, do you?'

'It looks to me uncommonly like it,' said Roger gravely. 'After all, he's the only person, so far as we know, who could have enlightened them about the safe.'

'But it's out of the question!' Alec burst out impulsively. 'Jefferson – I don't know anything about him, though I should certainly have set him down as quite a decent fellow and a sahib, even if he is a bit reserved. But Mrs Plant! My dear chap, you're absolutely off the rails there. Of all the obviously straightforward and honest people in the world, I should have said that Mrs Plant was the most. Oh, you *must* be on the wrong tack!'

'I only wish I were,' Roger returned seriously. 'Three hours ago I should have said that the idea of Mrs Plant being mixed up in a murder was not only unthinkable, but ludicrous. I've always thought her a charming woman, and, as you say, absolutely sincere. Certainly not a happy woman (one doesn't know anything about that husband of hers, by the way; he may be a bad egg); in fact, a woman with a good deal of sorrow in her life, I should say. But absolutely as straight as a die. Yet what can one think now? Facts speak louder than opinions. And the facts are only too plain.'

'I don't care,' said Alec obstinately. 'If you're trying to mix Mrs Plant up in this affair, you're making a hopeless mistake, Roger. That's all I've got to say.'

'I hope you're right, Alec,' Roger said dryly. 'By the way, I think I want to have a word with the lady. Oh, I'm not going to tax her with the murder or anything,' he added with a smile, observing the look on Alec's face. 'But I think she said at lunch that she was expecting to leave here this afternoon. Of course that's out of the question. She was the last person to see Stanworth alive, and she'll be wanted to give evidence at the inquest. The inspector must have forgotten to tell her. Let's go and see what she's got to say about it.'

Somewhat unwillingly Alec accompanied Roger on his quest. He did not attempt to make any secret of his distaste for this aspect of his new role. To hunt down a man who deserves no mercy and expects none is one thing; to hunt down a charming lady is very much another.

Mrs Plant was sitting in a garden chair on a shady part of the lawn. There was a book in her lap, but she was staring abstractedly at the grass before her and her thoughts were evidently very far away. Hearing their footsteps she glanced up quickly and greeted the two with her usual quiet, rather sad smile.

'Have you come to tell me that Inspector Mansfield has arrived?' she asked, perfectly naturally.

Roger threw himself casually on the ground just in front of her.

'No, he hasn't come yet,' he replied easily. 'Very hot out here, isn't it?'

'I suppose it is. But the heat doesn't worry me, I'm glad to say. I had enough of it in the Sudan to inure me to anything that this country can produce.'

'You're lucky then. Alec, why on earth don't you lie down and be comfortable? Never stand up when you can sit down instead. By the way, Mrs Plant, I suppose you'll be staying over for the inquest tomorrow, won't you?'

'Oh, no. I shall be off this afternoon, Mr Sheringham.'

Roger glanced up. 'But surely you'll be wanted to give evidence? You were the last person to see him alive, weren't you? In the hall, you know?'

'Oh, I – I don't think I shall be needed, shall I?' Mrs Plant asked apprehensively, paling slightly. 'The inspector didn't – he didn't say anything about it.'

'Perhaps he didn't know then that you were the last person,' said Roger carelessly, but watching her narrowly. 'And afterwards he must have forgotten to warn you; or else he was intending to do so this afternoon. But they're certain to need you, you know.'

It was very clear that this piece of news was highly unwelcome. Mrs Plant's hand was trembling in her lap, and she was biting her lip in an effort to retain her self – control.

'Do you really think so?' she asked, in a voice that she strove desperately to render unconcerned. 'But I haven't got anything of – of any importance to tell, you know.'

'Oh, no, of course not,' Roger said reassuringly. 'It's only a matter of form, you know. You'll just have to repeat what you told the inspector this morning.'

'Will they – Are they likely to ask me any questions, Mr Sheringham?' Mrs Plant asked, with a little laugh.

'Oh, they may ask you one or two, perhaps. Nothing very dreadful.'

'I see. What sort of questions, would you imagine?'

'About Mr Stanworth's manner, probably. Whether he was cheerful, and all that. And of course they'll want to know what he spoke to you about.'

'Oh, that was nothing,' Mrs Plant replied quickly. 'Just about – Oh, nothing of any importance whatever. Er – you will be giving evidence, too, won't you, Mr Sheringham?'

'Yes, unfortunately.'

Only the white knuckles of her clenched hand gave any hint of Mrs Plant's feelings as she asked lightly enough, 'And you're not going to give me away over that absurd panic of mine about my jewels this morning, are you? You promised, didn't you?'

'Of course not!' said Roger easily. 'Wouldn't dream of it!'

'Not even if they ask you?' Mrs Plant persisted, with a nervous little laugh.

'How could they ask me?' Roger smiled. 'Nobody knows anything about it except us three. Besides, I shouldn't think of giving you away.'

'Nor you, Mr Grierson?' she asked, turning to Alec.

Alec flushed slightly. 'Naturally not,' he said awkwardly.

Mrs Plant fumbled with the handkerchief in her hand and surreptitiously wiped her mouth.

'Thank you so much, both of you,' she said in a low voice.

Roger jumped suddenly to his feet.

'Hullo!' he exclaimed, putting an end to a difficult pause. 'Isn't that the inspector just going up to the front door? Let's go in and watch the safe being opened, shall we?'

chapter eleven

Lady Stanworth Exchanges Glances

Leaving Alec to accompany Mrs Plant to the house, Roger hurried on ahead with a muttered excuse. He was anxious not to miss a moment of the highly significant scene which was about to take place. As he reached the hall, Jefferson was in the act of greeting the perspiring inspector.

'I'm sorry you have had all this trouble, Inspector,' he was saying. 'It's too bad on a day like this.'

'It is a bit warm, sir,' the inspector admitted, mopping vigorously.

'I should have thought they might have provided you with a car or something. Hullo, Sheringham. Come to see the safe opened?'

'If the inspector has no objections,' Roger said.

'Me, sir? Not in the least. In fact, I think everybody concerned ought to be present. Not that I really expect to find anything particularly important, but you never know, do you?'

'Never,' said Roger gravely.

'Well, Lady Stanworth will be down in a minute, no doubt,' Jefferson remarked; 'and then we can see to it. You had no difficulty in getting the combination, Inspector?'

'None at all, sir. It was only a question of ringing up the makers. Whew! It *is* hot!'

Roger had been watching Jefferson carefully. There was no doubt that, whatever his feelings about the opening of the safe had been in the morning, he was now quite unperturbed. Roger was more convinced than ever that something of the first importance must have occurred to effect this radical change.

A slow tread overhead caused him to look up. Lady Stanworth was descending the stairs.

'Ah, here is Lady Stanworth,' the inspector observed, with a slight bow.

Lady Stanworth inclined her head coldly. 'You wish me to be present at this formality, Inspector?' she asked distantly.

The inspector looked slightly taken aback.

'Well, I think it would be better, my lady,' he replied, a trifle deprecatingly. 'As the only surviving relative of the deceased's, you know. But of course if you have any – '

'I was not a relative of Mr Stanworth's,' Lady Stanworth interrupted in the same tone. 'I thought I had made that clear to you this morning. He was my brother-in-law.'

'Quite so, quite so,' said the inspector apologetically. 'I should perhaps have said *connection*. It is usual for the nearest connection to be present when – '

'I ought to have warned you, perhaps, Lady Stanworth,' Jefferson put in evenly. 'But, unfortunately, I have not seen you to do so since before lunch; and I did not care to take the responsibility of disturbing you. The opening of the safe is, after all, a mere formality; and both the inspector and myself have no doubt that nothing of any importance will be found. Nothing whatever.'

Lady Stanworth looked hard at the last speaker for a moment, and when she spoke again the former coldness of her tone had completely disappeared.

'Of course I will come if you think it better, Inspector,' she said graciously. 'There is really no reason whatever why I should not do so.' And without more ado she led the way towards the library.

Roger brought up the rear of the little party. He was thinking furiously. He had watched the little exchange that had just taken place with feelings almost of bewilderment. It was so unlike Lady Stanworth to go out of her way to snub the poor inspector in that highly unnecessary manner. Why had she done so? And why had she been so very much on the high horse with regard to the opening of the safe? It seemed almost as if she had been really apprehensive of something, and had adopted this attitude in order to cloak her actual feelings. But if that were the case, what earthly reason could she have for apprehension? Roger asked himself despairingly.

Yet her sudden change of manner was no less remarkable. As soon as Jefferson had spoken, she had become as gracious as ever and all objections had been abruptly dropped. What was it Jefferson had said? Something about nothing of importance being found in the safe. Ah, yes. 'Both the inspector and myself have no doubt that nothing of importance will be found.' And myself! Now he came to think of it, Jefferson had certainly stressed those two words a little. Could it be that he had conveyed some kind of warning to her? Information of some sort? And if so, what? Obviously the same information that he and Mrs Plant had received during the morning. Was it possible then that Lady Stanworth herself could be in league with Mrs Plant and Jefferson? Surely this was making things altogether too complicated. Yet he could take his oath that *something* had passed between those two before Lady Stanworth finally descended the last few stairs so amicably.

Thus the gist of the thoughts that whirled confusedly through Roger's brain during the few seconds occupied by the journey to the library. As he passed the threshold he raised his eyebrows in mock despair and, shelving this fresh problem for the time being, prepared to give all his attention to present events.

Mrs Plant and Alec were already in the library; the former perfectly cool and collected, the latter, to Roger's eyes at any rate, somewhat ill at ease. It was clear, Roger reflected, with some uneasiness, that Alec did not at all like the highly ambiguous position in which he stood with regard to that lady. What would he say when he heard the possibility that his hostess also might not be unconcerned with this dark and mysterious business? It would be just like Alec to throw up the whole affair and insist on all cards being laid upon the table; and that would have broken Roger's heart just at the moment.

Inspector Mansfield was regrettably lacking in an appreciation of dramatic effects. He did not gaze around him from beneath lowered brows. He did not mutter to himself so that everyone could strain forward to catch his ominous words. He did not even make a speech.

All he did was to observe cheerfully, 'Well, let's get this business over,' and casually open the safe. He could not have made less fuss had it been a tin of sardines.

But in spite of the inspector's lamentable behaviour, drama was not altogether lacking. As the heavy door swung open, there was an involuntary catching of breath and heads were craned anxiously forward. Roger, watching the faces of the others instead of the centre of attraction, noted quickly that a flicker of anxiety flashed across the countenances of both Mrs Plant and Jefferson. 'Neither of 'em have seen inside, then,' he thought. 'Their information came from a third person. That's certain, anyway.'

But it was Lady Stanworth who held his attention most closely. Thinking herself unobserved for the moment, she had not troubled to hide her feelings. She was standing a little behind the others, peering between their heads. Her breath was coming quickly, and her bosom rising and falling almost tumultuously; her face was quite white. For a few seconds Roger thought she was going to faint. Then, as if she was reassured, the colour came back into her face and she sighed ever so softly.

'Well, Inspector?' she asked in normal tones. 'What is there?'

The inspector was rapidly scrutinising the contents.

'As I expected,' he replied, a trifle disappointedly. 'Nothing of any importance as far as I'm concerned, my lady.' He glanced quickly through a bundle of papers that he held in his hands. 'Share certificates; business documents; contracts; more share certificates.'

He replaced the bundle in the safe and took out a cash-box.

'Whew!' he whistled softly, as he opened it. 'Mr Stanworth kept plenty of ready money on hand, didn't he?'

Roger pricked up his ears and followed the direction of the inspector's gaze. Lying loosely at the bottom of the cash-box was a thick wad of banknotes. The inspector picked it out and flicked them over.

'Upwards of four thousand pounds, I should say,' he remarked with fitting awe. 'That doesn't look as if he was in financial difficulties, does it?'

'I told you I thought it most unlikely,' Jefferson said shortly.

Mrs Plant stooped and looked into the safe.

'Oh, there's my jewel-box,' she said, in tones of relief. 'On the bottom shelf.'

The inspector bent down and extracted a small case of green leather. 'This, madam?' he asked. 'You said this is yours?'

'Yes. I gave them to him to lock up for me yesterday morning. I never like to leave them lying about in my room if I can help it, you know.'

The inspector pressed the catch and the lid of the case flew open. A necklace, a bracelet or two, and a few rings were visible inside; pleasant little trinkets, but not of any remarkable value.

Roger exchanged glances with Alec. In the eyes of the latter there was a scarcely concealed derision which Roger found peculiarly difficult to bear in silence. If ever a look said, 'I told you so!' Alec's did at that moment.

'I suppose Lady Stanworth can identify these as yours, madam,' the inspector was saying. 'Purely as a matter of form,' he added, half apologetically.

'Oh, yes,' said Mrs Plant easily, picking the necklace and a few other things out of the case. 'You've seen me wearing these, haven't you, Lady Stanworth?'

There was a perceptible pause before Lady Stanworth answered; and it seemed to Roger that she was looking at Mrs Plant in rather an odd way. Then she said, naturally enough:

'Of course. And I remember the case, too. Yes, these belong to Mrs Plant, Inspector.'

'Then we may as well hand them over to her at once,' said the inspector, and Lady Stanworth nodded approvingly.

'Is that all you require, Inspector?' Jefferson asked.

'Yes, sir; quite. And I've had my journey for nothing, I'm afraid. Still, we have to go into everything, as you know.'

'Oh, naturally,' Jefferson murmured, turning away from the safe.

'And now I must get back and finish my report,' the inspector continued. 'The coroner will communicate with you this afternoon as soon as I've seen him again.'

'Oh, by the way, Inspector,' Mrs Plant put in, 'Mr Sheringham was telling me that I might be wanted to attend the inquest. Is that necessary?'

'I'm afraid so, madam. You were the last person to see Mr Stanworth alive.'

'Yes, but my – my evidence wouldn't be of the least importance, would it? The few words I had with him about those roses can't throw any light on the matter at all.'

'I'm very sorry, madam,' the inspector murmured, 'but in these cases the last person to see the deceased alive is invariably called, whether the evidence appears to be of any importance or not.'

'Oh! Then I must take it as quite certain that I shall have to attend?' Mrs Plant asked disappointedly.

'Quite, madam,' the inspector returned firmly, moving towards the door.

Roger hooked his arm through that of Alec and drew him out through the French windows.

'Well?' asked the latter with an undisguised grin. 'Still as sure as ever that those jewels weren't in the safe, Sherlock Sheringham?'

'Yes. I've been expecting a little subtle ridicule from you, Alec,' Roger said with mock humility. 'No doubt I deserve it.'

'I'm glad you're beginning to realise that,' retorted Alec pleasantly.

'Yes, for drawing the only possible conclusions from a given set of facts. Well, I suppose we shall have to go back to the beginning again, and start to draw some impossible ones instead.'

'Oh, Lord!' Alec groaned.

'But seriously, Alec,' said Roger with a change of tone, 'things are going very curiously. Those jewels ought not to have been in the safe at all, you know. Nor the money either, for that matter. It's all wrong.'

'Most annoying when things break rules like that, isn't it? Well, I suppose you'll allow now that Mrs Plant *was* speaking the truth this morning, after all.'

'I suppose I shall have to,' said Roger reluctantly. 'For the present, at any rate. But it's very, very extraordinary.'

'That Mrs Plant should have been speaking the truth? It seemed to me far more extraordinary that she should have been lying, as you were so jolly sure.'

'All right, Alec. Don't get rattled. No, I wasn't meaning that exactly. But that she should have been so remarkably agitated about those jewels of hers, as if she thought that somebody was going to steal them! And then that yarn of hers that she thought the police would take them and she wouldn't get them back. No, say what you like, Alec, it *is* extraordinary.'

'Women are extraordinary,' said Alec wisely.

'Humph! Certainly Mrs Plant is.'

'Well, at any rate, she's exonerated, I take it.'

'No, that she isn't,' said Roger with decision. 'That lady isn't free from suspicion yet by any means. After all, the matter of the jewels is only one of several curious circumstances. But look here, Alec; another remarkable thing has cropped up since I saw you last. I'm going to tell you, because I promised I'd share anything new with you at the very beginning. But I won't unless you'll promise to take it quite calmly, and not smite me with that great ham-fist of yours or throw yourself despairingly into a rose bush or anything. You know, you're a very difficult sort of person to work with on this sort of job, Alec.'

'Fire away!' Alec grunted. 'What's happened now?'

'You won't like it, but I can't help that. After all, I'm only telling you facts, not theories; and there's no getting away from them, however unwelcome they may be. It's about Lady Stanworth this time. Listen.'

And Roger embarked upon a voluble recital of The Strange Behaviour of Lady Stanworth.

chapter twelve

Hidden Chambers
and What-nots

'Oh!' said Alec carefully, when Roger had finished.

'You see? I carefully refrain from drawing any deduction. Aloud, at any rate. All I say is that it *looks* funny.'

'Lots of things seem to look funny to you, Roger,' Alec remarked tolerantly.

'About this case?' Roger retorted. 'You're quite right. Lots of things do. But let's put all these side issues behind us for the moment. There's one thing that I'm simply aching to set about.'

'Only one?' said Alec nastily. 'And what's that?'

'To find out how the murderer got away from the library last night. If we can solve that little problem, we've cleared up the last remaining difficulty as far as the committing of the murder goes.'

'Yes, I suppose we have,' Alec replied thoughtfully. 'But it seems to me that we've rather got our work cut out there, haven't we? I mean, it's pretty well impossible for a man to get out of a room like that and leave everything locked up behind him, you know.'

'On the contrary, that's just what it isn't; because he did it. And it's up to us to find out how.'

'Got any ideas about it?' Alec asked with interest.

'Not a one! At least, I can think of one very obvious way. We'll test that first, at any rate. The library's empty now, and I expect Jefferson will be pretty busy for the rest of the afternoon. We can sleuth away in peace.'

They turned their steps in the direction of the library.

'And what is the obvious solution to the library mystery?' Alec asked. 'I'm blessed if I can see one.'

Roger looked at him curiously. 'Can't you *really*?' he said.

'No, I'm dashed if I can.'

'Well – what about a secret door, then?'

'Oh!' Alec observed blankly. 'Yes, I didn't seem to think of that.'

'It's the only obvious way. And it's not outside the possibilities by any means in an old house like this. Especially in the library, which hasn't been pulled about so much as some of the other rooms.'

'That's true enough,' said Alec, quite excitedly. 'Roger, old sleuth, I really do believe you're on the track of something at last.'

'Thanks,' Roger returned dryly. 'I've been waiting for a remark like that for some hours.'

'Yes, but this really is interesting. Secret passages and – and hidden chambers and what-nots. Jolly romantic, and all that. I'm all in favour of unearthing it.'

'Well, here we are, and the scent ought to be strong. Let's get down to it.'

'What shall we do?' asked Alec, staring curiously round the walls as if he expected the secret door to fly suddenly open if he looked hard enough.

'Well, first of all, I think we'd better examine this panelling. Now, let's see; this wall where the fireplace is backs on to the drawing room, doesn't it? And this one behind the safe on to the storeroom and a little bit of the hall. So that if there is a door or anything, the probability is that it will be in one of those two walls; it's not likely to be in either of the outside ones. Well, I tell you what we'd better do. You examine the panelling in here, and I'll scout round on the other side of the walls and see if I can spot anything there.'

'Right-ho,' said Alec, beginning to scrutinise the fireplace wall with great earnestness.

Roger made his way out into the hall and thence to the drawing room. The dividing wall between that room and the library was covered with paper, and one or two china cabinets stood against it. After a cursory peep or two behind these, Roger mentally wrote that wall off, at any rate, as blameless. The storeroom, similarly, was so full up with trunks and lumber as to be out of the question.

Roger returned to the library, to find Alec industriously tapping panels.

'I say,' said the latter, 'several of these panels sound hollow.'

'Well, there's no way through either into the drawing room or the storeroom, I'm convinced,' Roger remarked, closing the door behind him. 'So that I don't think it's much use trying those walls haphazard.'

Alec paused. 'What about a secret chamber, though? That wouldn't necessarily need a way straight through. It might come out anywhere.'

'I thought of that. But the walls aren't thick enough. They're only about eighteen inches through. No, let's go and have a look at it from the outside. There might possibly be some way into the garden.'

They went out through the open windows and contemplated the red-brick walls attentively.

'Doesn't look very hopeful, does it?' said Alec.

'I'm afraid not,' Roger admitted. 'No, I fear that the secret-door theory falls to the ground. I thought it would somehow.'

'Oh? Why?'

'Well, this house doesn't belong to the Stanworths, you see, and they've only been here a month or so. I don't suppose they'd know anything about secret passages, even if there were any.'

'No, but the other fellow might.'

'The murderer? It isn't likely, is it?'

'I hate giving up the idea,' said Alec reluctantly. 'After all, it's the only possible explanation of his disappearance, as far as I can see.'

Roger suddenly smote his hands together. 'By Jove! There's one hope left. Idiot not to have thought of it before! The fireplace!'

'The fireplace?'

'Of course! That's where most of these old houses have their secret hiding places. It will be there if anywhere.'

He hurried back into the library, Alec close at his heels. There he stopped suddenly short.

'Oh, Lord, I was forgetting that the blessed place had been bricked in so very thoroughly.' He gazed at the modern intrusion without enthusiasm. 'That's hopeless, I'm afraid.'

Alec looked thoughtfully round the room. 'I don't think we've examined these walls enough, you know,' he remarked hopefully. 'There's plenty of scope in this panelling really.'

Roger shook his head. 'It's just possible, but I'm very much afraid that − ' He caught a sudden and violent frown from Alec, and broke off in mid-sentence. The door was opening softly.

The next moment Jefferson entered.

'Oh, hullo, you two,' he said. 'I've been looking for you. Can you manage to look after yourselves for the afternoon?

Lady Stanworth and Mrs Plant are in their rooms. Both naturally rather upset. And I've got to go into the town to see about a few things.'

'Oh, we'll be all right,' Roger said easily. 'Please don't bother about us.'

Jefferson glanced round.

'Looking for a book?' he asked.

'No,' said Roger quickly. 'As a matter of fact, I was studying this overmantel. I'm rather interested in that sort of thing − carving, and panelling, and old houses. This is really rather a wonderful room. What's the date, do you know? Early Jacobean, I should say.'

'Somewhere about that,' Jefferson said indifferently. 'I don't know the actual date, I'm afraid.'

'Very interesting period,' Roger commented. 'And there's usually a priest-hole or something like that in houses built at that time. Anything of the sort here? There ought to be, you know.'

'Can't say, I'm afraid,' Jefferson replied, a little impatiently. 'Never heard of one, at any rate. Well, I must be getting along.'

As the door closed behind him, Roger turned to Alec.

'I didn't expect anything, but I thought I might as well try it. He didn't give anything away, though, whether he knew or not. On the whole, I should say that he didn't know.'

'Why?'

'He was far too off-hand to be lying. If he wanted to put us off, he'd have elaborated somewhat, I fancy. Well, if we can't find our secret door, we must try other means of providing an exit for our man. That leaves us with one door and three windows. We'll try the door first.'

The door proved to be a massive piece of wood, with a large and efficient lock. Except where the socket in the lintel had been torn away in the efforts to force an entrance, it was still undamaged.

'Well, that's out of the question, at any rate,' Roger said with decision. 'I don't see how anybody could possibly have got out through that and left it locked on the inside, with the key still in the lock. It might have been done with a pair of pliers, if the end of the key projected beyond the lock on the other side. But it doesn't; so that's out of the question. French windows next.'

These were of the ordinary pattern, with a handle which shot a bolt simultaneously at the top and bottom. In addition there were small brass bolts at the bottom and top, both of which had been fastened when the window was opened that morning.

'It looks out of the question to me,' Roger muttered. 'It *is* out of the question. Even if he had been able to turn the handle (which he couldn't possibly have done), he couldn't have shot the bolts as well.'

'I'm blessed if he could,' said Alec with conviction.

Roger turned away.

'Then that leaves these two windows. I don't see how anyone could have left this little lattice one closed behind him. What about the sash one? That looks more hopeful.'

He climbed up on the window seat and examined the fastening attentively.

'Any luck?' asked Alec.

Roger stepped heavily on to the floor again. 'I regret to have to confess myself baffled,' he said disappointedly. 'There's an anti-burglar fitting on that window which would absolutely prevent the thing being fastened from the outside. I'm beginning to think the fellow must have been a wizard in a small way.'

'It seems to me,' said Alec weightily, 'that if the chap couldn't have got out, as we appear to have proved, then he could never have been in here at all. In other words, he doesn't exist, and old Stanworth did commit suicide, after all.'

'But I tell you that Stanworth *can't* have committed suicide,' said Roger petulantly. 'There's far too much evidence against it.'

Alec threw himself into a chair. 'Is there, though?' he asked argumentatively. 'As you put it, it's certainly consistent with murder. But it's equally consistent with suicide. Aren't you rather losing sight of that in your anxiety to make a murder of it? Besides, don't forget that your motive has fallen to the ground since the safe was opened. There wasn't a robbery here last night, after all.'

Roger was roaming restlessly about the room. At Alec's last words he paused in his stride and looked at his companion with some irritation.

'Oh, don't be childish, Alec,' he said sharply. 'Money and jewels aren't the only things that can be robbed. The motive still holds perfectly good if we've got to have a motive. It was robbery of something else; that's all. But why stick to robbery? Make it revenge, hatred, self-protection, anything you like, but take it from me that Stanworth *was* murdered. The evidence is *not* equally consistent with suicide. Think it over for yourself and you'll see; I can't bother to go through it all again. And if we can't find the way the chap got out, that's because we're a pair of idiots and can't see what must be lying under our noses, that's all.' And he resumed his stride again.

'Humph!' said Alec incredulously.

'Door, window, window, window,' Roger muttered to himself. 'It must be one of those four. There's simply no other way.'

He wandered impatiently from one to the other, trying desperately to put himself in the place of the criminal. What *would* he have done?

With some ceremony Alec filled and lighted his pipe. When it was in full blast he leaned back in his chair and allowed his eyes to rest approvingly on the cool greens of the gardens outside.

'Life's too short,' he remarked lazily. 'If it really was a clear case of murder, I'd be on the trail as strenuously as anyone. But really, old man, when you come to consider – calmly and sanely, I mean – how extraordinarily little you've got to go on and how you're twisting the most ordinary things, why I think even you will admit in a few weeks' time that when all's said and done we – '

'Alec!'

Something in Roger's tone caused Alec to turn round in his chair and look at him. He was leaning out of the lattice window, apparently intent on the garden outside.

'Well?' said Alec tolerantly. 'What is it now?'

'If you come here, Alec,' said Roger, very gently, 'I'll show you how the murderer got away last night.'

chapter thirteen

Mr Sheringham Investigates a Footprint

'Show me *what?*' Alec exclaimed, bounding out of his chair.

'How the murderer escaped,' Roger repeated, turning and smiling happily at his dumb-founded accomplice. 'It's extraordinarily simple, re-ally. That's why we never spotted it. Have you ever noticed, Alec, that it's always the simple things of life – plans, inventions, what you like – that are the most effective? Take, for instance – '

Alec seized his too voluble friend by the shoulder and shook him violently.

'*How* did the chap escape?' he demanded.

Roger pointed to the window through which he had been leaning.

'There!' he said simply.

'Yes, but how do you know?' cried the exasperated Alec.

'Oh, is that what you meant? Come, friend Alec.' Roger took his fellow-sleuth by the arm and pointed triumphantly to the window-sill. On the surface of the white paint were a few faint scratches. 'You see those? Now look at that!' And he indicated something on the flower bed beneath. 'I said it must be lying under our noses all the time,' he added complacently.

Alec leaned out of the window and looked at the bed. Just below the window was an unmistakable footprint, the toe pointing towards the window.

'You said *escaped*, didn't you?' he asked, withdrawing his head.

'I did, Alexander.'

'Well, I'm sorry to disappoint you and all that,' said Alec, in a tone that curiously belied his words, 'but nobody escaped this way. Someone got in. If you look again, carefully this time, you'll see that the toe is pointing towards the window; not the heel. That means that somebody stepped from the ground to the window-ledge, not vice versa.'

'Alec, you are on your day today, aren't you?' said Roger admiringly. 'Precisely the same thought occurred to myself at a first glance. Then, looking carefully, as you so kindly suggest, I noticed that the indentation of the heel is very much deeper than that of the toe, indicating that somebody stepped backwards from the window to the ground, after thoughtfully closing the window behind him. If he'd been stepping up, the toe would be deeper than the heel, as a moment's thought will show you, won't it?'

'Oh!' said the crestfallen Alec.

'Sorry to have to score off you in that blatant Sherlockian way,' Roger continued more kindly, 'but you did ask for it, you know. No, but seriously, Alec, this is most extraordinarily important. It clears up the last difficulty about murder.'

'But how did he close the window behind him?' asked Alec, still half incredulous.

'Oh! That's the neatest thing of all. And delightfully simple, although it took me a minute or two to discover it after I'd seen the footprint. Look! You see this handle, the ordinary type for this sort of window. It consists of an arm that fits into the lock and a heavy handle set at right angles to it, the whole moving on a central pivot; the weight of the handle end keeps the other end in position. Well, watch!'

Carefully arranging the handle so that the heavy end was balanced exactly above the pivot, Roger pushed the window sharply back into its frame. Immediately the handle was dislodged by the jar, and, with a little click, the fastener fell into place in its socket, the weight of the falling handle driving it well home.

'Well, I'm dashed!' Alec said.

'Neat, isn't it?' Roger said proudly. 'He stood on the sill outside, you see, and pulled it to behind him, having fixed the handle in position before he got out. I suppose it's a trick you could play with any lattice window, though I've never come across it before.'

'That's one to you, all right,' said the humbled Alec. 'I take back quite a lot of the unkind things I've said to you.'

'Oh, don't trouble to apologise,' Roger said magnanimously. 'Though I did warn you that I should turn out to be right in the end, you remember. Well, I don't think you'll trouble to dispute the fact of murder any more, will you?'

'Don't rub it in,' Alec protested. 'I did it for the best, like the doctor in the poem. Well, what's the next move?'

'Let's go out and have a look at that footprint at close range, shall we?' Roger suggested. 'There might be some others, too. Footprints! We *are* getting professional, aren't we?'

On a more careful inspection the footprint fully bore out Roger's contention that it must have been made by a man stepping backward from the sill. The heel end was nearly an inch and a half deep; the toe scarcely half an inch. The edges were slightly blurred where the earth had crumbled, but the mark was clearly that of a large foot.

'At least a ten boot,' Roger said, stooping over it. 'Possibly eleven. This may be very useful indeed, Alec.'

'It's a bit of luck, certainly,' Alec agreed.

Roger straightened up and began to search among the plants near the edge of the bed. After a moment he dropped on his knees on the grass border.

'Look!' he exclaimed excitedly. 'Here's another!'

He parted two little shrubs and peered between them. Alec saw another footprint, not so deep as the last, but quite plainly marked in the dry earth. The toe of this one was also pointing towards the window.

'Same fellow?' he asked, bending over it.

'Yes,' Roger replied, examining the print intently. 'The other boot. Let's see, this is well over a yard from the last one, isn't it? He must have stepped back on to the path in two big strides.' He rose to his feet and dusted the knees of his trousers. 'It's a pity we can't track him any farther,' he added disappointedly.

'Can you do anything more with these?' Alec asked with interest.

'I don't know. We ought to take accurate measurements of them some time, I suppose. Oh, and there's something else I should very much like to do.'

95

'What's that?'

'Get hold of a specimen boot from every male person in the house and grounds and fit them into these prints,' Roger exclaimed, raising his voice slightly in his excitement. 'Yes, that's what we ought to do if we possibly can.'

Alec was pondering.

'But look here, wouldn't you say that these footprints meant that the fellow was someone outside the house? They show him getting away from the place after Stanworth had been killed, don't they? If the chap had been someone inside the house, why should he have troubled to get out so elaborately through the window, when all he'd got to do was to walk out by the door? After all the other things he'd done to make it look like suicide, it wouldn't really be necessary to leave the door locked on the inside, would it?'

'You mean we're not likely to find a boot in the house to correspond with these prints?'

'Not if the chap were someone from outside, no. What do you think?'

'Oh, yes, I agree. I think in all probability it was someone not belonging to the household. You're quite right about the existence of these footprints all pointing to that conclusion. But we don't actually *know*, do we? And I believe in eliminating all possibilities, however remote. If we can get a chance to try everyone's boots out and they don't fit, then we know quite definitely that everybody in this house is free from suspicion of committing the crime itself; though not from suspicion of other things, by the way.'

'What other things?' Alec asked interestedly.

'Being an accessory after the fact. After, certainly; and not improbably before, as well, some of them. It seems to me, Alec,' Roger added pathetically, 'that three quarters of this household seem to be accessories after the fact! It isn't fair.'

'Humph!' said Alec. This was trespassing upon ground which he had no wish to cover. He felt thankful that at any rate Barbara Shannon's mysterious behaviour had not come to Roger's ears. What would the latter have said had he heard of that? Accessory after the fact seemed mild in comparison.

'Hullo! What's up?' he asked, suddenly catching sight of Roger. That gentleman was listening intently, his head on one side. At Alec's words he held up his finger warningly.

'Thought I heard someone in the library!' he whispered. 'You creep up to the lattice window and look through. I'll try the French ones. Carefully!'

Enjoying himself thoroughly, he made his way stealthily to the side of the French windows and peeped cautiously round them. He had his reward. The library door was closing softly.

He hurried back to Alec. 'Did you see?' he asked, in a voice thick with suppressed excitement. 'Did you see?'

Alec nodded. 'Somebody was going out of the library,' he said.

'Yes, but did you see who it was, man?'

Alec shook his head. 'No, I'm afraid I didn't. Got here too late.'

The two looked at each other in silence.

'The question is, were we overheard?' Roger said at last.

'Good Lord!' Alec exclaimed in dismay. 'Do you think we were?'

'Impossible to say. I hope to goodness we weren't, though. It would rather give things away, wouldn't it?'

'Hopelessly!' said Alec with fervour.

Roger looked at him curiously. 'Why, Alexander, you're actually getting quite keen on the chase at last!'

'It's – it is rather exciting,' Alec confessed, almost apologetically.

'That's the spirit. Well, come off that bed and let's get farther away from the house to discuss what's to be done next. It's not safe to talk near these windows, evidently. Hullo, you've made rather a mess of the bed. Steady! Don't step on our two particular prints.'

Alec glanced ruefully at the bed, which was now embellished with several extra footprints.

'I'd better smooth mine out,' he said hastily. 'They look a bit suspicious, all round that window, don't they? Anyone can see that we've been mucking about here.'

'Yes, do,' Roger said approvingly. 'But hurry up, and for goodness' sake, don't let anybody see you. That would be worse still.'

'And now, Sherlock Sheringham,' said Alec, when they had gained the security of the lawn, 'what do you propose? Isn't it time you disguised yourself, or something? I'm sure the best detectives always do that at about this stage of the proceedings.'

'Don't be ribald, friend Alec,' Roger said reprovingly. 'This is a very serious business, and we're getting along with it very nicely. I think our next move is fairly clear, isn't it? We embark on the quest of the Mysterious Stranger.'

'What mysterious stranger?'

'I mean, we make some inquiries round about as to whether any stranger was seen near the place last night. The lodge, the station, the village, and the rest of it.'

'That seems a sound scheme.'

'Yes, but before we start there's just one other thing I want to do. You saw how productive the contents of the waste-paper basket were. I should like to have a look at yesterday's as well.'

'Haven't they been destroyed?'

'No, I don't think so. I made some inquiries while you were otherwise engaged just now, saying that I had thrown away a letter I meant to keep, and as far as I can make out the contents of all the waste-paper baskets are emptied on to an ash pit at the back of the house, where they lie till William sees fit to use them up in a bonfire. I want to have a peep at that ash pit before we start. Not that I really expect to find anything, but you never know.'

'How do we get there?'

'We'll go round the front of the house; it's somewhere on the farther side, I think. We'd better get a move on; we've got no time to waste.'

'I'm game,' said Alec, quite enthusiastically.

They set off.

In front of the house the car was standing, the chauffeur lounging negligently at the wheel as if he had been there some time.

Roger whistled softly.

'Hullo, hullo, hul-*lo!*' he said softly. 'What's this?'

'It's the car,' replied the ever literal Alec.

'I said you'd make a great detective one day, if you ever took it up seriously, Alec. No, you goop! What's the car doing here? Who's it waiting for?'

'Better ask the chauffeur, I should think,' said Alec, quite unruffled.

'I will.'

Alec slapped his pockets.

'Dash it all! I've left my pipe somewhere. In the library, I think. I'll run back for it while you're speaking to the chauffeur; that'll give you a chance to dawdle. Won't be a minute.'

He jog-trotted round the angle of the house, and Roger sauntered towards the chauffeur.

When Alec reappeared, pipe in mouth, two or three minutes later, Roger was waiting for him near the car. There was a look of mingled apprehension and triumph on his face.

'Ah, here you are!' he exclaimed in a loud voice. 'Well, we'd better be off if we want anything like a decent long walk before tea.'

Alec opened his mouth to speak, but caught a warning look and was silent. Roger took his arm and drew him at a rapid pace down the drive. It was not till they had turned a corner and the house was securely hidden from view that he spoke again.

'In here,' he observed briskly, and plunged into the thick bushes which bordered the drive on either side.

In some bewilderment Alec followed. 'What's the idea?' he asked, as he rejoined his companion.

'A little game of hide-and-seek. You heard what I fog-horned to you just now? That was for the benefit of the chauffeur; so that just in case anybody were to ask him what Messrs Grierson and Sheringham are up to this afternoon, he has his answer pat. Now I want to see just how long it is after the disappearance of the two said gentlemen that that car leaves its anchorage. You see, the chauffeur told me that he is waiting to take Jefferson into Elchester, Alec.'

'I expect that's right,' Alec replied intelligently. 'Jefferson said he'd got to go in, you remember.'

'He's been waiting nearly half an hour, Alec.'

'Has he? Yes, probably he has. It must be getting on for that since Jefferson came into the library.'

'Therefore Jefferson intended to go into Elchester half an hour ago, Alec. And he didn't go, Alec. And he's been in the house all that time instead, Alec. And somebody whom we couldn't see came into the library and went away very quietly indeed, Alec. And can you put two and two together, Alec?'

'Do you mean that – that it was Jefferson who came into the library that time?'

'Amazing!' observed Roger admiringly. 'I can't think how the man does it. It must be something to do with wireless. Yes, Alec; you're quite right. I most certainly do think it was Jefferson who came into the library that time. But don't you see the other significance? Why didn't he go into Elchester half an hour ago? He was surely quite ready when he came and told us. Was it because I somehow roused his suspicions, asking him about priest-holes and things, and he stayed behind to spy on us and find out what we were up to?'

'The Lord knows!' said Alec helplessly.

'Well, it looks like it, doesn't it? It looks as if Jefferson is getting suspicious. Uncommonly suspicious. I don't like it. Things are going to get awkward if they get wind of our little game. We shan't be able to investigate in peace any longer.'

'Dashed awkward,' Alec agreed feelingly.

'Hush!' Roger crouched down hastily behind a bush, and Alec followed suit. As they did so, there came the noise of an approaching car, and the big blue Sunbeam swept past them and down the drive.

Roger glanced at his watch.

'Humph! Started four minutes after we did. It all fits in, doesn't it? But there's one thing that really is worrying me badly.'

'What's that?'

They scrambled through the undergrowth and headed for the house once more. Roger turned impressively to Alec.

'Did he or did he not hear what we were saying outside that window? And if he did, how much?'

chapter fourteen

Dirty Work at the Ash Pit

The ash pit proved easy to locate. It lay among some outhouses and was surrounded on three sides by mellow old red-brick walls, the space within which was filled with a depressed-looking mass of rotting vegetable matter, old paper, and tins. The smell that hung heavily about it was not a nice one.

'Have we got to search that?' Alec asked, eyeing the view with considerable disfavour.

'We have,' Roger returned, and plunged happily into the smell. 'Can't expect to get through a job like ours without a certain amount of dirty work, you know.'

'Personally, I prefer my dirty work at the crossroads,' Alec murmured, following his intrepid leader with the greatest reluctance. 'They're cleaner. Dirty work at the ash pit doesn't seem to appeal to me in the least.' He began gingerly to handle the cleanest pieces of paper he could see, which happened to be old newspapers.

Roger was rooting contentedly among a heap of scraps and shreds in the middle. 'These on the top seem to be yesterday's collection all right,' he announced. 'Yes, here's the envelope from a letter of mine that came by the first post. Hum! Nothing in this lot, as far as I can see.'

'What exactly are we looking for?' Alec asked after a short pause, glancing with some interest at the county cricket page of a newspaper three weeks old.

'What am *I* looking for, you mean? Come on, you lazy blighter. This is the waste-paper basket heap, over here. You won't find anything among those tins and newspapers. I don't know what I'm looking for.'

'There won't be anything here,' Alec urged earnestly. 'Let's chuck it, and go off to make those inquiries.'

'I'm afraid you're right,' said Roger reluctantly. 'I've gone back about a week here, and haven't struck anything of the faintest interest. Below this everything pretty well rotted away, too. Still, I'll just – Hullo! What's this?'

'What?'

Roger had straightened up abruptly and was scrutinising with bent brows a grimy piece of paper he held in his hand. The next moment he whistled softly.

'Here is something, though!' he exclaimed, and scrambled to dry land. 'Here, what do you make of this?'

He handed the paper to Alec, who studied it carefully. It was very wet and limp, but a few traces of writing in pencil could still be made out on its surface, while here and there an isolated word or phrase stood out fairly legibly.

'It looks like a letter,' Alec said slowly. 'Hullo, did you see this? "Frightened almost out of my…" Out of my life, that must be.'

Roger nodded portentously. 'That's exactly what caught my eye. The writing's Stanworth's; I can recognise that. But I shouldn't say it was a letter. He wouldn't write a letter in pencil. It's probably some notes; or it may be the rough draft of a letter. Yes, that's more likely. Look, you can make that bit out – see? "Serious dang – " Serious danger, my boy! Alec, we're on the track of something here.' He took the paper from the other's hands and studied it afresh.

'Can't see who it's addressed to, can you?' Alec asked excitedly.

'No, worse luck; the first line or two has absolutely gone. Wait a minute, there's something here. "This n-e-i-" and the last two letters look like o-d. A long word. What's that?' He pointed with a quivering finger.

'N-e-i-g, isn't it?' said Alec. 'And that's an r. Neighbourhood!'

'By Jove, so it is! "This neighbourhood." And here's something else. "That b-r-u-t…" "That brute – " '

'Prince!'

'Prince?'

'The next word. See? You can make it out quite distinctly.'

'So it is! Good for you, Alec. "That brute Prince." Good Lord, do you realise what this means?' Roger's excitement was showing signs of becoming uncontrollable; his eyes were sparkling and he was breathing as if he had just run a hundred yards in eleven seconds.

'It's jolly important,' Alec concurred, beaming. 'I mean, it shows that – '

'Important!' Roger almost howled. 'Don't you see, man? It means that we know the murderer's name!'

'*What?*'

'It's put the game right in our hands. Stanworth was murdered by a man called Prince, whom he knew to be in the neighbourhood and – But let's go somewhere rather more secluded and study this document some more.'

The nearest outhouse offering a safe refuge, they withdrew hastily and scrutinised their find more closely. After ten minutes' concentrated effort they found themselves in possession of the following:

'... that brute Prince...this neighbourhood...serious danger...fright of my life this morning on chancing to...be locked up...'

'I think that's absolutely all that's decipherable, without a magnifying glass, at any rate,' Roger said at length, folding up the precious paper and stowing it carefully away in his pocketbook. 'But it's plain enough, isn't it? So forward!' He marched out of the shed and turned in the direction of the drive.

'Where to now?' asked the faithful Alec, hurrying after him.

'To find Master Prince,' Roger returned grimly.

'Ah! You think he's still about here?'

'I think it's quite probable. He's been in communication with Jefferson this morning, hasn't he? At any rate, we can soon find out.'

'What exactly have you deduced then?'

'Well, there's precious little deduction needed; the thing speaks for itself. Stanworth, for some reason still unknown to us, had cause to fear a man named Prince. To his surprise and terror he chanced to encounter him unexpectedly one morning about a week ago in this neighbourhood, and knew at once that he was in serious danger. He comes home at once, makes a rough draft of a letter, and then writes off to some other person telling him all about it and asking, probably, for help; at the same time expressing his conviction that Prince ought to be locked up.'

'It's curious,' Alec mused.

'Fishy, you mean? Yes, but we've had a suspicion for some time that there was something fishy going on behind the scenes in all this, haven't we? Not only with regard to the behaviour of the other people in the house, but even possibly in connection with old Stanworth himself. But we're hot on the trail this time, I think.'

'What's your plan of campaign?' Alec asked, as they turned into the drive.

'Well, we must make a few discreet inquiries. In fact, our course will be much the same as we contemplated before, except that our field of action has luckily been narrowed down very considerably. Instead of chasing about after some nebulous stranger, we've now got a definite goal. We had a pretty good idea of what he looks like before, but now we even know the blighter's name. Oh, this is going to be too easy.'

'How do you mean – we had a pretty good idea of what he looks like?'

'Well, haven't we? We know he must be strong, because of what happened in the library; Stanworth was no weakling, remember. Then the size of his footprints shows that he was a large man, probably tall. I can't tell you the colour of his hair or how many false teeth he's got; but we've got a good working idea of his appearance for all that.'

'But what are you going to do, if you do succeed in finding him? You can't go up to him and say, "Good afternoon, Mr Prince. I believe you murdered Mr Stanworth at two o'clock this morning." It – it isn't done.'

'You leave all that to me,' Roger returned largely. 'I'll think of something to say to him all right.'

'I'm sure you will,' Alec murmured with conviction.

'In the meantime, here's the lodge. What about seeing if William's in? He lives here, doesn't he? Or Mrs William. They might have opened the gates to this man Prince last night.'

'Right-ho. But be discreet.'

'Really, Alec!' said Roger with dignity, as he tapped on the lodge door.

William's wife was a round-faced, apple-cheeked old lady with a pair of twinkling blue eyes that looked as if they saw something humorous in most of the things upon which they rested; as no doubt they did, considering that they belonged to the wife of William.

'Good afternoon, gentlemen,' she said, with a little old-fashioned bob. 'Would it be me you were wanting?'

'Good afternoon,' Roger replied with a smile. 'We were wondering if William happened to be at home.'

'Me 'usband? Lor', no, sir; he's never at home at this time. He's got his work to do.'

'Oh, I suppose he's about the garden somewhere, is he?'

'Yes, sir. Cuttin' pea-sticks in the orchard, I think he is. Was it anything important?'

'Oh, no; nothing important. I'll call around and see him later on.'

'Shocking business this, sir; about the master,' Mrs William began volubly. 'Shocking! Such a thing's never been known at Layton Court before, not in my time it 'asn't; nor ever before that, so far as I've 'eard tell. An' did you see the corpse, sir? Shot hisself in the 'ead, didn't he?'

'Yes, shocking,' said Roger hastily. 'Shocking! By the way, I was expecting a friend last night rather late, but he never turned up. You didn't see anything of him here I suppose, did you?'

'About what time would that be, sir?'

'Oh, somewhere about eleven o'clock, I should think; or even later.'

'No, sir; that I didn't. William an' me was both on us in bed and asleep before half-past ten.'

'I see. And you close the gates when you lock up for the night, don't you?'

'That we do, sir. Unless there's orders come down to the contrary. They was shut near after ten o'clock last night, an' not opened till Halbert (that's the showfure) came down early this mornin'. Was your friend coming by motor car, sir?'

'I don't know. It depended. Why?'

'Because there's always the little gate at the side left open, which people on foot can come in by. All I can tell you, sir, is that nobody came to my knowledge, which he naturally wouldn't 'ave done if he never came up to the house, would he? Not without he got lost in the drive, which isn't very likely in a manner of speaking.'

'No, I'm afraid he can't have come at all. In any case, you say that, up to the time you went to bed, no stranger at all came in? Absolutely nobody?'

'No, sir. Nobody to my knowledge.'

'Oh, well; that quite settles it. By the way, only yesterday afternoon poor Mr Stanworth was asking me to do him a favour the next time I went for a walk. It was to call in and see someone called Prince for him, and – '

'Prince?' Mrs William interrupted with unexpected energy. 'Don't you go going anywhere near *him*, sir.'

'Why not?' Roger asked eagerly, flashing a look of triumph at Alec.

Mrs William hesitated. 'You do mean Prince, sir? John?'

'Yes, John; that's right. Why mustn't I go anywhere near him?'

'Because he's dangerous, sir,' said Mrs William vehemently. 'Downright dangerous! In fact' – she lowered her voice significantly – 'it's my opinion that he's a little mad.'

'Mad?' Roger echoed in surprise. 'Oh, come; I don't think that can be the case, can it?'

'Well, look how he went for Mr Stanworth that time, sir. You know about that, of course?'

Roger hurriedly checked a whistle. 'I've heard something about it,' he said glibly. 'Er – attacked him, didn't he?'

'That he did, sir. And all for no reason at all. In fact, if one of Mr Wetherby's farm hands hadn't luckily been by, he might 'ave done Mr Stanworth a power of harm. Of course they did their best to hush it up; it gives the place a bad name if them things get about. But *I* heard on it all right.'

'Indeed? I had no idea it was as bad as that. There was – how shall I put it? – bad blood between them?'

'Well, you might call it that, sir. He seemed to take a dislike to Mr Stanworth the very first time 'e saw him, like.'

'Rather a drastic way of showing it,' Roger laughed. 'Perhaps he has got a screw loose, as you say. He hasn't been here long then?'

'Oh, no. Not more'n a matter of three weeks or so, sir.'

'Well, I think I shall risk it. What I wanted to ask you was the quickest way of getting there.'

'To Mr Wetherby's? Why, you can't go quicker than follow the road through the village, sir; that takes you straight there. It's about a mile an' a half from here, or maybe a trifle more.'

'Mr Wetherby's; yes. Let me see, that's – ?'

'Hillcrest Farm, sir. A very nice gentleman he is, too. Him an' Mr Stanworth was getting quite friendly before – before – '

'Yes,' said Roger hurriedly. 'Well, thank you very much. I'm so sorry to have kept you all this time.'

'You're welcome, sir, I'm sure,' rejoined Mrs William smilingly. 'Good afternoon, sir.'

'Good afternoon.'

Mrs William popped back into her lodge again, and the two struck into the main road.

Roger's pent-up emotions burst forth as soon as they were out of earshot. '*There!*' he exclaimed. 'What do you think of that, eh?'

'Extraordinary!' Alec ejaculated, hardly less excited.

'But what a bit of luck just to hit on possibly the one person who would have been willing to give us all the information. Luck? It's positively uncanny. Well, I never guessed that detecting was as easy as this.'

'We're going straight after this man Prince, then?'

'You bet we are. We want to catch our bird before he flies.'

'You think he intends flying?'

'Most probably, I should say,' Roger replied, striding along the dusty road at top speed. 'He's only been in the place three weeks, you see, so he evidently came with the full intention of doing what he has done; now the job's accomplished there's no need for him to stay any longer. Oh, he's a clever one, is Master Prince. But not quite clever enough.'

'He attacked Stanworth once before apparently and in broad daylight.'

'Yes, didn't she bring that out beautifully? I could have screamed with excitement. It all fits together, doesn't it? "Seemed to take a dislike to him at first sight, like." Ah, Mrs William, that wasn't first sight; not by a long chalk. I expect that happened after Stanworth wrote his letter; otherwise he'd have mentioned it.'

'It may have been in one of the bits that have disappeared.'

'That's true; there were some long gaps. Look here, I'll tell you what we'd better do – call in at the village pub on our way and see if we can get any more information out of the landlord. He's sure to know everything that happens round here.'

'That seems a sound scheme,' Alec agreed readily.

'In the meantime, let's marshal our facts – that's the correct phrase, isn't it? This man Prince has managed to obtain employment of some kind on the farm of a Mr Wetherby, who appears to be a gentleman farmer. That was a cunning move of his, by the way; gives a reason for his presence in the neighbourhood, you see. He came here for some definite purpose connected with Stanworth; I don't say murder necessarily, that may not have been intended at first. The very first time he saw Stanworth his feelings were so much for him that he went for the old man baldheaded. The affair was hushed up, but there's certain to have been some gossip about it.'

'Silly thing to do, that,' Alec commented.

'Yes, very; showed his hand too soon. Still, there you are; he did it. And now let us devote all our energies to reaching this scorching village. Time's precious, and I want to ruminate a little.'

They walked rapidly down the winding white road into the village and made for the local public house. Time was, indeed, so precious that no considerations of temperature could be allowed to interfere with their expenditure of it.

chapter fifteen

Mr Sheringham Amuses
an Ancient Rustic

After the blazing sun and the dust, the cool bar of the old-fashioned little village inn, with its sanded floor and its brasses gleaming in the soft twilight, was remarkably welcome.

Roger buried his nose thankfully in his tankard before getting to business.

'My word, that's good!' he observed in heartfelt tones to the landlord, setting the tankard down half empty on the polished counter. 'There's nothing like beer for thirst, is there?'

'That's true enough, sir,' replied the landlord heartily, both because it was good for trade and because he thoroughly believed it. 'And you can't have too much of it on a day like this, I'm thinking,' he added, with an eye to the former consideration.

Roger looked about him appreciatively.

'Nice little place you've got here.'

'Not so bad, sir. There ain't a better bar parlour within ten miles, though I say it as shouldn't. You two gentlemen come far today?'

'Elchester,' said Roger briefly. He did not wish to divulge the fact that he was staying at Layton Court, having no desire to waste time in parrying the stream of questions that would inevitably result from this information.

'Ah, then, you would have a thirst on you and all,' the landlord remarked approvingly.

'We have,' agreed Roger, finishing up the contents of his tankard, 'so you can fill these up again for us.'

The landlord replenished the tankards and leaned confidentially over the counter.

'You heard the noos? There ain't half been goings on round these parts this morning. Up at Layton Court. You'd pass it on the left coming from Elchester; nigh on a mile back. Gentleman shot hisself there, they say. The showver, 'e told me about it. Came in for a glass o' beer, 'e did, same as what you two gentlemen might be doing now, an' told me all about it. Wasn't 'arf put out about it, 'e wasn't. Wanted the day off tomorrow, an' now he can't ask for it, what with having to cart the police an' everyone backwards and forwards an' all.'

Roger hurriedly subdued the involuntary smile that had risen to his lips on learning Albert's personal view of the tragedy. It would have made a striking epitaph, he felt. 'Sacred to the memory of John Brown, who died, greatly regretted by everybody, especially his chauffeur, who wanted the day off.'

'Yes, I did hear something about it,' he replied carelessly. 'Shocking affair. And how do you find business round here?'

'Mustn't complain, I suppose,' said the landlord guardedly; 'this bein' the only public in the village, y'see. An' good drinkers they are round these parts, too,' he added with enthusiasm.

'That's fine. I like a man who can appreciate good beer when he gets it. And I suppose you get quite a few strangers in here from time to time as well?'

'No, none too many,' said the landlord regretfully. 'We lie a bit off the chief roads here, y' see. Not but what a few walking gentlemen such as yourselves don't drop in now and then, for all that.'

'Yes, I suppose you get a walking gentleman now and then,' Roger replied vaguely, wondering what exactly constituted a walking gentleman, and whether he was the opposite to a running gentleman. 'How often would that be?'

'Well, sir, that depends, don't it?' said the landlord cautiously, evidently determined to be entrapped into no rash statements. 'Yes, that depends.'

'Does it? Well, take a special day. How many strangers came in yesterday, for instance?'

'Lor' bless you, sir, we don't get 'em in like that; not so many in a day. In a month, more like. Why, I don't suppose there's been a stranger in this bar before you gents come in not for a matter o' nearly a week.'

'You don't say!'

'I do, sir,' retorted the landlord with much earnestness. 'I do an' all.'

'Well, I should have thought you'd have got plenty in a cosy little place like this. Anyhow, you can be sure that I shall warn all my friends to come and pay you a visit if they happen to be in the neighbourhood. Better beer I've never tasted anywhere.'

'It *is* good beer,' the landlord admitted, almost reluctantly. 'Thank you kindly, sir. And anything I can do in return for you and your friends, I'm sure I'll be most happy.'

'Well, you can do something now, as a matter of fact,' Roger rejoined caressingly. 'We've come over from Elchester to see Prince – er John, you know. Up at Hillcrest Farm.'

The landlord nodded. 'Aye; I know.'

'So if you could put us on the right road from here, we should be very grateful.'

'Turn to the left when you get out of here and go straight on, sir,' returned the landlord promptly. 'You can't miss it. First farm on the right – ' and side past the crossroads.'

'Thanks very much. Let me see, I've never actually met Prince before, but he's pretty easy to recognise, I understand. Big fellow, isn't he?'

'Aye, that 'e is. Matter o' nigh on six feet from the top of his 'ead down; when he 'olds 'is 'ead up, that is.'

'Ah, stoops a bit, does he?'

'Well, you might call it that, sir. 'Angs 'is 'ead, in a manner of speakin'. You know 'ow they do.'

'Oh, yes; quite. Strong chap, too, isn't he?'

'''E is, an' all. It 'ud take all of six men to 'old him, if 'e did get rampageous.'

'Pretty quiet usually, then, is he?'

'Oh, aye. 'E's quiet enough.'

'But no fool, I gather. I mean, he's pretty intelligent, isn't he?'

111

The landlord chuckled hoarsely. 'Lor' bless you, no. Prince ain't no fool. 'E's a clever devil, all right. Cunning, you might call 'im. Nor you wouldn't be far wrong, neither.'

'Oh? In what way?'

'Oh, pretty nigh every way,' said the landlord vaguely. 'But it's a pity you two gents should have 'ad this walk out today. Prince was in Helchester 'isself yesterday.'

'Oho!' observed Roger softly, with a side glance at Alec. 'He was, was he?'

'Aye, at the Hagricultooral Show, 'e was.'

'Oh? What was he doing there?'

'Showin'.'

'Showing himself, was he?'

'Aye, that 'e was. An' took a prize, too.'

'What a pity we didn't know that; it would have saved us a journey today. By the way, you don't know what time he came back, do you? Mr Wetherby was there, too, I suppose?'

'Mr Wetherby was there, but Prince didn't come back with 'im. I see Mr Wetherby pass by 'ere on 'is mare soon after seven o'clock. Prince wouldn't 'ave come till a deal later than that. But they'll tell you up at the farm better nor I can about that.'

'Oh, well, it isn't really of the least importance, so long as I can see him up there now.'

'He's up there now right enough, sir. You ask any of the men up there an' they'll show you.'

Roger finished up the remains of his beer and put the tankard down on the counter with a business-like air.

'Well, Alec,' he said briskly. 'Time we were getting along if we're ever to get back to Elchester today.'

'You really are rather marvellous, you know, Roger,' Alec observed, as they set out along the road once more.

'I know I am,' Roger said candidly. 'But why particularly?'

'Carrying on a chat with the landlord like that. I couldn't have done it to save my life. I shouldn't know what to say.'

'I suppose it comes naturally,' Roger replied complacently. 'I'm a bit of what our American friends call a mixer. As a matter of fact, I thoroughly enjoy a yap with somebody like that; friend William, for instance. And it all comes in useful, you know; local colour and so on. But what about the information I was able to extract, eh?'

'Yes, we got a few more details, didn't we?'

'Highly important ones, too. What do you make of Master Prince showing on his own account at Elchester? That puts him in rather an independent position, doesn't it? And he wasn't back till late last night, you see. It all tallies.'

'Yes, we seem to be on the right track this time.'

'Of course we're on the right track. How could we be anything else? The evidence is overwhelming. As a matter of fact,' Roger added thoughtfully, 'I believe I can make a pretty good guess as to what actually happened last night.'

'Oh? What?'

'Why, friend Prince, naturally somewhat elated at winning a prize at the show, got drinking with some of the new pals he must have picked up here and had a couple of drops too much. On his way back he passes Layton Court and either rattles the side door and notices it ajar; in any case, walks in and up to the French windows, which are open. Stanworth, who we know was mortally afraid of him, jumps at his appearance and threatens him with a revolver. In the struggle, Stanworth is shot, either on purpose or accidentally. That sobers friend Prince up more than a little, and, with the cunning we know him to possess, he sets the stage for us to find the next morning. How's that?'

'It's quite possible,' Alec admitted. 'But what I want to know is – how are we going to tackle Prince now?'

'Wait and see what happens. I shall get into conversation with him and try to get him to account for his movements last night. If he gets obstreperous, we shall simply have to lay him out; that's all. You'll come in useful there, by the way.'

'Humph!' Alec observed.

'In any case,' Roger concluded enthusiastically, 'it's going to be dashed exciting. You can take my word for that.'

There was no mistaking Hillcrest Farm. It lay on the top of a sharp rise just as the landlord had described it. The two instinctively slackened their steps as they approached, as if unconsciously reconnoitring the scene of battle.

'I don't want to enlist Wetherby just yet,' Roger murmured. 'I think we ought to try and tackle him ourselves. And we don't want to give the alarm in any case, or arouse any suspicions. That's why I didn't put hundreds more questions to that landlord. What do you think?'

'Oh, absolutely. What about asking that old chap if he knows where Prince is?'

'Yes, I will.' Roger strolled over towards the spot where an ancient rustic was clipping one of Mr Wetherby's hedges. 'I want to speak to Mr Prince,' he confided to the ancient. 'Can you tell me where I shall find him?'

'Sir?' queried the other, curving a large and horny hand round an equally large and horny ear.

'I want to speak to Mr Prince,' Roger repeated loudly. 'Where is he?'

The ancient did not move. 'Sir?' he remarked stolidly.

'Prince!' bawled Roger. 'Where?'

'Oh, *Prince*! 'E's in the next field alongside. Up 'tother end I seed 'im last, not above five minutes back.'

The horny palm ceased to function as an ear trumpet and became a receptacle for a spare shilling of Roger's, and the two moved on. In the side of the next field was set a sturdy gate. Roger swung himself easily over it, the light of battle in his eyes. Alec followed suit, and they advanced together up the centre of the field.

'I can't see anyone here, can you?' Roger remarked, when they had gone some little distance. 'Perhaps he's gone somewhere else.'

'Nothing but a cow in that corner. Is there any other way out of the field? He didn't get over that gate into the road within the last five minutes. We should have seen him.'

Roger halted and gazed round carefully. 'Yes, there's a – Hullo! What's the matter with that cow? She seems very interested in us.'

The cow, a large, powerful-looking animal, had indeed quitted its corner and was advancing purposefully in their direction. Its head was swaying curiously from side to side and it was emitting a noise not unlike the hoot of a steamer.

'My God!' Alec shouted suddenly. 'That isn't a cow; it's a bull! Run like hell!'

Roger needed no second invitation; he set off at top speed in the wake of the flying Alec. The bull, observing this disappointing procedure, thundered after them. It was an exciting race while it lasted. The result, some six seconds later, was as follows:

1. Mr A Grierson.
2. Mr R Sheringham.
3. Bull.

Distance between first and second, ten yards; between second and third, one five-barred gate (taken by the second in his stride).

' 'Strewth!' Roger observed with feeling, and collapsed incontinently into a ditch.

A hoarse and grating noise caused them to look up. The noise emanated from the ancient. He was laughing.

'Nearly 'ad you that time, gents,' he croaked joyfully. 'Ain't seen him go fer anyone like that not since he went fer that Mr Stanfoerth, or whatever 'e calls 'isself – 'im from Layton Court. I ought to 'ave warned 'ee. You want ter be very careful o' that there Prince John.'

chapter sixteen

Mr Sheringham Lectures on Neo-Platonism

'Alec,' interrupted Roger plaintively, 'if you say one more word to me about bulls, cows, or any other farmyard impedimenta, I shall burst at once into loud tears. I warn you.'

They were walking once more along the white, dusty road; but the springy exhilaration of the outward journey had gone out of their steps. A short but pithy conversation with the ancient rustic, conducted mostly in ear-splitting yells, had speedily shown the crestfallen Roger the precise nature of the wild goose (or should it be wild bull?) he had been chasing. Alec, it might be noticed in passing, was not being at all kind about it.

'If ever anything could have been more obvious!' Roger pursued mournfully. 'My reasoning was perfectly sound. It almost looks as if Mrs William and that idiot of a landlord were trying deliberately to deceive me. Why couldn't they have said straight out that the disgusting animal was a bull and have done with it?'

'I don't expect you gave them a chance,' Alec remarked with an un-disguised grin.

Roger gave him a dignified look and relapsed into silence.

But not for long. 'So here we are, back again at the precise point we had reached before we ever came across that miserable piece of paper,' he resumed unhappily. 'A whole valuable hour wasted.'

'You've had some exercise, at any rate,' Alec pointed out kindly. 'Jolly good for you, too.'

'The point is, what are we going to do next?'

'Go back to tea,' said Alec promptly. 'And talking about wasting valuable time, I believe that's all we're doing at all with regard to this business. If such a clear clue as that fizzles out in this way, why shouldn't the whole thing be equally a mare's nest? I don't believe there ever *was* a murder, after all. Stanworth committed suicide.'

'Let's see,' Roger went on, completely disregarding this interruption, 'we were setting out to get on the trail of a Mysterious Stranger, weren't we? Well, that's where we shall have to take the thing up from. Luckily I kept my wits about me enough to put a few questions about strangers to those two, and we drew a blank. We will now visit the station.'

'Oh, no!' Alec groaned. 'Tea!'

'Station!' returned Roger firmly; and station it was.

But even the station did not prove any more fruitful. On the plea of making inquiries for a friend, Roger succeeded in extracting with some difficulty, from a very bucolic porter, the information that only half-a-dozen trains in a day stopped there (the place was indeed little more than a halt), and none at all after seven o'clock in the evening. The earliest in the morning was soon after six, and no passengers had been picked up so far as he knew. No, he hadn't seen a stranger arrive yesterday; leastways, not to notice one like.

'After all, it's only what we might have expected,' Roger remarked philosophically, as they set off homewards at last.

'If the fellow came by train at all, he'd probably go to Elchester. He's no fool, as we knew very well.'

Alec, now that the prospect of tea and shade was definitely before him, was ready to discuss the matter rather more amicably.

'You're quite sure now that he is a stranger, then?' he asked. 'You've given up the idea that it's anybody actually in this neighbourhood?'

'I'm nothing of the sort,' Roger retorted. 'I'm not sure of any blessed thing about him, except that he wears large boots, is strong, and is no ordinary criminal; and that he corresponds closely with the quite distinct mental picture I had formed of the late lamented Mr John Prince. He may be a stranger to the neighbourhood, and he may not. We know that he was still in it during the morning, because he managed to communicate with the occupants of the household. But as for anything more definite than that, we simply can't say, not knowing his motive. By Jove, I do wish we could discover that! It would narrow things down immensely.'

'I tell you something that never seems to have occurred to us,' Alec remarked suddenly. 'Why shouldn't it have been just an ordinary burglar, who got so panic-stricken when he found he'd actually killed his householder that he hadn't the nerve to complete what he came for and simply hurried off? That seems to me as probable as anything, and it fits the facts perfectly.'

'Ye-es; we did rather touch on the burglar idea at the very beginning, didn't we? Do you realise that it was only five hours ago, by the way? It seems more like five weeks. But that was before the curious behaviour of all these other people impressed itself upon us.'

'Upon you, you mean. I still think you're making ever so much too much of that side of it. There's probably some perfectly simple explanation, if we only knew it. I suppose you mean Jefferson and Mrs Plant?'

'*And* Lady Stanworth!'

'And Lady Stanworth, then. Well, dash it all, you can't expect them to take us into their confidence, can you? And that is the only way in which their part can be cleared up. Not that it seems to me in the least worth clearing up. I don't see that it could possibly have anything to do with the murder. Good Lord, it's practically the same thing as accusing them of the murder itself! I ask you, my dear chap, *can* you imagine either Mrs Plant or Lady Stanworth – we'll leave Jefferson out for the moment – actually plotting old Stanworth's murder! It's really too ludicrous. You ought to have more sense.'

'This particular topic always seems to excite you, Alexander,' observed Roger mildly.

'Well, I mean, it's so dashed absurd. You can't really believe anything of the sort.'

'Perhaps I don't. Anyhow, we'll shelve it till something more definite crops up. It's quite hot enough already, without making each other still more heated. Look here, let's give the whole thing a rest till we get back. It will clear our brains. I'll give you a short lecture on the influence of the Platonic ethics on Hegelian philosophy instead, with a few sidelights on neo-Platonism.' Which, in spite of Alec's spirited protests, he at once proceeded to do.

In this way the time passed pleasantly and instructively till they had passed the lodge gates once more.

'So you see,' concluded Roger happily, 'that while in medieval philosophy this mysticism is in powerful and ultimately successful opposition to rationalistic dogmatism, with its contemptuous disregard for all experience, the embryonic science of the fifteenth and sixteenth centuries was actually in itself a logical development of neo-Platonism in this same opposition to barren rationalism.'

'Was it?' said Alec gloomily, registering a secret but none the less fervent prayer that he might never hear the word neo-Platonism again as long as he lived. 'I see.'

'You do? Good. Then let us seek out and have speech with friend William.'

'Are you going to give him a short lecture on rationalistic dogmatism?' Alec asked carefully. 'Because if so, I'm going indoors.'

'I'm afraid it would be wasted on William,' Roger replied seriously. 'William, I feel sure, is a dogmatist of the most bigoted type if ever there was one; and to lecture to him on the futility of dogma would be as ineffective as to harangue a hippopotamus on the subject of drawing-room etiquette. No, I just want to sound William a little. Not that I think it will really be of much help to us, but just at present I'm turning every stone I can see.'

In due course William was run to earth in a large greenhouse. He was mounted unhappily on an exceedingly rickety pair of steps and engaged in tying up a vine. On seeing Roger he hastily descended to firm ground. William did not believe in taking chances.

'Good afternoon, William,' said Roger brightly.

'Arternoon, sir,' William responded suspiciously.

'I've just been having a chat with your wife, William.'

William grunted noncommittally.

'I was telling her that a friend of mine, whom I expected to come up to the house to see me last night, never turned up; and I was wondering if you'd seen anything of him down at the lodge.'

William ostentatiously busied himself with a small plant.

'Never see'd no one,' he observed with decision.

'No? Never mind, then. It doesn't really matter. That's an interesting job you've got on hand, William. You take a plant out of its pot, sniff its roots and put it back again; is that it? Now what operation do you call that in the science of horticulture?'

William hastily relinquished the plant and glowered at his interlocutor.

'Some folks mayn't have no work to do,' he remarked darkly; 'but other folks 'ave.'

'Meaning yourself, I take it?' Roger said approvingly. 'That's right. Work away. Nothing like it, is there? Keeps you cheerful and bright and contented. Great thing, work, I agree with you.'

A flicker of interest passed across William's countenance. 'What did that there Mr Stanworth want to shoot hisself for, eh?' he demanded suddenly.

'I don't know, to tell you the truth,' said Roger, somewhat taken aback at the unexpectedness of this query. 'Why, have you got any ideas about it?'

'I don't 'old with it meself,' said William primly. 'Not with sooeycide.'

'You're absolutely right, William,' Roger replied warmly. 'If more people were like you, there'd be – there'd be less suicides, undoubtedly. It's an untidy habit, to say the least.'

'It ain't acting right,' William pursued firmly. 'That's what it ain't.'

'You put it in a nutshell, William; it isn't. In fact, it's acting all wrong. By the way, William, somebody or other was telling me that a stranger had been seen about the grounds during the last day or two. You noticed him by any chance?'

'Stranger? What sort of a stranger?'

'Oh, the usual sort; a head and four pairs of fingers, you know. This particular one, they said, was a rather large man. Have you seen a rather large strange man round the house lately?'

William cogitated deeply.

'I 'ave an' all.'

'Have you, though? When?'

William cogitated again. 'It 'ud be a matter of ha'-past eight last night,' he announced at last. 'Ha'-past eight it 'ud be, as near as anything. I was a-settin' out in front o' the lodge, an' up he walks, bold as brass, an' nods at me an' goes on up the drive.'

Roger exchanged glances with Alec.

'Yes, William?' he said warmly. 'A man you'd never seen before? A fairly large man?'

'A very large man,' William corrected meticulously.

'A very large man. Excellent! Go on. What happened?'

'Well, I says to the missus, "Oo's that?" I says. "A-walkin' up the drive as if he owned the place." ' William pondered.

' "As if he *owned* the place," I says,' he repeated firmly.

'And a very good thing to say, too. Well?'

' "Oh, 'im?" she says. " 'E's the cook's brother," she says. "I was inter-juiced to 'im at Helchester the other day," she says. "At least, she *says* 'e's 'er brother," she says.' A strange rasping noise in his throat appeared to indicate that William was amused. ' "At least, she *says* 'e's 'er brother," she says,' he repeated with much enjoyment.

'Oh!' Roger exclaimed, somewhat dashed. 'Oh, did she? And did you see him again, William?'

'That I did. Back 'e come nigh on a quarter of a hower later, an' cook with 'im, a-hangin' on 'is arm like what she ought to have known better not to 'ave done,' William rejoined, suddenly stern. 'I don't 'old with it meself, I don't,' added this severe moralist. 'Not at 'er age, I don't.' His expression relaxed reminiscently. ' "At least, she *says* 'e's 'er brother," she says,' he added, with a sudden rasp.

'I see,' said Roger. 'Thank you, William. Well, I suppose we mustn't interrupt you any more. Come on, Alec.'

Slowly and sadly they made their way back to the house.

'William got his own back then, if he only knew it,' Roger said with a wry smile. 'I did think for a moment that we might be getting at something at last.'

'You really are a hell of an optimist, Roger,' Alec observed wonderingly.

Their path took them past the library, and as they reached the bed in which the footprints had been discovered Roger instinctively paused. The next moment he darted forward and stared with incredulous eyes at the bed.

'Good Lord!' he exclaimed, clutching Alec's arm and pointing with an excited finger. 'Look! They've gone, both of them! They've been smoothed out!'

'Great Scott, so they have!'

The two gazed at each other with wide eyes.

'So Jefferson *did* hear what we were talking about!' Roger almost whispered. 'I have an idea that things are going to get rather exciting very soon, after all.'

chapter seventeen

Mr Grierson Becomes Heated

But however much Jefferson might guess of their activities, certainly nothing was visible in his manner as Roger and Alec entered the drawing room, twenty minutes late for tea. He greeted them in his usual curt, rather brusque way, and asked casually how they had managed to amuse themselves. Lady Stanworth was not present, and Mrs Plant was seated behind the tea tray.

'Oh, we went for a stroll through the village; but it was too hot to be pleasant. Thanks, Mrs Plant. Yes, milk and sugar, please. Two lumps. You got through your business in Elchester all right? I saw you starting.'

'Yes. Got off infernally late. Had to rush things. However, I managed to get everything done all right.'

'Have they arranged about the inquest yet, by the way?' Alec asked suddenly.

'Yes. Tomorrow morning at eleven, here.'

'Oh, they're going to hold it here, are they?' said Roger. 'Which room will you put them in? The library?'

'No. I think the morning room's better.'

'Yes, I think it is.'

'Oh, I do wish it were over!' Mrs Plant remarked with an involuntary sigh.

'You don't seem to be looking forward to the ordeal,' Roger said quickly, with a slight smile.

'I hate the idea of giving evidence,' Mrs Plant replied, almost passionately. 'It's horrible!'

'Oh, come. It isn't as bad as all that. It's not like a law case, you know. There'll be no cross-examination or anything like that. The proceedings will be purely formal, I take it, eh, Jefferson?'

'Purely,' Jefferson said, lighting a cigarette with deliberation. 'Don't suppose the whole thing will last more than twenty minutes.'

'So you see there won't be anything very dreadful in it, Mrs Plant, May I have another cup of tea, please?'

'Well, I wish it were over; that's all,' Mrs Plant said with a nervous little laugh, and Roger noticed that the hand which held his cup shook slightly.

Jefferson rose to his feet.

'Afraid I shall have to leave you chaps to your own resources again,' he remarked abruptly. 'Lady Stanworth hopes you'll do whatever you like. Sorry to appear so inhospitable, but you know what things are like at this sort of time.'

He walked out of the room.

Roger decided to put out a small feeler.

'Jefferson doesn't seem extraordinarily upset really, does he?' he said to Mrs Plant. 'Yet it must be rather a shock to lose an employer, with whom one's been so many years, in this tragic way.'

Mrs Plant glanced at him, as if rather questioning the good taste of this remark. 'I don't think Major Jefferson is the sort of man to show his real feelings before comparative strangers, do you, Mr Sheringham?' she replied a little stiffly.

'Probably not,' Roger replied easily. 'But he seems singularly unperturbed about it all.'

'He is a very imperturbable sort of person, I imagine.'

Roger tried another tack. 'Had you known Mr Stanworth long, Mrs Plant?' he asked conversationally, leaning back in his chair and pulling his pipe out of his pocket. 'You don't mind if I smoke, do you?'

'Please do. Oh, no; not very long. My – my husband knew him, you know.'

'I see. A curious habit that of his, asking comparative, or, in my case at any rate, complete strangers down to these little gatherings, wasn't it?'

'I think Mr Stanworth was a very hospitable man,' Mrs Plant replied tonelessly.

'Very! A most excellent fellow in every way, didn't you think?' Roger asked with enthusiasm.

'Oh, most,' said Mrs Plant in a curiously flat voice.

Roger glanced at her shrewdly. 'You don't agree with me, Mrs Plant?' he said suddenly.

Mrs Plant started.

'I?' she said hurriedly. 'Why, of course I do. I thought Mr Stanworth a – a very nice man indeed. Charming! Of course I agree with you.'

'Oh, I'm sorry. I thought for the moment that you didn't seem very enthusiastic about him. No earthly reason why you should be, of course. Everybody has their likes and dislikes, don't they?'

Mrs Plant glanced quickly at Roger, and then looked out of the window. 'I was simply thinking how – how tragic the whole thing is,' she said in a low voice.

There was a short silence.

'Lady Stanworth didn't seem to be on very good terms with him, though, did she?' Roger remarked carelessly, prodding at the tobacco in his pipe with a match-stalk.

'Do you think so?' Mrs Plant returned guardedly.

'She certainly gave me that impression. In fact, I should have gone farther. I should have said that she positively disliked him.'

Mrs Plant looked at the speaker with distaste. 'There are secrets in every household, I suppose,' she said shortly. 'Don't you think that it is a little impertinent for outsiders to probe into them? Especially under circumstances like these.'

'That's one for me,' Roger smiled, quite unabashed. 'Yes, I suppose it is, Mrs Plant. The trouble is, you see, that I simply can't help it. I'm the most curious person alive. Everything interests me, especially every human thing, and I've just got to get to the bottom of it. And you must admit that the relations between Lady Stanworth, of all people, and the – shall we say? – somewhat plebeian Mr Stanworth, are uncommonly interesting to a novelist.'

'Everything is "copy" to you, you mean?' Mrs Plant retorted, though less uncompromisingly. 'Well, if you put it like that I suppose you may have a certain amount of reason; though I don't admit the justification for all that. Yes, I believe Lady Stanworth did not get on very well with her brother-in-law. After all, it's only to be expected, isn't it?'

'Is it?' asked Roger quickly. 'Why?'

'Well, because of the circumstances of – ' Mrs Plant broke off abruptly and bit her lip. 'Because of the blood and water idea, I suppose. They were utterly unlike each other in every way.'

'That isn't what you were going to say. What had you got in mind when you corrected yourself?'

Mrs Plant flushed slightly.

'Really, Mr Sheringham, I – '

Alec rose suddenly from his chair. 'I say, it's awfully hot in this room,' he remarked abruptly. 'Come into the garden and get some air, Roger, I'm sure Mrs Plant will excuse us.'

Mrs Plant flashed a grateful look at him.

'Certainly,' she said, in somewhat agitated tones. 'I – I think I shall go upstairs and lie down for a little myself. I have rather a headache.'

The two men watched her go out of the room in silence. Then Alec turned to Roger.

'Look here,' he said heatedly, 'I'm not going to let you bully that poor little woman like this. It's a bit too thick. You get a lot of damned silly notions into your head about her, and then you try to bully her into confirming them. I'm not going to stand for it.'

Roger shook his head in mock despair.

'Really, Alexander,' he said tragically, 'you are a difficult person, you know. Extraordinarily difficult.'

'Well, it's getting past a joke,' Alec retorted a little more calmly, though his face was still flushed with anger. 'We can do what we want without bullying women.'

'And just when I was getting along so nicely!' Roger mourned. 'You make a rotten Watson, Alec. I can't think why I ever took you on in the part.'

'A jolly good thing for you that you did,' Alec said grimly. 'I can see fair play, at any rate. And trying to trick a woman who's got nothing to do with the thing at all into a lot of silly admissions is *not* playing the game.'

Roger took the other's arm and led him gently into the garden.

'All right, all right,' he said in the tones of one soothing a fractious child. 'We'll try other tactics, if you're so set on it. In any case, there's no need to get excited. The trouble is that you've mistaken your century, Alec. You ought to have lived four or five hundred years ago. As a heavy-weight succourer of ladies in distress you could have challenged all corners with one lance tied behind your back. There, there!'

'Oh, it's all very well for you to laugh,' returned the slightly mollified Alec, 'but I'm perfectly right, and you know it. If we're going on with this thing, we're not going to make use of any dashed underhand sneaky little detective tricks. If it comes to that, why don't you tackle Jefferson, if you're so jolly keen on tackling someone?'

'For the simple reason that the excellent Jefferson would certainly not give anything away, my dear Alec; whereas there's always the chance that a woman will. But enough! We'll confine ourselves to sticks and stones, and leave the human element out of account; or the feminine part of it, at any rate. But for all that,' Roger added wistfully, 'I would like to know what's going on amongst that trio!'

'Humph!' Alec grunted disapprovingly.

They paced for a time in silence up and down the edge of the lawn, which ran parallel with the back of the house.

Roger's thoughts were racing. The disappearance of the footprints had caused him drastically to rearrange his ideas. He had now no doubt at all that Jefferson not only knew all about the crime itself, but that he was in all probability an actual participator in it. Whether his part had been an active one and he had been present in the library at the time, was impossible to say; probably not, Roger inclined to think. But that he had helped to plan it and was now actively concerned in endeavouring to destroy all traces of it was surely beyond all disbelief. That meant one accomplice, at least, within the house.

But what was really worrying Roger far more than the question of Jefferson's share in the affair was the possible inclusion of the two women who seemed somehow to be mixed up with it. On the face of things no doubt it was, as Alec so strongly held, almost incredible that either Mrs Plant or Lady Stanworth could be a party to a murder. Yet it was impossible to dispute the facts. That there was a distinct understanding between Jefferson and Lady Stanworth seemed as certain to Roger as that there had been a murder in the house instead of a suicide. And a similar understanding between Mrs Plant and Jefferson appeared to be even more strongly established. Added to which there was her suspicious behaviour in the library that morning; for in spite of the fact that her jewels had been in the safe, after all, Roger was still no less firmly convinced that this excuse for her presence in the library was a lie. Furthermore, Mrs Plant certainly knew very much more about Stanworth and his relations with his secretary and sister-in-law than she was willing to admit; it was a pity that she had checked herself just in time after tea, when she appeared to have been on the point of allowing something of real importance to slip past her guard.

Yes; though he was no more willing to believe it than was Alec himself, Roger could see no loophole through which to escape from the assumption that both Mrs Plant and Lady Stanworth were as deeply implicated as Jefferson himself. It was most unfortunate that Alec should have chosen to adopt such a highly prejudiced view of the matter; this was just the sort of thing for which nothing was required so much as impartial discussion. Roger covertly eyed the face of his taciturn companion and sighed softly.

The back of the house did not run in a single straight line. Between the library and the dining room, where was the small room which was used for storing trunks and lumber, the wall was set back a few feet and formed a shallow recess; and this space was occupied by a little shrubbery of laurels. As the two passed this shrubbery, a small blue object, lying on the ground at the outer edge, caught the sun's rays and the gleam of it attracted Roger's attention. Carelessly and half unconsciously, he strolled towards it.

Then something in its particular shade of blue struck a sudden note in his memory, and he stared at it curiously.

'What's that little blue thing by the roots of those laurels, Alec?' he asked, frowning at it. 'It seems vaguely familiar somehow.'

He stepped across the path and picked it up. It was a piece of blue china.

'Hullo!' he said eagerly, holding it up so that Alec could see it. 'Do you realise what this is?'

Alec joined him on the path and looked at the piece of china without very much interest.

'Yes, it's a bit of broken plate or something.'

'Oh, no, it isn't! Don't you recognise the colour? It's a bit of the missing vase, my boy. I wonder – By Jove, I wonder if the rest is in here.'

He dropped on his hands and knees and peered among the laurels. 'Yes, I believe I can see some other bits farther in. I'll investigate, if you'll keep an eye open to see that nobody is coming.' And he crawled laboriously into the little shrubbery.

A few moments later he returned by the same route. In his hands were several more pieces of the vase.

'It's all in there,' he announced triumphantly. 'Right back by the wall. You see what must have happened?'

'The fellow threw it in there,' said Alec wisely.

'Exactly. I expect he put the pieces in his pocket when he collected them, in order to chuck them away somewhere as soon as he got clear. Methodical sort of bird, isn't he?'

'Yes,' Alec agreed, looking at Roger with some surprise. 'You seem quite excited about it.'

'I am!' Roger said emphatically.

'Why? It's what we expected, isn't it? More or less. I mean, if the vase was broken and the pieces disappeared, it's a pretty reasonable assumption that he threw them away somewhere, isn't it?'

Roger's eyes sparkled. 'Oh, perfectly. But the point is *where* he threw them. Doesn't it occur to you, Alec, that this place is not on the route between the lattice window and the quickest way out of the grounds? In other words, the drive. Also, doesn't it occur to you that if he wanted to throw them where nobody would be likely to find them, the best place to do it would be that thick undergrowth on either side of the drive – especially as he would be passing along it on his way out? Don't those points seem rather significant to you?'

'Well, perhaps it is a little curious, now you come to mention it.'

'A little curious!' Roger repeated disgustedly. 'My dear chap, it's one of the most significant things we've struck yet. What's the inference? I don't say it's correct, by the way. But what *is* the inference?'

Alec pondered.

'That he was in a deuce of a hurry?'

'That he was in a deuce of a fiddlestick! He'd have gone on straight down the drive if that is all. No! The inference to my way of thinking is that he never was going down the drive at all.'

'Oh? Where was he going, then?'

'Back into the house again! Alec, it's beginning to look as if that Mysterious Stranger of ours may be going the same way as Mr John Prince.'

chapter eighteen

What the Settee had to Tell

Alec stared incredulously. 'Back into the *house?* But – but what on earth would he want to be going back into the house for?'

'Ah, now you're asking me something. I haven't the least idea. I don't even know that he was going back into the house. All I say is that that is the only inference I can draw from the fact of these pieces of vase being where they are. It's possibly quite wrong.'

'But look here, if he wanted to go into the house again, why on earth should he have taken the trouble to climb out of the window like that? Why didn't he just go out of the library door?'

'Obviously because he wanted to leave all ways into or out of the library fastened on the inside, in order to further the idea of suicide.'

'But why should he have gone back into the house at all? That's what I can't understand.'

'Well,' Roger remarked very casually, 'supposing he lived there?'

'*What?*'

'I said, supposing he lived there. He'd want to go up to bed, wouldn't he?'

'Good Lord, you're surely not suggesting that somebody in the house murdered old Stanworth, are you?' Alec asked in horrified tones.

Roger relit his pipe with some care.

'Not necessarily, but you keep asking me why he should want to get back into the house, and I give you the most obvious explanation. As a matter of fact, I should say that he probably wanted to communicate with somebody inside before making his escape.'

'Then you don't think it was somebody from inside the house who killed Stanworth?' Alec asked with some relief.

'Heaven only knows,' Roger replied laconically. 'No, perhaps on second thoughts I don't. We mustn't forget that Jefferson couldn't find those keys this morning. Unless that was a blind, by Jove! I never thought of that. Or he might have forgotten something important and wanted to get at the safe again, not realising that he'd put the keys back in the wrong pocket.'

'I suppose,' Alec said slowly, 'that Jefferson is the only person inside the house that you would suspect of having done it?'

'No, I'm hanged if he is,' Roger retorted with energy.

'Oh! Who else then?'

'I'm suspecting everybody at present; put it like that. Everybody and everything within these four walls.'

'Well, look here, don't forget your promise, mind. No decisive steps to be taken without me, eh?'

'Yes, but look here, Alec,' Roger said seriously, 'you really mustn't stand out unnecessarily if I might want to take steps that don't altogether meet with your approval. We're playing a very grave game, you know, and we can't treat it as a joy-trip and only do the bits we like and leave out all the nasty part.'

'Yes,' Alec said, a little reluctantly. 'I see that. I won't make a fuss about anything unnecessarily. But we must go on working together.'

'Right!' Roger answered promptly. 'That's a bargain, then. Well, look here, there's one thing we ought to have done earlier, but it quite slipped my memory. We must have a look for that possible second cartridge case. Personally I don't believe there is one; I think there was one shot fired from each revolver. But it's a possibility, and we ought not to overlook it.'

'Rather a tall order, isn't it? It might be anywhere in the whole grounds.'

'Yes, but there's only one place that it's any use to search – the library. If we can't find it there, we'll give it up.'

'Very well.'

'Oh, Alexander,' Roger observed unhappily, as they strolled back to the library. 'Alexander, we're very terribly handicapped in this little problem, as Holmes would call it.'

'In what way particularly?'

'Not knowing the motive for the murder. If we could only get at that, it would simplify matters tremendously. Why, I dare say we could put our hands on the criminal at once. That's the way all these murder cases are solved, both in real life and in fiction. Establish your motive, and work back from that. We're groping utterly in the dark, you see, till we've found that.'

'And you haven't any idea of it at all? Not even a guess?'

'Not a one. Or, rather, too many. It's impossible to say with a man like Stanworth. After all, what do we know about him, beyond that he was a cheery old gentleman and kept an excellent cellar? Nothing! He might have been a lady-killer, and it may be a case of the jealous husband, with Lady Stanworth and Jefferson in the know after it had happened, and hushing it up for the sake of the name.'

'I say, that's a good idea! Do you really think it was that? I shouldn't be a bit surprised.'

'It's possible, but I shouldn't say it was likely. He was rather too old to be acting as Lothario, wasn't he? Or again it might have been somebody whom he ruined in business (I shouldn't say his methods were any too scrupulous) and a somewhat drastic revenge, with the other two also knowing what had happened and keeping quiet about it for reasons that we don't know anything about. But what's the use? There are a hundred theories, all equally possible and plausible, to fit the very meagre array of facts that we've got in our possession.'

'We are in a bit of a fog, yes,' Alec agreed as they entered the library.

'But there's rather more light I think, already, than an hour or two ago,' Roger replied cheerfully. 'No, when all's said and done, we haven't done so badly as yet, what with luck and certain other things which modesty forbids me to mention. And now for this cartridge case, and let's pray that we shan't be interrupted.'

For some minutes they searched diligently in silence. Then Alec scrambled up from his knees beside the little typist's table and inspected his hands ruefully.

'No sign of it,' he said, 'and I'm in a filthy mess. I don't think it can be in here, do you?'

Roger was investigating the cushions of the big settee.

'Afraid not,' he replied. 'I hardly expected it, but – Hullo, what's this?'

He drew out a small piece of white material from between two of the loose cushions and inspected it with interest.

Alec strolled across the room and joined him. 'It looks like a woman's handkerchief,' he said carefully.

'More than that, Alexander; it *is* a woman's handkerchief. Now what on earth is a woman's handkerchief doing in Stanworth's library?'

'I expect she left it here,' Alec remarked wisely.

'Alec, this is positive genius! I see it all now. She must have left it here. And there was I thinking that she'd sent it by post, with special instructions for it to be placed between those cushions in case she ever wanted to find it there!'

'You are funny, aren't you?' Alec growled wearily.

'Occasionally,' Roger admitted modestly, 'quite. But reverting to the handkerchief, I wonder whether this is going to prove rather important. What do you think?'

'How could it?'

'I'm not quite sure yet, but I have a sort of feeling. It all depends on several things. Whose handkerchief it is, for instance, and when this settee was tidied up last, and when the owner of the handkerchief admits she was in here last, and – Oh, quite a large number of things.' He sniffed at the handkerchief delicately. 'H'm! I seem to know that scent, at all events.'

'You do?' Alec asked eagerly. 'Who uses it?'

'That unfortunately I don't appear to remember for the moment,' Roger confessed reluctantly. 'Still, we ought to be able to find that out with a few discreet inquiries.'

He put the handkerchief carefully in his breast pocket, crumpling it into a small ball so as to retain as much of the scent as possible.

'But I think the first thing to do,' he continued, when it was safely bestowed, 'is to examine this settee rather more minutely. You never know what you're going to find, apparently.'

Without disturbing the cushions further, he began a careful scrutiny of the back and arms. It was not long before he found himself rewarded.

'Look!' he exclaimed suddenly, pointing at a place on the left arm. 'Powder! See? Face powder, for a sovereign. Now I wonder what on earth that's got to tell us, if we only know how to read it.'

Alec bent and examined the place. A very faint smudge of white powder stood out upon the black surface of the cloth.

'You're sure that's face powder?' he asked, a little incredulously. 'How can you tell?'

'I can't,' Roger admitted cheerfully. 'It might be French chalk. But I'm sure it is face powder. Let me see, face powder just on the inner curve of the arm; what does that mean? Or talking about arms, perhaps it's arm powder. They do powder their arms, don't they?'

'I don't know. Probably.'

'Well, you ought to,' Roger said severely. 'You're engaged, aren't you?'

'No,' Alec replied mournfully. After all, Roger would have to know some time that the engagement had been broken off.

Roger stared at him in amazement. 'No? But you got engaged to Barbara yesterday, didn't you?'

'Yes,' said Alec, still more mournfully. 'But we broke it off today. Or postponed it, rather, It may be on again in a month or so, I hope.'

'But why, in the name of goodness?'

'Oh, for – for certain reasons,' Alec said lamely. 'We decided it was the best thing to do. Er – private reasons, you know.'

'Good Lord, I'm awfully sorry to hear it, old man,' said Roger genuinely. 'I hope things will come all right for you in the end; and if there's anything in the world that I can do, you know you've only got to say the word. There isn't a couple anywhere that I'd sooner see fixed up than you and Barbara. You're quite the nicest two people I know.' Roger was in the habit of disregarding the convention that a man should never under any circumstances display emotion in the presence of another man, just as heartily as he violated all other conventions.

Alec flushed with pleasure. 'Thanks awfully, old chap,' he said gruffly. 'I knew I could rely on you. But really, there isn't anything you could possibly do. And things will come out all right, I feel sure.'

'Well, I sincerely hope so, or I'll wring young Barbara's neck for her,' said Roger; and both men knew that the topic was closed, until or unless Alec himself chose to reopen it.

'And about this powder?' Alec prompted.

'Ah, yes. I hadn't finished with the settee, had I? Well, let's see if there's anything more to be found first.'

He bent over the couch again, only to look up the next instant.

'See this?' he said, indicating a long fair hair in the angle between the arm and the back. 'There *has* been a woman sitting here recently. This confirms the face powder. What an extraordinarily lucky thing that we thought of searching the place for that cartridge case. It would never have done to have missed this. I have an idea that this woman is going to be more useful to us than fifty cartridge cases.' And taking a letter out of his pocket he drew out the sheet of paper and carefully placed the hair in the envelope. 'They always do this in books,' he explained, observing Alec's interested gaze, 'so I suppose it's the right thing to do.'

'And what are you going to do next?' Alec asked, as the envelope followed the handkerchief into Roger's breast pocket. 'You've only got about half an hour before dinner time, you know.'

'Yes. I'm going to try and find out if I can when this settee was last tidied up; that seems to me the point on which everything depends. After that I've got to spot the owner of the handkerchief.'

'By the scent? There are no initials on it.'

'By the scent. This is the sort of occasion when being a dog must come in so useful,' Roger added reflectively.

chapter nineteen

Mr Sheringham Loses and Wins the Same Bet

At the top of the stairs the two parted, Alec going to his own room and Roger to his. Arrived there, the latter did not proceed immediately with his changing; for some moments he leaned, deep in thought, on the window-sill overlooking the garden. Then, as if he had come to a decision, he crossed the room briskly and rang the bell.

A cheerful, plump young person answered it and smiled questioningly. Roger was always a favourite with servants; if not always with gardeners.

'Oh, hullo, Alice. I say, I seem to have lost my fountain pen. You haven't seen it about anywhere, have you?'

The girl shook her head. 'No, sir, that I haven't. It wasn't in here when I did the room this morning, I'm sure.'

'H'm! That's a nuisance. I've missed it since last night. The last time I remember having it was in the library a short time before dinner. I wonder if I can have left it in there. Do you do the library?'

'Oh, no, sir. I only do the bedrooms. Mary does the downstairs rooms.'

'I see. Well, do you think I could have a word with Mary, if she's not too busy? Perhaps you could send her up here?'

'Yes, sir. I'll tell her at once.'

'Thank you, Alice.'

In due course Mary made her appearance.

'I say, Mary,' Roger remarked confidentially, 'I've lost my fountain pen, and Alice tells me that she hasn't come across it in here. Now the last time I had it was in the library yesterday, some time between tea and dinner; I've been looking round for it in there, but I can't see it. I suppose you haven't tidied up the library since then, or seen anything of it?'

'Yes, sir, I tidied up the library last night while they were in at dinner. And little did I think when I was doing it that – '

'Yes, quite so,' Roger put in soothingly. 'Shocking business! But what did the tidying up consist of, Mary? I mean, if it was only cursory you might not have noticed the pen. What did you do exactly?'

'Well, sir, I put the chairs straight and tidied up the cigarette ends in the hearth and emptied the ashtrays.'

'What about the settee? I remember sitting on the settee with the pen in my hand.'

'It wasn't there then, sir,' Mary said with decision. 'I took up all the cushions and shook them, and there wasn't anything there. I should have noticed it if there had been.'

'I see. You did the settee quite thoroughly, in fact? Brushed it, and all that sort of thing?'

'Yes, sir. I always run a brush over the settee and the armchairs of an evening. They get so terribly dusty with all those windows, and that black rep shows the dust up something awful.'

'Well, thank you, Mary. I suppose I must have left it somewhere else, after all. By the way, you haven't done the library at all today, have you?'

'No, sir,' Mary replied with a little shiver. 'Nor wouldn't like to; not alone, at all events. Creepy, I should call it, sir, with that poor gentleman sitting there all night like a – '

'Yes, yes,' said Roger with mechanical haste. 'Shocking! Well, I'm sorry to have brought you all this way for nothing, Mary; but if you ever come across it, you might let me know.'

'Yes, sir,' Mary said with a pleasant smile. 'Thank you, sir.'

'And that is that!' Roger murmured confidentially to the closing door.

He completed his changing as rapidly as possible and, hurrying along to Alec's room, recounted the facts he had just learnt.

'So you see,' he concluded, 'that woman must have been in the library some time after dinner. Now who was it? Barbara was with you in the garden, of course; so she's out of the running. That leaves Mrs Shannon, Mrs Plant, and Lady Stanworth – if it *was* somebody in the house, by the way,' he added thoughtfully. 'I never thought of that.'

Alec paused in the act of tying his black tie to look round interrogatively.

'But what's all this getting at?' he asked. 'Is there any particular reason why one of those three shouldn't have been in the library yesterday evening?'

'No, not exactly. But it rather depends on who it is. If it was Lady Stanworth, for instance, I shouldn't say there was anything in it; unless she specifically denied that she went into the library at all. On the other hand, if it was someone from outside the household it might be decidedly important. Oh, it's too vague to explain, but what I feel is that this is the emergence of a new fact – the presence of a woman in the library yesterday evening. And a woman sitting down at that, not just passing through. Therefore, like every other fact in the case, it has got to be investigated. It may turn out to be absolutely in order. On the other hand, it may not. That's all.'

'It's certainly vague, as you say,' Alec commented, fastening his waistcoat. 'And when do you expect to spot the woman?'

'Possibly the end of dinner. I shall sniff delicately and unobtrusively at Lady Stanworth and Mrs Plant, and if it isn't either of them, it may be Mrs Shannon. If that's the case, of course there's no importance to be attached to it at all; but if it isn't any of them, I don't know what I shall do. I can't go dashing all over the county, sniffing at strange women, can I? It might lead to all sorts of awkward complications. Hurry up, Alexander, the bell went at least five minutes ago.'

'I'm ready,' Alec said, glancing at his well flattened hair in the mirror with approval. 'Lead on.'

The others were already waiting for them when they arrived in the drawing room, and the party went in to dinner at once. Lady Stanworth was present, to all appearances unmoved, but even more silent than usual; and her presence laid an added constraint on the little gathering.

Roger tried hard to keep the ball rolling, and both Mrs Plant and Jefferson did their best in their respective ways to second him, but Alec for some reason was almost as quiet as his hostess. Glancing now and again at his preoccupied face, Roger concluded that the role of amateur detective was proving highly uncongenial to that uncompromisingly straightforward young man. Probably the introduction of this new feminine question regarding the ownership of the handkerchief was upsetting him again.

'Did you notice,' Roger remarked casually, addressing himself to Jefferson, 'when the inspector was questioning us this morning, how very difficult it is to remember the things that have occurred, even only twenty-four hours before, if they were not sufficiently important to impress one in any way?'

'Yes, I know what you mean,' Jefferson agreed. 'Noticed it often myself.'

Roger glanced at him curiously. It was a strange position, this sort of armed and forced friendliness between Jefferson and himself. If the former had heard much of that conversation by the lattice window, he must know Roger for his enemy; and in any case the disappearance of the footprint showed that he was thoroughly on his guard. Yet not the faintest trace of this appeared in his manner. He behaved towards both of them exactly as he always had done; no more and no less. Roger could not help admiring the man's nerve.

'Especially as regards movements,' he resumed conversationally. 'I often have the very greatest trouble in remembering exactly where I was at a certain time. Last night wasn't so difficult, because I was in the garden from the end of dinner till I went up to bed. But take your case, for instance, Lady Stanworth. I'm prepared to bet quite a reasonable sum that you couldn't say, without stopping to think, exactly what rooms you visited yesterday evening between the end of dinner and going up to bed.'

Out of the tail of his eye Roger noticed a quick look flash between Lady Stanworth and Jefferson. It was as if the latter had warned her of the possibility of a trap.

'Then I am afraid you would lose your bet, Mr Sheringham,' she replied calmly, after a momentary pause. 'I remember perfectly. From the dining room I went into the drawing room, where I sat for about half an hour. Then I went into the morning room to discuss certain of the accounts with Major Jefferson, and after that I went upstairs.'

'Oh, that's altogether too easy,' Roger laughed. 'It's not playing fair. You ought to have visited far more rooms than that to make the game a success. What about you, then, Mrs Plant? Shall I transfer the bet to you?'

'You'd lose again if you did,' Mrs Plant smiled. 'I was only in one room, worse still. I stayed in the drawing room the whole time till I met you in the hall on my way upstairs. There! What was the bet, by the way?'

'I shall have to think of that. A handkerchief, I think, don't you? Yes, I owe you a handkerchief.'

'What a poor little bet!' Mrs Plant laughed. 'I wouldn't have taken it if I'd known it was going to be so unremunerative.'

'Well, I'll throw in a bottle of scent to go with it, shall I?'

'That would be better, certainly.'

'Better stop there, Sheringham,' Jefferson put in. 'She'll have got on to gloves before you know where you are.'

'Oh, I'm drawing the line at scent. What's your favourite brand, by the way, Mrs Plant?'

'*Amour des Fleurs*,' Mrs Plant replied promptly. 'A guinea a bottle!'

'Oh! Remember, I'm only a poor author.'

'Well, you asked for my favourite, so I told you. But that isn't the one I generally use.'

'Ah, now we're getting warmer. Something about elevenpence a bottle is more like my mark.'

'I'm afraid you'll have to pay just a little more than that. *Parfum Jasmine*; nine and sixpence. And it will serve you right.'

'I shan't bet with *you* again, Mrs Plant,' Roger retorted with mock severity. 'I hate people who win bets against me. It isn't fair.'

For the rest of dinner Roger seemed to be a little preoccupied.

As soon as the ladies had left the room, he strolled over to the open French windows which, like those of the library on the other side, led out on to the lawn.

'I think a smoke in the open air is indicated,' he observed carelessly. 'Coming, Alec? What about you, Jefferson?'

'No rest for me, I'm afraid,' Jefferson replied with a smile. 'I'm up to the eyes in it.'

'Straightening things up?'

'Trying to; they're in a dreadful muddle.'

'Finances, you mean?'

'Yes, that and everything. He always managed his own affairs and this is the first time I've seen his passbooks and the rest. As he appeared to have accounts at no less than five different banks, you can understand something of what I've got to wade through.' Jefferson's manner was perfectly friendly and open, almost frank.

'That's funny. I wonder why he did that. And have you found any reason for his killing himself?'

'None,' said Jefferson candidly. 'In fact, the whole thing absolutely beats me. It's the last thing you'd have expected of old Stanworth, if you'd known him as well as I did.'

'You knew him pretty well, of course?' Roger asked, applying a match to his cigarette.

'I should say so. I was with him longer than I like to remember,' Jefferson replied with a little laugh that sounded somewhat bitter to Roger's suspicious ears.

'What sort of a man was he really? I thought him quite a good sort; but then I'd probably only seen one side of him.'

'Oh, everyone has their different sides, don't they?' Jefferson parried. 'I don't suppose Stanworth was very unlike anyone else.'

'Why did he employ an ex-prize-fighter as a butler?' Roger asked suddenly, looking the other straight in the face.

But Jefferson was not to be caught off his guard.

'Oh, a whim I should think,' he said easily. 'He had plenty of whims like that.'

'It seems funny to meet with a butler called Graves in real life,' Roger said with a little smile. 'They're always called Graves on the stage, aren't they?'

'Oh, that isn't his real name. He's really called Bill Higgins, I believe. Mr Stanworth couldn't face the name of Higgins, so he called him Graves instead.'

'It's a pity. Higgins is an admirably original name for a butler. Besides, it harmonises much more with the gentleman's general air of ruggedness, doesn't it? Well, what about this breath of air we promised ourselves, Alec? See you later no doubt, Jefferson.'

Jefferson nodded amicably, and the two strolled out on to the lawn. It was only just beginning to get dusk, and the light was still strong.

'I've found out who the handkerchief belongs to, Alec,' Roger said in a low voice.

'Have you? Who?'

'Mrs Plant. I was almost certain before we sat down to dinner, but what she said clinched it. That scent is jasmine right enough.'

'And what are you going to do?'

Roger hesitated. 'Well, you heard what she said,' he replied, almost apologetically. 'She didn't actually deny it, because I never asked her; but she wouldn't admit to being in the library at all yesterday evening.'

'But surely it's a perfectly innocent thing to be in the library?' Alec protested. 'Why, Stanworth wasn't even there.

He was out in the garden with you. Why shouldn't she have been in the library?'

'And, equally, why shouldn't she acknowledge it?' Roger retorted quickly.

'It may have slipped her memory. That's nothing. You were saying yourself how difficult it is to remember exactly where one's been.'

'It's no use, Alec,' Roger said gently. 'We've got to clear this up. It may be innocent enough; I only hope it is! On the other hand, it may be exceedingly important for us to find out just exactly why Mrs Plant was in that library, and what she was doing there. You must see that we can't leave it as it is.'

'But what do you propose to do? Tackle her about it?'

'Yes. I'm going to ask her point-blank if she was in the library last night or not, and see what she says.'

'And if she denies it?'

Roger shrugged his shoulders. 'That remains to be seen,' he said shortly.

'I don't like it,' Alec frowned. 'In fact, I hate it. It's a beastly position. Look here, Roger,' he said with sudden earnestness, 'let's chuck the whole thing! Let's assume, as the police are doing, that old Stanworth committed suicide and leave it at that. Shall we?'

'You bet we won't!' Roger said grimly. 'I'm not going to leave a thing half threshed out like that; especially not such an interesting thing as this. You can back out if you like; there's no reason for you to be mixed up with it if you don't want. But I'm most decidedly going on with it.'

'Oh, if you do, I shall, too,' Alec replied gloomily. 'But I'd much rather we both chucked it.'

'That's out of the question,' Roger said briskly. 'Couldn't dream of it. Well, if you're going to stick to it with me, you'd better be present at my chat with Mrs Plant. Let's stroll round to the drawing room and see if we can find an excuse to speak with her alone.'

'All right, then,' Alec agreed unhappily. 'If we must.'

Luck was on their side. Mrs Plant was alone in the drawing room. Roger drew a chair up so as to face her squarely and commented casually on Lady Stanworth's absence. Alec turned his back on them and gazed moodily out of the window, as if washing his hands of the whole affair.

'Lady Stanworth?' Mrs Plant repeated. 'Oh, she's gone in to help Major Jefferson, I think. In the morning room.'

Roger looked at her steadily. 'Mrs Plant,' he said in a low voice, 'you're quite certain you won that bet of ours at dinner, aren't you?'

'Certain?' asked Mrs Plant uneasily. 'Of course I am. Why?'

'You didn't forget any room that you went into yesterday evening by any chance?' Roger pursued firmly. 'The morning room, the storeroom, or – the library, for instance?'

Mrs Plant stared at him with wide eyes. 'What do you mean, Mr Sheringham?' she asked in somewhat heightened tones. 'Of course I didn't forget.'

'You went into none of those rooms, then?'

'Certainly not!'

'H'm! The bet was a bottle of scent and a handkerchief, wasn't it?' Roger remarked musingly, feeling in his pocket. 'Well, here's the handkerchief. I found it where you left it – on the couch in the library!'

chapter twenty

Mrs Plant Proves Disappointing

For a moment Mrs Plant sat perfectly rigid. Then she put out her hand and mechanically took the handkerchief that Roger was still holding out to her. Her face had gone quite white and her eyes were wide with terror.

'Please don't be alarmed,' said Roger gently, touching her hand reassuringly. 'I don't want to frighten you, or anything like that; but don't you think it would be better if you told me the truth? You might get into very serious trouble with the police, you know, if it came out that you had been concealing any important fact. Really, I only want to help you, Mrs Plant.'

The colour drained back into her face at that, though her breath still came in gasps and she continued to stare at him fearfully.

'But – but it wasn't anything – important,' she said jerkily. 'It was only – ' She paused again.

'Don't tell me if you'd rather not, of course,' Roger said quickly. 'But I can't help feeling that I might be able to advise you. It's a serious matter to mislead the police, even in the most trivial details. Take your time and think it over.' He rose to his feet and joined Alec at the window.

When Mrs Plant spoke again, her composure was largely restored.

'Really,' she said, with a nervous little laugh, 'it's absurd for me to make such a fuss over a trifle, but I have got a horror of giving evidence – morbid, if you like, but none the less genuine. So I tried to minimise my last conversation with Mr Stanworth as much as possible, in the hope that the police would attach so little importance to it that they wouldn't call on me to give evidence.'

Roger seated himself on the arm of a chair and swung his leg carelessly.

'But you'll be called in any case, so why not tell exactly what happened?'

'Yes, but – but I didn't know that then, you see; not when I made my statement. I didn't think they'd call me at all then. Or I hoped they wouldn't.'

'I see. Still, I think it would be better not to conceal anything as things are, don't you?'

'Oh, yes. I quite see that now. Quite. It's very good of you to help me like this, Mr Sheringham. When – when did you find my handkerchief?'

'Just before I went up to change for dinner. It was between two of those loose cushions on the couch.'

'So you knew I must have been in the library? But how did you know what time I was there?'

'I didn't. In fact, I don't know,' Roger smiled. 'All I know is that it must have been after dinner, because the maid always tidies the room at that time.'

Mrs Plant nodded slowly. 'I see. Yes, that was clever of you. I didn't leave anything else there, did I?' she added, again with that nervous little laugh.

'No, nothing else,' Roger replied smoothly. 'Well, have you thought it over?'

'Oh, of course I'll tell you, Mr Sheringham. It's really too ridiculous. You remember when you passed us in the hall? Well, Mr Stanworth was speaking to me about some roses he'd had sent up to my room. And then I asked him if he'd put my jewels in his safe for me, as I – '

'But I thought you said this morning that you asked him that the other day?' Roger interrupted.

Mrs Plant laughed lightly. She was quite herself again.

'Yes, I did; and I told the inspector it was yesterday morning. Wasn't it dreadful of me? That's why I was so upset when you told me this afternoon that I should have to give evidence. I was so afraid they'd ask me a lot of questions and find out that I was in the library, after all, when I hadn't said anything about it, and that I had told the inspector a lie about the jewels. In fact, you frightened me terribly, Mr Sheringham. I had dreadful visions of passing the rest of my days in prison for telling fibs to the police.'

'I'm very sorry,' Roger smiled. 'But I didn't know, did I?'

'Of course you didn't. It was my own fault. Well, anyhow, Mr Stanworth very kindly said he'd be delighted to put them away safely for me, so I ran upstairs to get them and brought them down into the library. Then I sat on the couch and watched him put them in the safe. That's all that happened really, and I quite see now how absurd it was of me to conceal it.'

'H'm!' said Roger thoughtfully. 'Well, it certainly isn't vastly important in any case, is it? And that's all?'

'Every bit!' Mrs Plant replied firmly. 'Now what do you advise me to do? Admit that I made a mistake when I was with the inspector and tell the truth? Or just say nothing about it? It may be very silly of me, but I really can't see that it makes the least difference either way. The incident is of no importance at all.'

'Still, it's best to be on the safe side, I think. If I were you I should take the inspector aside before the proceedings open tomorrow and tell him frankly that you made a mistake, and that you took your jewels in to Mr Stanworth in the library last night before saying good night to him.'

Mrs Plant made a wry face. 'Very well,' she said reluctantly, 'I will. It's horrid to have to admit that one was wrong; but you're probably right. Anyhow, I'll do that.'

'I think you're wise,' Roger replied, getting to his feet again. 'Well, Alec, what about that stroll of ours? I'm afraid it will have to be a moonlit one now.' He paused in the doorway and turned back. 'Good night, Mrs Plant, if I don't see you again; I expect you will be turning in fairly early. Sleep well, and don't let things worry you, whatever you do.'

'I'll try not to,' she smiled back. 'Good night, Mr Sheringham, and thank you very much indeed.' And she heaved a heartfelt sigh of relief as she watched his disappearing back.

The two made their way out on to the lawn in silence.

'Hullo,' Roger remarked, as they reached the big cedar, 'they've left the chairs out here. Let's take advantage of them.'

'Well?' Alec demanded gruffly when they were seated, disapproval written large in every line of him. 'Well? I hope you're satisfied now.'

Roger pulled his pipe out of his pocket and filled it methodically, gazing thoughtfully into the soft darkness as he did so.

'Satisfied?' he repeated at last. 'Well, hardly. What do you think?'

'I think you scared that wretched woman out of her wits for absolutely nothing at all. I told you ages ago you were making a mistake about her.'

'You're a very simple-minded young man I'm afraid, Alec,' Roger said, quite regretfully.

'Why, you surely don't mean to say you disbelieve her?' Alec asked in astonishment.

'H'm! I wouldn't necessarily say that. She *may* have been speaking the truth.'

'That's awfully good of you,' Alec commented sarcastically.

'But the trouble is that she certainly wasn't speaking the whole of it. She's got something up her sleeve, has that lady, whatever you choose to think, Alec. Didn't you notice how she tried to pump me? How did I know what time she'd been in there? Had she left anything else there? When did I find the handkerchief? No, her explanation sounds perfectly reasonable, I admit, as far as it goes. But it doesn't go nearly far enough. It doesn't explain the powder on the arm of the couch, for instance; and I noticed at dinner that she doesn't powder her arms. But there's one thing above all that it leaves entirely out of the reckoning.'

'Oh?' Alec asked ironically. 'And what may that be?'

'The fact that she was crying when she was in the library,' Roger replied simply.

'How on earth do you know that?' said the dumbfounded Alec.

'Because the handkerchief was just slightly damp when I found it. Also it was rolled up in a tight little ball, as women do when they cry.'

'Oh!' said Alec blankly.

'So you see there is still a lot for which Mrs Plant did most certainly not account, isn't there? As to what she did say, it may be true or it may be not. In gist I should say that it was. There's only one thing that I'm really doubtful about, and that's the time when she said she was in the library.'

'What makes you doubt that?'

'Well, in the first place I didn't hear her come upstairs immediately to fetch her jewels, as I almost certainly should have done. And, secondly, didn't you notice that she carefully asked me if I knew what time she was there, before she gave a time at all? In other words, after I had let out like an idiot that I didn't know what time she was there, she realised that she could say what time she liked, and as long as it didn't clash with any of the known facts (such as Stanworth being out in the garden with me) it would be all right.'

'Splitting hairs?' Alec murmured laconically.

'Possibly; but nice, thick, easily splittable ones.'

For a time they smoked in silence, each engaged with his own thoughts. Then:

'Who would you say was the older, Alec,' Roger asked suddenly, 'Lady Stanworth or Mrs Shannon?'

'Mrs Shannon,' Alec replied without hesitation. 'Why?'

'I was just wondering. But Lady Stanworth looks older; her hair is getting quite grey. Mrs Shannon's is still brown.'

'Yes, I know Mrs Shannon looks the younger of the two; but I'm sure she's not, for all that.'

'Well, what age would you put Jefferson at?'

'Lord, I don't know. He might be any age. About the same as Lady Stanworth, I should imagine. What on earth are you asking all this for?'

'Oh, just something that was passing through my mind. Nothing very important.'

They relapsed into silence once more.

Suddenly Roger slapped his knee. 'By Jove!' he ejaculated. 'I wonder if we dare!'

'What's up now?'

'I've just had a brain wave. Look here, Alexander Watson, it seems to me that we've been tackling this little affair from the wrong end.'

'How's that?'

'Why, we've been concentrating all our energies on working backwards from suspicious circumstances and people. What we ought to have done is to start farther back and work forwards.'

'Don't quite get you.'

'Well, put it another way. The big clue to any murder must after all be supplied by the victim himself. People don't get murdered for nothing – except by a chance burglar, of course, or a homicidal maniac; and I think we can dismiss both of those possibilities here. What I mean is, find out all you can about the victim and the information ought to give you a lead towards his murderer. You see? We've been neglecting that side of it altogether. What we ought to have been doing is to collect every possible scrap of information we can about old Stanworth. Find out exactly what sort of a character he had and all his activities, and then work forwards from that. Get me?'

'That seems reasonable enough,' Alec said cautiously. 'But how could we find out anything? It's no good asking Jefferson or Lady Stanworth. We should never get any information out of them.'

'No, but we've got the very chance lying close to our hand to find out pretty nearly as much as Jefferson knows,' Roger said excitedly. 'Didn't he say that he was going through all Stanworth's papers and accounts and things in the morning room? What's to prevent us having a look at them, too?'

'You mean, nip in when nobody's about and go through them?'

'Exactly. Are you game?'

Alec was silent for a moment.

'Hardly done, is it?' he said at last. 'Fellow's private papers and all that, I mean, what?'

'Alec, you sponge-headed parrot!' Roger exclaimed, in tones of the liveliest exasperation. 'Really, you are a most maddening person! Here's a chap murdered under your very nose, and you're prepared to let the murderer walk away scot-free because you think it isn't 'done' to look through the wretched victim's private papers. How remarkably pleased Stanworth would be to hear you, wouldn't he?'

'Of course if you put it like that,' Alec said doubtfully.

'But I do put it like that, you goop! It's the only way there is of putting it. Come, Alec, do try and be sensible for once in your life.'

'All right then,' Alec said, though not with any vast degree of enthusiasm. 'I'm game.'

'That's more like it. Now look here, my bedroom window is in the front of the house and I can see the morning-room window from it. You go to bed in the ordinary way, and sleep, too, if you like (all the better, in case Jefferson should take it into his head to have a look in at you); and I'll sit up and watch for the morning-room light to go out. I'm safe enough in any case, as I can always pretend to be working; I'll put my things out, in fact. Then I'll wait for an hour after it's out, to give Jefferson plenty of time to get to sleep; and then I'll come along and rouse you, and we'll creep down at our leisure. How about that?'

'Sounds all right,' Alec admitted.

'Then that's settled,' Roger said briskly. 'Well, I think the best thing for you to do is to go to bed at once, yawning loudly and ostentatiously. It will show that you have gone, for one thing; and also it will show that we're not powwowing together out here. We've got to remember that those three, in spite of their fair words and friendliness, are bound to be regarding us with the greatest suspicion. They don't know how much we know, and of course they daren't give themselves away by trying to find out. But you can be sure that Jefferson has warned the others about that footprint; and I expect that as soon as our backs were turned just now, Mrs Plant ran into the morning room and recounted our conversation to them. That's why I pretended to be taken in by her explanation.'

The bowl of Alec's pipe glowed red in the darkness.

'You're still convinced, then, in spite of what she said, that those three are in league together?' he asked after a moment's pause.

'Run along to bed, little Alexander,' said Roger kindly, 'and don't be childish.'

chapter twenty – one

Mr Sheringham Is Dramatic

Long after Alec's not altogether willing departure, Roger sat smoking and thinking. On the whole, he was not sorry to be alone. Alec was proving a somewhat discouraging companion in this business. Evidently his heart was not in it; and for one so situated the ferreting out of facts and the general atmosphere of suspicion and distrust that is inevitably attendant on such a task, must be singularly distasteful. Roger could not blame Alec for his undisguised reluctance to see the thing through, but he also could not help thinking somewhat wistfully of the enthusiastic and worshipping prototypes whose mantle Alec was at first supposed to have inherited. Roger felt that he could have welcomed a little enthusiasm and worshipping at the end of this eventful and very strenuous day.

He began to try to arrange methodically in his mind the data they had collected. First with regard to the murderer. He had made an effective escape from the house only, in all probability as it seemed, to enter it again by another way. Why? Either because he lived there, or because he wished to communicate with somebody who did. Which of these? Heaven only knew!

He tried another line of attack. Which of the minor puzzles still remained unsolved? Chiefly, without doubt, the sudden change of attitude on the part of Mrs Plant and Jefferson before lunch. But why need they have been apprehensive at all, if the murderer had been able to communicate with them after the crime had been committed? Perhaps the interview had been a hurried one, and he had forgotten to reassure them on some particularly vital point. Yet he had been able to do so in the course of the next morning. This meant that, up till lunch time at any rate, he had still been in the neighbourhood. More than that, actually on the premises, as it seemed. Did this point more definitely to the probability of his being one of the household? It seemed feasible; but who? Jefferson? Possibly, though there were several difficult points to get over if this were the case. The women were obviously out of the question. The butler? Again possibly; but why on earth should the man want to murder his master?

Yet the butler was a strange figure, there was no getting away from that. And as far as Roger could judge, there had been no love lost between him and Stanworth. Yes, there was undoubtedly a mystery of some kind connected with that butler. Jefferson's explanation of why Mr Stanworth should have employed a prize-fighting butler did not strike one as quite satisfactory.

Then why had Mrs Plant been crying in the library? Roger strove to remember some scenes in which she and Stanworth had been thrown into contact. How had they behaved towards each other? Had they seemed friendly, or the reverse? As far as he could recollect, Stanworth had treated her with the same casual good-fellowship which he showed to everybody; while she – Yes, now he came to think of it, she had never appeared to be on particularly good terms with him. She had been quiet and reserved when he was in the room. Not that she was really ever anything else but quiet and reserved under any circumstances; but yes, there had been a subtle change in her manner when he was about. Obviously she had disliked him.

Clearly there was only one hope for finding the answer to these riddles, and that was to investigate Stanworth's affairs. In all probability even that would prove futile; but as far as Roger could see there was no other way to try with even a moderate chance of success. And while he was racking his brains out here, Jefferson was sitting in the morning room surrounded by documents which Roger would give anything to see.

A sudden idea occurred to him. Why not beard the lion in his den and offer to give Jefferson a hand with his task? In any case, that would form a direct challenge, the answer to which could not fail to be interesting.

With Roger to think was, in nine cases out of ten, to leap into precipitate action. Almost before the thought had completed its passage through his mind, he was on his feet and striding eagerly towards the house.

Without troubling to knock he burst open the door of the morning room and walked in. Jefferson was seated in front of the table in the centre of the room, surrounded, as Roger's mind's eye had seen him, with papers and documents. Lady Stanworth was not present.

He glanced up as Roger entered.

'Hullo, Sheringham,' he said in some surprise. 'Anything I can do for you?'

'Well, I was smoking out there in the garden with nothing to do,' Roger remarked with a friendly smile, 'when it occurred to me that instead of wasting my time like that I might be giving you a hand here; you said you were up to the eyes in it. Is there anything I can do to help?'

'Damned good of you,' Jefferson replied, a little awkwardly, 'but I don't really think there's anything. I'm trying to tabulate a statement of his financial position. Something like that is sure to be wanted when the will's proved, or whatever the rigmarole is.'

'Well, surely there's something I can do to help you out, isn't there?' Roger asked, sitting on a corner of the table. 'Add up tremendous columns of figures, or something like that?'

Jefferson hesitated and glanced round at the papers in front of him. 'Well,' he said slowly.

'Of course if there's anything particularly private in Stanworth's affairs – !' Roger remarked airily.

Jefferson looked up quickly. 'Private? There's nothing particularly private about them. Why should there be?'

'Then make use of me by all means, my dear chap. I'm at a loose end, and only too glad to give you a hand.'

'Of course if you put it like that, I should be only too pleased,' Jefferson replied, though not without a certain reluctance. 'H'm! I was just wondering what would be the best job for you to tackle.'

'Oh, anything that comes along, you know.'

'Well, look here, I tell you what you might do,' Jefferson said suddenly. 'I want a statement made out showing his holdings in the various companies of which he was a director, with the approximate value of the shares, their yield for the last financial year, his director's fees, and all the rest of it. Manage that, could you?'

'Like a shot,' said Roger with great cheerfulness, concealing his disappointment at the comparative un-importance of the task allotted to him. Such details as these could be obtained from any work of reference on the subject; he had hoped for a little insight into something that was rather less public property.

Still, half a bun was better than no cake, and he settled down at the opposite side of the table and set to work willingly enough on the data with which Jefferson supplied him. From time to time he tried to peep surreptitiously at some of the documents in which the latter was immersed, but Jefferson was guarding them too jealously and Roger could obtain no clear idea of their contents.

An hour later he sat back in his chair with a sigh of relief.

'There you are! And a very charming and comprehensive statement, too.'

'Thanks very much,' Jefferson said, taking the statement which Roger was holding out to him. 'Damned good of you, Sheringham. Saved me a lot of trouble. And you've done it in about a quarter of the time I should have taken. Not my sort of line, this game.'

'So I should imagine,' Roger observed with studied carelessness. 'In fact, it's always surprised me that you should have taken a job like this secretaryship on at all. I should have put you down as a typical open-air man, if you'll allow me to say so. The type of Englishman that won our colonies for us, you know.'

'No option,' Jefferson said, with a return to his usual curt manner. 'Not my choice, I assure you. Had to take what I could jolly well get.'

'Rotten, I know,' Roger replied sympathetically, watching the other curiously. In spite of himself and what he felt he knew he could not help a mild liking for this abrupt, taciturn person; a typical soldier of the wordless, unsocial school. It struck Roger at that moment that Jefferson, whom he had been inclined to regard at first as something of a sinister figure, was in reality nothing of the sort. The man was shy, exceedingly shy, and he endeavoured to hide this shyness behind a brusque, almost rude manner; and as always in such a case, this had produced an entirely mistaken first impression of the man himself behind the manner. Jefferson was downright; but it was the downrightness of honesty, Roger felt, not of villainy.

Roger began, half unconsciously, to rearrange some of his ideas. If Jefferson was concerned in Stanworth's death, then it would be because there was a very excellent reason for that death. All the more reason to probe into Stanworth's affairs.

'Going to stay down here long, Jefferson?' he asked, with an obvious yawn.

'Not very. Just got to finish off this job I'm on now. You turn in. Must be getting pretty late.'

Roger glanced at his watch. 'Close on twelve. Right, I think I will, if you're sure there's nothing else I can do?'

'Nothing, thanks. I shall have a go at it before breakfast myself. Got to get cleared up in here by eleven. Well, good night, Sheringham, and many thanks.'

Roger sought his room in a state of some perplexity. This new conclusion of his with regard to Jefferson was going to make things very much more complicated instead of more simple. He felt a strong sympathy with Jefferson all of a sudden. He was not a clever man; certainly he was not the brains of the conspiracy. What must his feelings be when he knew, as indeed he must know, that Roger was tracking out things that would, in ninety-nine cases out of a hundred and with only very ordinary luck, have remained undiscovered for ever? How must he regard the net which he could see spread to catch him, and with him − whom?

Roger dragged a chair up to the open window, and sat down with his feet on the sill. He felt he was getting maudlin. This had every appearance of a thoroughly cold-blooded crime, and here he was feeling sorry already for one of its chief participants. Yet it was because Jefferson, as he saw now that the scales had suddenly fallen from his eyes, was such a fine type of man − the tall, thin, small-headed type that is the real pioneer of our race − and because he himself genuinely liked all three members of that suspicious trio, that Roger, without necessarily giving way to maudlin sentiment, was yet unable to stifle his very real regret that everything should point so decisively to their guilt.

Still, it was too late to back out now. He owed it to himself, if not even to them, to see the thing through. Roger could sympathise more fully now with Alec's feelings on the matter. Curious that he should after all have come round in the end to that much-derided point of view of Alec's!

He began to review the personal element in the light of this new revelation. How did it help? If Jefferson was an honest man and would only kill because nothing short of killing would meet some unknown case, then what was most likely to have produced such a state of affairs? What is the mainspring that actuates three quarters of such drastic deeds? Well, the answer to that was obvious enough. A woman.

How did that apply in this case? Could Jefferson be in love with some woman, whose happiness or peace had been threatened in some mysterious way by Stanworth himself, and if so, who was the woman? Lady Stanworth? Mrs Plant? Roger uttered an involuntary exclamation. Mrs Plant!

That, at any rate, would fit in with some of the puzzling facts. The powder on the arm of the couch, for instance, and the wet handkerchief.

Roger's imagination began to ride free. Mrs Plant was in the library with Stanworth; he was bullying her, or something. Perhaps he was trying to force some course of action upon her which was repugnant to her. In any case, she weeps and implores him. He is adamant. She hides her face against the arm of the couch and goes on weeping. Jefferson enters, sees at a glance what is happening and kills Stanworth in the madness of his passion with as little compunction as one would feel towards a rat. Mrs Plant looks on in horror; tries to interfere, perhaps, but without effect. As soon as the thing is done she becomes as cool as ice and sets the stage for suicide.

Roger jumped to his feet and leaned out over the sill.

'It fits!' he murmured excitedly. 'It all fits in!' Glancing downwards, he noticed that the morning-room light had been extinguished and made a note of the time. It was past one. He sank back in his chair and began to consider whether the other pieces of the puzzle would slip as neatly into this general scene – the safe incident, the change of attitude, Lady Stanworth, and so on. No, this was not going to be quite so easy.

At the end of the hour he was still uncertain. The main outline still seemed convincing enough, but all the details appeared hardly so glib.

'I'm getting addled,' he murmured aloud, as he rose from the chair. 'Better give this side of it a rest for a little.'

He made his way softly out of the room and crept along the passage to Alec's bedroom.

Alec sat abruptly up in bed as the door opened.

'That you, Roger?' he demanded.

'No, this is Jefferson,' Roger said, hastily shutting the door behind him. 'And very nicely you'd have given things away if it had been, Alexander Watson. And you might try and moderate your voice a bit. The sound of a foghorn in the middle of the night is bound to make people wonder. Ready?'

Alec got out of bed and put on his dressing gown.

'Right-ho.'

As quietly as possible they stole downstairs and into the morning room. Roger drew the thick curtains together carefully before switching on the light.

'Now for it!' he breathed excitedly, eyeing the crowded table with eagerness. 'That little pile there I've already been through, so you needn't bother about those.'

'Already?' Alec asked in surprise.

'Yes, in company with my excellent friend, Major Jefferson,' Roger grinned, and proceeded to explain what he had been doing.

'You've got some cheek,' Alec commented with a smile.

'Yes, and I've got something more than that,' Roger retorted. 'I've got a thoroughly sound working idea as to who killed Stanworth and under what circumstances. I can tell you, friend Alec, I've been uncommonly busy these last two hours or so.'

'You have?' said Alec eagerly. 'Tell me.'

Roger shook his head. 'Not at the moment,' he said, sitting down in Jefferson's chair. 'Let's get this little job safely done first. Now look here, you go through these miscellaneous documents, will you? I want to study the passbooks first of all. And I'll tell you one thing I've discovered. The income from those various businesses of his didn't amount to a quarter of what he must have been spending. He cleared just over two thousand out of all five of them last year, and I should say that he's been living at the rate of at least ten thousand a year. And besides all that, he's been investing heavily as well. Where does all the extra cash come from? That's what I want to find out.'

Alec began to wade obediently through the sheaf of papers that Roger had indicated, while the latter picked out the passbooks and glanced at them.

'Hullo!' he exclaimed suddenly. 'Two of these accounts are in his own name, and the other three appear to be in three different names. Jefferson never said anything about that. Now I wonder what the devil that means?'

He began to pore over them methodically, and for some time there was silence in the room. Then Roger looked up with a frown.

'I don't understand these at all,' he said slowly. 'The dividends are all shown in his own two passbooks, and various checks and so on; but the other three seem to be made up entirely of cash payments, on the credit side at any rate. Listen to this: Feb. 9th, £100; Feb. 17th, £500; Mar. 12th, £200; Mar. 28th, £350; and then April 9th, £1,000. What on earth do you make of that? All in cash, and such nice round sums. Why a thousand pounds in cash?'

'Seems funny, certainly,' Alec agreed.

Roger picked up another of the books, and flicked the pages through carefully.

'This is just the same sort of thing. Hullo, here's an entry of £5,000 paid in cash. £5,000 in cash! Now why? What does it mean? Does your pile throw any light on it?'

'No, these are only business letters. There doesn't appear to be anything out of the ordinary here at all.'

Roger still held the book mechanically in his hand, but he was staring blankly at the wall.

'Nothing but cash,' he murmured softly; 'all sorts of sums between £10 and £5,000; each sum a multiple of ten, or some other round figure; no shillings or pence; and *cash!* That's what worries me. Why cash? I can't find a single check marked on the credit side of these three books. And where in the name of goodness did all this cash come from? There's absolutely nothing to account for it, as far as I can make out. It's not the proceeds of any sort of business, apparently. Besides, the debit side shows nothing but checks drawn to self. He paid it in as cash and he drew it out himself. Now what on earth does all this mean?'

'Don't ask me,' said Alec helplessly.

Roger stared at the wall in silence for a few minutes. Suddenly, his mouth opened, and he whistled softly.

'By – Jove!' he exclaimed, transferring his gaze to Alec. 'I believe I've got it. And doesn't it simplify things, too? Yes, it *must* be right. It makes everything as clear as daylight. Good lord! Well, I'm damned!'

'Out with it, then!'

Roger paused impressively. This was the most dramatic moment he had yet encountered, and he was not going to spoil it by any undue precipitation.

He smote the table softly with his fist by way of preparation. Then:

'Old Stanworth was a professional blackmailer!' he said in vibrant tones.

chapter twenty – two

Mr Sheringham Solves the Mystery

It was past ten o'clock on the following morning, and Roger and Alec were engaged in taking a constitutional in the rose garden after breakfast before the inquest proceedings opened. Roger had refused to say anything further on the previous evening – or, rather, in the small hours of the same morning. All he had done was to remark that it was quite time they were in bed, and that he wanted a clear head before discussing the affair in the light of this new revelation of Stanworth's character. He remarked this not once, but many times; and Alec had perforce to be contented with it.

Now, with pipes in full blast, they were preparing to go further into the matter.

Roger himself was complacently triumphant.

'Mystery?' he repeated, in answer to a question of Alec's. 'There isn't any mystery now. I've solved it.'

'Oh, I know the mystery about Stanworth is cleared up,' said Alec impatiently; to tell the truth, Roger in this mood irritated him not a little. 'That is, if your explanation is the right one, which I'm not disputing at the moment.'

'Thank you very much.'

'But what about the mystery of his death? You can't have solved that.'

'On the contrary, Alexander,' Roger rejoined, with a satisfied smile; 'that is exactly what I have done.'

'Oh? Then who killed him?'

'If you want it in a single word,' Roger said, not without a certain reluctance, 'Jefferson.'

'*Jefferson?*' Alec exclaimed. 'Oh, rot!'

Roger glanced at him curiously. 'Now that's interesting,' he commented. 'Why do you say "rot" like that?'

'Because – ' Alec hesitated. 'Oh, I don't know. It seems such rot to think of Jefferson committing a murder, I suppose. Why?'

'You mean, you don't think it's the sort of thing he would do?'

'I certainly don't!' Alec returned with emphasis.

'Do you know, Alec, I'm beginning to think you're a better judge of character than I am. It's a humiliating confession, but there you are. Tell me, have you always thought that about Jefferson, or only just recently?'

Alec considered. 'Ever since this business cropped up, I think. It always seemed fantastic to me that Jefferson could be mixed up with it. And the two women as well, for that matter. No, Roger, if you're trying to fix it on Jefferson, I'm quite sure you're making a bad mistake.'

Roger's complacency was unshaken.

'If the case were an ordinary one, no doubt,' he replied. 'But you've got to remember that this isn't. Stanworth was a blackmailer, and that alters everything. You may murder an ordinary man, but you execute a blackmailer. That is, if you don't kill him on the spur of the moment, carried away by madness or exasperation. You'd do that sort of thing on your own account, wouldn't you? Well, how much more so are you going to do it on behalf of a woman, and that a woman with whom you're in love? I tell you, Alec, the whole thing is as plain as a pikestaff.'

'Meaning that Jefferson is in love?'

'Precisely.'

'Who with?'

'Mrs Plant.'

Alec gasped. 'Good Lord, how on earth do you know that?' he asked incredulously.

'I don't,' Roger replied with a pleased air. 'But he must be. It's the only explanation. I deduced it.'

'The devil you did!'

'Yes, I'd arrived at that conclusion even before we discovered the secret of Stanworth's hidden life. That clears up absolutely everything.'

'Does it? I admit it seems to make some of the things more understandable, but I'm dashed if I can see how it makes you so sure that Jefferson killed him.'

'I'll explain,' Roger said kindly. 'Jefferson was secretly in love with Mrs Plant. For some reason or other Mrs Plant was being blackmailed by Stanworth unknown to Jefferson. He has a midnight interview with her in the library and demands money. She weeps and implores him (hence the dampness of the handkerchief) and lays a face on the arm of the couch as women do (hence the powder in that particular place). Stanworth is adamant; he must have money. She says she hasn't got any money. All right, says Stanworth, hand your jewels over then. She goes and gets her jewels and gives them to him. Stanworth opens the safe and tells her that is where he keeps his evidence against her. Then he locks the jewels up and tells her she can go. Enter Jefferson unexpectedly, takes in the situation at a glance, and goes for Stanworth bald-headed. Stanworth fires at him and misses, hitting the vase. Jefferson grabs his wrist, forces the revolver round and pulls the trigger, thus shooting Stanworth with his own revolver without relaxing the other's grip on it. Mrs Plant is horror-struck; but, seeing that the thing is done, she takes command of the situation and arranges the rest. And that,' Roger concluded, with a metaphorical pat on his own back, 'is the solution of the peculiar events at Layton Court.'

'Is it?' Alec said, with less certainty. 'It's a very pretty little story, no doubt, and does great credit to your imagination. But as to being the solution – well, I'm not so sure about that.'

'It seems to me to account for pretty well everything,' Roger retorted. 'But you always were difficult to please, Alec. Think. The broken vase and the second bullet; how the murder was committed; the fact that the murderer went back into the house again; the agitation about the safe being opened; Mrs Plant's behaviour in the morning, her reluctance to give evidence (in case she let out anything of what really happened, you see), and her fright when I sprang on her the fact that I knew she'd been in the library, after all; the disappearance of the footprints; the presence of the powder and the dampness of the handkerchief; Lady Stanworth's indifference to her brother-in-law's death (I expect he had some hold over her, too, if the truth were known); the employment of a prize-fighter as a butler, obviously a measure of self-protection; the fact that I heard people moving about late that night; everything! All cleared up and explained.'

'Humph!' said Alec noncommittally.

'Well, can you find a single flaw in it?' Roger asked, in some exasperation.

'If it comes to that,' Alec replied slowly, 'why was it that both Mrs Plant and Jefferson suddenly had no objection to the safe being opened, after they'd both shown that they were anxious to prevent it?'

'Easy!' Roger retorted. 'While we were upstairs, Jefferson opened the safe and took out the documents. It would only take a minute, after all. Any objection to that?'

'Did the inspector leave the keys behind? I thought he put them in his pocket.'

'No, he left them on the table, and Jefferson put them in *his* pocket. I remember noticing that at the time, and wondering why he did it. Now it's obvious, of course.'

'Well, what about that little pile of ashes in the library hearth? You suggested that it might be the remains of some important documents, and you thought that Jefferson looked uncommonly relieved at the idea.'

'My mistake at the time,' Roger said promptly. 'As for the ashes, they might have been anything. I don't attach any importance to them.'

'But you did!' Alec persisted obstinately.

'Yes, excellent but sponge-headed Alexander,' Roger explained patiently, 'because I thought at first that they *were* important. Now I see that I was mistaken, and they *aren't*. Are you beginning to grasp the idea?'

'Well, tell me this, then,' Alec said suddenly. 'Why the dickens didn't Jefferson get the documents out of the safe directly after Stanworth's death, instead of waiting till the next morning and getting so agitated about it?'

'Yes, I thought of that. Presumably because they were both so flustered at what had happened that they forgot all about the documents in their anxiety to cover up their traces and get away.'

Alec sniffed slightly. 'Rather unlikely that, isn't it? Not natural, as you're always so fond of saying.'

'Unlikely things do happen sometimes, however. This one did, for instance.'

'Then you're absolutely convinced that Jefferson killed Stanworth, and that's how it all happened, are you?'

'I am, Alexander.'

'Oh!'

'Well, aren't you?'

'No,' Alec said uncompromisingly. 'I'm not.'

'But dash it all, I've proved it to you. You can't shove all my proofs on one side in that offhand way. The whole thing stands to reason. You can't get away from it.'

'If you say that Jefferson killed Stanworth,' Alec proceeded with obstinate deliberation, 'then I'm perfectly sure you're wrong. That's all.'

'But *why*?'

'Because I don't believe he did,' said Alec, with an air of great wisdom. 'He's not the sort of fellow to do a thing like that. I suppose I've got a sort of intuition about it,' he added modestly.

'Intuition be hanged!' Roger retorted, with a not unjustified irritation. 'You can't back your blessed intuition against proofs like the ones I've just given you.'

'But I do,' Alec said simply. 'Every time,' he added, with a careful attention to detail.

'Then I wash my hands of you,' said Roger shortly.

For a time they paced side by side in silence. Alec appeared to be pondering deeply, and Roger was undisguisedly huffy. After all, it is a little irksome to solve in so ingenious yet so convincing a way a problem of such apparently mysterious depth, only to be brought up against a blank wall of disbelief founded on so unstable a foundation as mere intuition. One's sympathy is certainly with Roger at that moment.

'Well, anyhow, what are you going to do about it?' Alec asked, after some minutes' reflection. 'Surely you're not going to tell the police without troubling to verify anything further, are you?'

'Of course not. In fact, I haven't made up my mind whether I shall tell the police at all yet.'

'Oh!'

'It depends largely on what the two of them – Jefferson and Mrs Plant – have to tell me.'

'So you're going to tackle them about it, are you?'

'Of course.'

There was another short silence.

'Are you going to see them together?' Alec asked.

'No, I shall speak to Mrs Plant first, I think. There are one or two minor points I want to clear up before I see Jefferson.'

Alec reflected again. 'I shouldn't, Roger, if I were you,' he said quite earnestly.

'Wouldn't what?'

'Speak to either of them about it. You're not at all sure whether you're really right or not; after all, it's only guesswork from beginning to end, however brilliant guesswork.'

'Guesswork!' Roger repeated indignantly. 'There isn't any guesswork about it! It's – '

'Yes, I know; you're going to say it's deduction. Well, you may be right or you may not; the thing's too deep for me. But shall I tell you what I think about it? I think you'd be wise to drop the whole thing just as it is. You think you've solved it; and perhaps you have. Why not be content with that?'

'But why this change of mind, Alexander?'

'It isn't a change of mind. You know I've never been keen on it from the very beginning. But now that Stanworth's turned out to be such a skunk, why – '

'Yes, I see what you mean,' Roger said softly. 'You mean that if Jefferson did kill Stanworth, he was perfectly right to do so and we ought to let him get away with it, don't you?'

'Well,' Alec said awkwardly, 'I wouldn't go so far as to say that, but – '

'But I don't know that *I* wouldn't,' Roger interrupted. 'That's why I said just now that I hadn't decided whether I'd tell the police or not. It all depends on whether things did happen as I imagine, or not. But the thing is, I must find out.'

'But must you?' Alec said slowly. 'As things are at present, whatever you may think, you don't actually *know*. And if you do find out for certain, it seems to me that you'll be deliberately saddling yourself with a responsibility which you might wish then that you hadn't been so jolly eager to adopt.'

'If it comes to that, Alec,' Roger retorted, 'I should have said that to take no steps to find out the truth now we're so near it is deliberately to shirk that very responsibility. Wouldn't you?'

Alec was silent for a moment.

'Hang that!' he said with sudden energy. 'Leave things as they are, Roger. There are some things of which it's better that everyone should remain in ignorance. Don't go and find out a lot of things that you'd give anything afterwards not to have discovered.'

Roger laughed lightly. 'Oh, I know it's the right thing to say, "Who am I to take the responsibility of judging you? No, it is not for me to do so. I will hand you over to the police, which means that you will inevitably be hanged. It's a pity, because my personal opinion is that your case is not murder, but justifiable homicide; and I know that a jury, directed by a judge with his eye on the asinine side of the law, would never be allowed to take that view. That's why I so much regret having myself to place a halter round your neck by handing you over to the police. But how is such a one as me to judge you?" That's what they always say in story-books, isn't it? But don't you worry, Alec. I'm not a spineless nincompoop like that, and I'm not in the least afraid of taking the responsibility of judging a case on its own merits; in fact, I consider that I'm very much more competent to do so than are twelve thick-headed rustics, presided over by a somnolent and tortuous-minded gentleman in an out-of-date wig. No, I'm going to follow this up to the bitter end, and when I've got there I'll take counsel with you as to what we're going to do about it.'

'I wish to goodness you'd leave it alone, Roger,' said Alec, almost plaintively.

chapter twenty – three

Mrs Plant Talks

The inquest, in spite of the snail-like deliberation demanded by all legal processes, did not occupy more than an hour and a half. The issue was never in the least doubt, and the proceedings were more or less perfunctory. Fortunately the coroner was not of a particularly inquisitive disposition and was quite satisfied with the facts as they stood; he did not waste very much time, beyond what was absolutely necessary, in probing into such matters as motive. Only the minimum possible number of witnesses were called, and though Roger listened carefully, no new facts of any description came to light.

Mrs Plant gave her evidence clearly and without a tremor; Lady Stanworth's statuesque calm was as unshaken as ever. Jefferson was in the witness box longer than anyone else, and told his story in his usual abrupt, straightforward manner.

'You'd never think, to see and hear him, that his whole evidence is nothing but a pack of lies, would you?' Roger whispered to Alec.

'No, I wouldn't; and what's more I don't,' retorted that gentleman behind his hand. 'It's my belief that he thinks he's telling the truth.'

Roger groaned gently.

As far as minor witnesses went, Graves, the butler, and Roger were both called to corroborate Jefferson's tale of the breaking down of the door; and the former was questioned regarding his discovery of the confession, while Roger told of the locked windows. Alec was not even called at all.

The verdict, 'Suicide during temporary insanity,' was inevitable.

As they left the morning room Roger caught Alec's arm.

'I'm going to try and get hold of Mrs Plant now, before lunch,' he said in a low voice. 'Do you want to be present, or not?'

Alec hesitated. 'What exactly are you going to do?' he asked.

'Tax her with having been blackmailed by Stanworth, and invite her to tell me the truth about the night before last.'

'Then I don't want to be there,' Alec said with decision. 'The whole thing absolutely sickens me.'

Roger nodded approvingly. 'I think it's better that you shouldn't be, I'm bound to say. And I can tell you afterwards what happened.'

'When shall I see you, then?'

'After lunch. I'll have a word with you before I tackle Jefferson.'

He edged away from Alec and intercepted Mrs Plant, who was on the point of ascending the staircase. Jefferson and Lady Stanworth were still talking with the coroner in the morning room.

'Mrs Plant,' he said quietly, 'can you spare me a few minutes? I want to have a little chat with you.'

Mrs Plant glanced at him sharply.

'But I'm just going up to finish my packing,' she objected.

'What I have to say is very much more important than packing,' Roger returned weightily, unconsciously regarding her from beneath lowered brows.

Mrs Plant laughed nervously. 'Dear me, Mr Sheringham, you sound very impressive. What is it that you want to speak to me about?'

'If you will come out into the garden where we shall not be overheard, I will tell you.'

For a moment she hesitated, with a longing glance up the staircase as if she wished to escape from something peculiarly unwelcome. Then with a little shrug of her shoulders she turned into the hall.

'Oh, very well,' she said, with an assumption of lightness. 'If you really make such a point of it.'

Roger piloted her out through the front door, picking up a couple of folding garden chairs as he passed through the hall. He led the way into a deserted corner of the rose garden that could not be overlooked from the house, and set up his chairs so that they faced one another.

'Will you sit down, Mrs Plant?' he said gravely.

If he had been trying to work up an atmosphere with a view to facilitating further developments, Roger appeared to have succeeded. Mrs Plant seated herself without a word and looked at him apprehensively.

Roger sat down with deliberation and gazed at her for a moment in silence. Then:

'It has come to my knowledge that you were not speaking the truth to me yesterday about your visit to the library, Mrs Plant,' he said slowly.

Mrs Plant started. 'Really, Mr Sheringham!' she exclaimed, flushing with indignation and rising hurriedly to her feet. 'I fail to understand what right you have to insult me in this gross way. This is the second time you have attempted to question me, and you will allow me to say that I consider your conduct presumptuous and impertinent in the highest degree. I should be obliged if you would kindly refrain from making me the target for your abominable lack of manners in future.'

Roger gazed up at her unperturbed.

'You were really there,' he continued impressively, 'for the purpose of being blackmailed by Mr Stanworth.'

Mrs Plant sat down so suddenly that it seemed as if her knees had collapsed beneath her. Her hands gripped the sides of her chair till the knuckles were as white as her face.

'Now look here, Mrs Plant,' Roger said, leaning forward and speaking rapidly, 'there's been something very funny going on here, and I mean to get to the bottom of it. Believe me, I don't mean you any harm. I'm absolutely on your side, if things are as I believe them to be. But I must know the truth. As a matter of fact, I think I know pretty well everything already; but I want you to confirm it for me with your own lips. I want you to tell me the plain, unvarnished truth of what happened in Stanworth's library the night before last.'

'And if I refuse?' almost whispered Mrs Plant, through bloodless lips.

Roger shrugged his shoulders. 'You leave me with absolutely no alternative. I shall have to tell the police what I know and leave the rest in their hands.'

'The *police?*'

'Yes. And I assure you I am not bluffing. As I said, I think I know almost everything already. I know, for instance, that you sat on the couch and begged Mr Stanworth to let you off; that you cried, in fact, when he refused to do so. Then you said you hadn't any money, didn't you? And he offered to take your jewels instead. Then – Oh, but you see. I'm not pretending to know what I don't.'

Roger's bow, drawn thus at a venture, had found its target. Mrs Plant acknowledged the truth of his deductions by crying incredulously, 'But how do you know all this, Mr Sheringham? How can you possibly have found it out?'

'We won't go into that at the moment, if you don't mind,' Roger replied complacently. 'Let it suffice that I do know. Now I want you to tell me in your own words the whole truth about that night. Please leave out nothing at all; you must understand that I can check you if you do so, and if you deceive me again – !' He paused eloquently.

For a few moments Mrs Plant sat motionless, gazing into her lap. Then she raised her head and wiped her eyes.

'Very well,' she said in a low voice. 'I will tell you. You understand that I am placing not only my happiness, but literally my whole future in your hands by doing so?'

'I do, Mrs Plant,' Roger said earnestly. 'And I assure you I will not abuse your confidence, although I am forcing it in this way.'

Mrs Plant's eyes rested on a bed of roses close at hand. 'You know that Mr Stanworth was a blackmailer?' she said.

Roger nodded. 'On a very large scale, indeed.'

'Is that so? I did not know it; but it does not surprise me in the least.' Her voice sank. 'He found out somehow that before I was married I – I – '

'There's not the least need to go into that sort of detail, Mrs Plant,' Roger interposed quickly. 'All that concerns me is that he *was* blackmailing you; I don't want to know why.'

Mrs Plant flashed a grateful look at him.

'Thank you,' she said softly. 'Well, I will just say that it was in connection with an incident which happened before I was married. I have never told my husband about it (it was all past and done with before I ever met him), because I knew that it would break his heart. And we are devotedly in love with each other,' she added simply.

'I understand,' Roger murmured sympathetically.

'Then that devil found out about it! For he was a devil, Mr Sheringham,' Mrs Plant said, looking at Roger with wide eyes, in which traces of horror still lingered. 'I could never have imagined that anyone could be so absolutely inhuman. Oh! It was hell!' She shuddered involuntarily.

'He demanded money, of course,' she went on after a minute in a calmer voice; 'and I paid him every penny I could. You must understand that I was willing to face any sacrifice rather than that my husband should be told. The other night I had to tell him that I had no more money left. I lied when I told you what time I went into the library. He stopped me in the hall to tell me that he wanted to see me there at half-past twelve. That would be when everyone else was in bed, you see. Mr Stanworth always preserved the greatest secrecy about these meetings.'

'And you went at half-past twelve?' Roger prompted sympathetically.

'Yes, taking my jewels with me. I told him that I had no more money. He wasn't angry. He never was. Just cold and sneering and horrible. He said he'd take the jewels for that time, but I must bring him the money he wanted – two hundred and fifty pounds – in three months' time.'

'But how could you, if you hadn't got it?'

Mrs Plant was silent. Then gazing unseeingly at the rose bed, as if living over again that tragic interview, she said in a curiously toneless voice, 'He said that a pretty woman like me could always obtain money if it was necessary. He said he would introduce me to a man out of whom I – I could get it, if I played my cards properly. He said if I wasn't ready with the two hundred and fifty pounds within three months he would tell my husband everything.'

'My God!' said Roger softly, appalled.

Mrs Plant looked him suddenly straight in the face.

'That will show you what sort of a man Mr Stanworth was, if you didn't know,' she said quietly.

'I didn't,' Roger answered. 'This explains a good deal,' he added to himself. 'And then, I suppose, Jefferson came in?'

'Major Jefferson?' Mrs Plant repeated, in unmistakable astonishment.

'Yes. Wasn't that when he came in?'

Mrs Plant stared at him in amazement.

'But Major Jefferson never came in at all!' she exclaimed. 'What ever makes you think that?'

It was Roger's turn to be astonished.

'Do I understand you to say that Jefferson never came in at all while you were in the library with Stanworth?' he asked.

'Good gracious, no,' Mrs Plant replied emphatically. 'I should hope not! Why ever should he?'

'I – I don't really know,' Roger said lamely. 'I thought he did. I must have been mistaken.' In spite of the unexpectedness of her denial, he was convinced that Mrs Plant was telling the truth; her surprise was far too genuine to have been assumed. 'Well, what happened?'

'Nothing. I – I implored him not to be so hard and to be content with what I had paid him and give me back the evidence he'd got, but – '

'Where did he keep the evidence, by the way? In the safe?'

'Yes. He always carried the safe about with him. It was supposed to be burglar-proof.'

'Was it open while you were there?'

'He opened it to put my jewels in before I went.'

'And did he leave it open, or did he lock it up again?'

'He locked it before I left the room.'

'I see. When would that be?'

'Oh, past one o'clock, I should say. I didn't notice the time very particularly. I was feeling too upset.'

'Naturally. And nothing of any importance occurred between his – his ultimatum and your departure upstairs?'

'No. He refused to give way an inch, and at last I left off trying to persuade him and went up to bed. That is all.'

'And nobody else came in at all? Not a sign of anybody else?'

'No; nobody.'

'Humph!' said Roger thoughtfully. This was decidedly disappointing; yet somehow it was impossible to disbelieve Mrs Plant's story. Still, Jefferson might have come in later, having heard something of what had taken place from outside the room. At any rate, it appeared that Mrs Plant herself could have had no hand in the actual murder, whatever provocation she might have received.

He decided to sound her a little farther.

'In view of what you've told me, Mrs Plant,' he remarked rather more casually, 'it seems very extraordinary that Stanworth should have committed suicide, doesn't it? Can you account for it in any way?'

173

'No, I certainly can't. It's inexplicable to me. But, Mr Sheringham, I am so thankful! No wonder I fainted when you told us after breakfast. I suddenly felt as if I had been let out of prison. Oh, that dreadful, terrible feeling of being in that man's power! You can't imagine it; or what an overwhelming relief it was to hear of his death.'

'Indeed I can, Mrs Plant,' Roger said with intense sympathy. 'In fact, what surprises me is that nobody should ever have killed him before this.'

'Do you imagine that people never thought of that?' Mrs Plant retorted passionately. 'I did myself. Hundreds of times! But what would have been the use? Do you know what he did – in my case, at any rate, and so in everyone else's, I suppose? He kept the documentary evidence against me in a sealed envelope addressed to my husband! He knew that if ever he met with a violent death the safe would be opened by the police, you see; and in that case they would take charge of the envelope, and presumably many other similar ones, and forward them all to their destinations. Just imagine that! Naturally nobody dared kill him; it would only make things worse than before. He used to gloat over it to me. Besides, he had always a loaded revolver in his hand when he opened the safe, in my presence at any rate. I can tell you, he took no chances. Oh, Mr Sheringham, that man was a fiend! Whatever can have induced him to take his own life, I can't conceive; but believe me, I shall thank God for it on my bended knees every night as long as I live!'

She sat biting her lip and breathing heavily in the intensity of her feelings.

'But if you knew the evidence was kept in the safe, why weren't you frightened when it was being opened by the inspector?' Roger asked curiously. 'I remember glancing at you, and you certainly didn't seem to be in the least perturbed about it.'

'Oh, that was after I'd had his letter, you see,' Mrs Plant explained readily. 'I was before, of course; terribly frightened. But not afterwards, though it did seem almost too good to be true. Hullo! isn't that the lunch bell? We had better be going indoors, hadn't we? I think I have told you all you can want to know.' She rose to her feet and turned towards the house.

Roger fell into step with her.

'Letter?' he said eagerly. 'What letter?'

Mrs Plant glanced at him in surprise. 'Oh, don't you know about that? I thought you must do, as you seemed to know everything. Yes, I got a letter from him saying that for certain private reasons he had decided to take his own life, and that before doing so he wished to inform me that I need have no fears about anything, as he had burnt the evidence he held against me. You can imagine what a relief it was!'

'Jumping Moses!' Roger exclaimed blankly. 'That appears to bash me somewhat sideways!'

'*What* did you say, Mr Sheringham?' asked Mrs Plant curiously.

Roger's dazed and slightly incoherent reply is not recorded.

chapter twenty – four

Mr Sheringham
Is Disconcerted

Roger sat through the first part of lunch in a species of minor trance. It was not until the necessity for consuming a large plateful of prunes and tapioca pudding, the two things besides Jews that he detested most in the world, began to impress itself upon his consciousness, that the power of connected thought returned to him. Mrs Plant's revelation appeared temporarily to have numbed his brain. The one thing which remained dazzlingly clear to him was that if Stanworth had written a letter announcing his impending suicide, then Stanworth could not after all have been murdered; and the whole imposing structure which he, Roger, had erected, crumbled away into the sand upon which it had been founded. It was a disturbing reflection for one so blithely certain of himself as Roger.

As soon as lunch was over and the discussion regarding trains and the like at an end, he hurried Alec upstairs to his bedroom to talk the matter over. It is true that Roger felt a certain reluctance to be compelled thus to acknowledge that he had been busily unearthing nothing but a mare's nest; but, on the other hand, Alec must know sooner or later, and at that moment the one vital necessity from Roger's point of view was to talk. In fact, the pent-up floods of talk in Roger's bosom that were striving for exit had been causing him something very nearly approaching physical pain during the last few minutes.

'Alexander!' he exclaimed dramatically as soon as the door was safely shut. 'Alexander, the game is up!'

'What do you mean?' Alec asked in surprise. 'Have the police got on the trail now?'

'Worse than that. Far worse! It appears that old Stanworth was never murdered at all! He did commit suicide, after all.'

Alec sat down heavily in the nearest chair. 'Good Lord!' he exclaimed limply. 'But what on earth makes you think that? I thought you were so convinced that it was murder.'

'So I was,' Roger said, leaning against the dressing table. 'That's what makes it all the more extraordinary, because I really am very seldom wrong. I say it in all modesty, but the fact is indisputable. By all the laws of average, Stanworth ought to have been murdered. It really is most inexplicable.'

'But how do you know he wasn't?' Alec demanded. 'What's happened since I saw you last to make you alter your mind like this?'

'The simple fact that Mrs Plant received a note from old Stanworth, saying that he was going to kill himself for private reasons of his own or something.'

'Oh.'

'I can tell you, it knocked me upside down for the minute. Anything more unexpected I couldn't have imagined. And the trouble is that I don't see how we can possibly get round it. A note like that is a very different matter to that statement.'

'You know, I'm not sure that I'm altogether surprised that something like this has turned up,' Alec said slowly. 'I was never quite so convinced by the murder idea as you were. After all, when you come to look at all the facts of the case, although they certainly seemed to be consistent with murder, were no less consistent with suicide, weren't they?'

'So it appears,' Roger said regretfully.

'It was simply that you'd got the notion of murder into your head – more picturesque, I suppose – and everything had to be construed to fit it, eh?'

'I suppose so.'

'In fact,' Alec concluded wisely, 'it was an *idée fixe*, and everything else was sacrificed to it. Isn't that right?'

'Alexander, you put me to shame,' Roger murmured.

'Well, anyhow, that shows you what comes of muddling in other people's affairs,' Alec pointed out severely. 'And it's lucky you hit on the truth before you made a still bigger idiot of yourself.'

'I deserve it all, I know,' Roger remarked contritely to his hair-brush.

It was Alec's turn to be complacent now, and he was taking full advantage of it. As he lay back leisurely in his chair and smoked away placidly, he presented a perfect picture of 'I told you so!' Roger contemplated him in rueful silence.

'And yet – !' he murmured tentatively, after a few moments' silence.

Alec waved an admonitory pipe.

'Now, then!' he said warningly.

Roger exploded suddenly. 'Well, say what you like, Alec,' he burst out, 'but the thing is dashed queer! You can't get away from it. After all, our inquiries haven't resulted in nothing, have they? We did establish the fact that Stanworth was a blackmailer. I forgot to tell you that, by the way. We were perfectly right; he had been blackmailing Mrs Plant, the swine, and jolly badly, too. Incidentally, she hadn't the least idea that his death might be anything else than suicide, and Jefferson didn't come into the library while she was there; so I was wrong in that particular detail. I'm satisfied she was telling the truth, too. But as for the rest – well, I'm dashed if I know what to think! The more I consider it, the more difficult I find it to believe that it was suicide, after all, and that all those other facts could have been nothing but mere coincidences. It isn't reasonable.'

'Yes, that's all very well,' Alec said sagely. 'But when a fellow actually goes out of his way to write a letter saying that – '

'By Jove, Alec!' Roger interrupted excitedly. 'You've given me an idea. *Did* he write it?'

'What do you mean?'

'Why, mightn't it have been typed? I haven't seen the thing yet, you know, and when she mentioned a letter it never occurred to me that it might not be a handwritten one. If it was typed, then there's still a chance.' He walked rapidly towards the door.

'Where are you going to now?' Alec asked in surprise.

'To see if I can get a look at this blessed letter,' Roger said, turning the handle. 'Mrs Plant's room is down this passage, isn't it?'

With a quick glance up and down the passage, Roger hurried along to Mrs Plant's bedroom and tapped on the door.

'Come in,' said a voice inside.

'It's me, Mrs Plant,' he replied softly. 'Mr Sheringham. Can I speak to you a minute?'

There came the sound of rapid footsteps crossing the floor and Mrs Plant's head appeared at the door.

'Yes?' she asked, not without a certain apprehension. 'What is it, Mr Sheringham?'

'You remember that letter you mentioned this morning? From Mr Stanworth, I mean. Have you still got it, by any chance, or have you destroyed it?'

He held his breath for her reply.

'Oh, no. Of course I destroyed it at once. Why?'

'Oh, I just wanted to test an idea. Let me see.' He thought rapidly. 'It was pushed under your door or something, I suppose?'

'Oh, no. It came by post.'

'Did it?' said Roger eagerly. 'You didn't notice the postmark, did you?'

'As a matter of fact I did. It seemed so funny that he should have taken the trouble to post it. It was posted from the village by the eight-thirty post that morning.'

'The village, was it? Oh! And was it typewritten?'

'Yes.'

Roger held his breath again. 'Was the signature written or typewritten?'

Mrs Plant considered.

'It was typewritten, as far as I remember.'

'Are you sure of that?' Roger asked eagerly.

'Ye-es, I think so. Oh, yes; I remember now. The whole thing was typewritten, signature and all.'

'Thank you very much, Mrs Plant,' Roger said gratefully. 'That's all I wanted to know.'

He sped back to his own room.

'Alexander!' he exclaimed dramatically, as soon as he was inside. 'Alexander, the game is on again!'

'What's up now?' Alec asked with a slight frown.

'That letter sounds like a fake, just the same as the confession. It was all typewritten, even the signature, and it was posted from the village. Can you imagine a man in his sane senses deliberately going down to the village to post his letter, when all he had to do was to push it under her door?'

'He might have had others to post as well,' Alec hazarded, blowing out a great cloud of smoke. 'Would Mrs Plant's be the only one?'

'H'm! I never thought of that. Yes, he would. But still, it's rather unlikely that he should have posted hers as well, I should say. By the way, it was that letter which accounted for her change of attitude before lunch. She knew then that she had nothing to fear from the opening of the safe, you see.'

'Well, how do matters stand now?'

'Exactly as they did before. I don't see that this really affects it either way. It's only another instance of the murderer's cunning. Mrs Plant, and possibly, as you say, one or two others, might raise awkward questions at Stanworth's sudden death; therefore their apprehensions must be allayed. All that it really does as far as we are concerned, is to confirm the idea that the murderer must have a very intimate knowledge of Stanworth's private affairs. Of course it shows that the safe *was* opened that night, and it brings our old friends, the ashes in the hearth, into prominence once more as being in all probability the remains of the blackmailer's evidence. Curious that that first guess of mine should have turned out to be so near the truth, isn't it?'

'And what about Jefferson?' Alec asked quietly.

'Ah, yes, Jefferson. Well, I suppose this affair of the letter and the fact that he did not break in on Mrs Plant and Stanworth in the library that night and consequently was not helped by that lady – I suppose all this gives him credit for rather more brains than I had been willing to concede him; but otherwise I don't see that his position is affected.'

'You mean, you still think he killed Stanworth?'

'If he didn't, can you tell me who did?'

Alec shrugged his shoulders. 'I've told you I'm convinced you're barking up the wrong tree. It's no good going on repeating it.'

'Not a bit,' Roger said cheerfully.

'So what are you going to do?'

'Exactly what I was before. Have a little chat with him.'

'Rather ticklish business, isn't it? I mean, when you're so very uncertain of your ground.'

'Possibly. But so was Mrs Plant for that matter. I think I shall be able to handle friend Jefferson all right. I shall be perfectly candid with him, and I'm willing to wager a small sum that I shall be back here within half an hour with his confession in my pocket.'

'Humph!' Alec observed sceptically. 'Are you going to accuse him directly of the murder?'

'My dear Alec! Nothing so crude as that. I shan't even say in so many words that I know a murder has been committed. I shall simply ask him a few pointed and extremely pertinent questions. He'll see the drift of them all right; Master Jefferson is no fool, as we have every reason to know. Then we shall be able to get down to things.'

'Well, for goodness' sake do bear in mind the possibility (I won't put it any stronger than that) that Jefferson never did kill Stanworth at all, and walk warily.'

'Trust me for that,' Roger replied complacently. 'By the way, did I tell you that Mrs Plant received that letter just before going into lunch? It caught the eight-thirty post from the village.'

'Did it?' Alec said without very much interest.

'By Jove!' Roger exclaimed suddenly. 'What an idiot I am! That's conclusive proof that Stanworth couldn't have posted it himself, isn't it? Fancy my never spotting that point before!'

'What point?'

'Why, the first post out from the village is five o'clock. That letter must have been posted between five and eight-thirty – four hours or more after Stanworth was dead!'

chapter twenty – five

The Mystery Finally Refuses to Accept Mr Sheringham's Solution

Roger had no time to waste. Mrs Plant, Alec, and himself were all to leave by the train soon after five o'clock; the car would be ready to take them into Elchester at half-past four. Tea was to be at four, and the time was already close on three. He had an hour left in which to disentangle the last remaining threads. As he stood for a moment outside the morning-room door it seemed to Roger as if even this narrow margin were half an hour more than he needed.

Jefferson was still at work among the piled-up papers. He glanced up abstractedly as Roger entered the room and then smiled slightly.

'Come to offer me a hand again?' he asked. 'Devilish good of you, but I'm afraid there's absolutely nothing I can turn over to you this time.'

Roger drew a chair up to the other side of the table and seated himself deliberately.

'As a matter of fact, I hadn't,' he said slowly. 'I wanted to ask you one or two questions, Jefferson, if you would be good enough to answer them.'

Jefferson looked slightly surprised.

'Questions? All right, fire away. What can I tell you?'

'Well, the first thing I want to ask you,' Roger shot out, 'is – where were you at the time that Stanworth died?'

A look of blank astonishment was followed in Jefferson's face by an angry flush.

'And what the devil has that got to do with you?' he asked abruptly.

'Never mind for the moment what it has to do with me,' Roger replied, his heart beating a little faster than usual. 'I want you to answer that question.'

Jefferson rose slowly to his feet, his eyes glittering ominously. 'Do you want me to kick you out of the room?' he said in a strangely quiet voice.

Roger leaned back in his chair and watched him unmoved.

'Do I understand that you refuse to answer?' he said evenly. 'You refuse to tell me where you were between, say, one and three o'clock on the morning that Stanworth died?'

'Most decidedly I do. And I want to know what the hell you think that has to do with you?'

'It may have nothing and it may have everything,' Roger said calmly. 'But I advise you to tell me, if not for your own sake at least for the lady's.'

If this was a chance shot, it had certainly got home. Jefferson's face took on a deeper tinge and his eyes widened in sheer fury. He clenched his fists till the knuckles showed up white and menacing.

'Damn you, Sheringham, that's about enough!' he muttered, advancing towards the other. 'I don't know what the devil you think you're playing at, but – '

A sudden bluff darted into Roger's mind. After all, what was a man like Jefferson doing as secretary to a man like Stanworth? He decided to risk it.

'Before you do anything rash, Jefferson,' he said quickly, 'I'd like to ask you another question. What was Stanworth blackmailing you for?'

There are times when bluff pays. This was one of them. Jefferson stopped short in his stride, his hands fell limply to his sides and his jaw drooped open. It was as if he had been struck by a sudden and unexpected bullet.

'Sit down and let's talk things over quietly,' Roger advised, and Jefferson resumed his seat without a word.

Roger reviewed the situation rapidly in his mind.

'You see,' he began in conversational tones, 'I know quite a lot of what's been going on here, and in the circumstances I really have no alternative but to find out the rest. I admit that it places me in rather an awkward situation, but I can't see that I can very well do anything else. Now what I suggest, Jefferson, is that we both put our cards on the table and talk the thing over as two men of the world. Do you agree?'

Jefferson frowned. 'You don't appear to give me much option, do you? Though what it has to do with you, I'm really hanged if I can see.'

It was on Roger's lips to retort that Jefferson would very probably be hanged if he didn't, but fortunately he was able to control himself.

'I should have thought that would have been obvious,' he said smoothly. 'I can hardly leave things as they are, can I? Still, we'll pass over that for the present. Now Stanworth was, as I know, a blackmailer, and there can be no doubt as to that affecting the situation in no small degree.'

'What situation?' Jefferson asked in puzzled tones.

Roger glanced at him shrewdly. '*The* situation,' he said firmly. 'I think we both understand to what I am referring.'

'I'm blessed if I do,' Jefferson retorted.

'Of course if you take up that attitude—!' Roger said tentatively. 'Still, perhaps it's a little early to get down to brass tacks,' he added, after a moment's pause. 'We'll confine ourselves to the other aspect for a time, shall we? Now Stanworth, I take it, had some definite hold over you. Would you mind telling me exactly what that was?'

'Is this necessary?' Jefferson demanded shortly. 'My private affair, you know. Why the deuce should you want to concern yourself in it?'

'Don't talk like that, Jefferson, please. You must see what course you'll force on me if you do.'

'Damned if I do! What course?'

'To put the whole thing in the hands of the police, naturally.'

Jefferson started violently. 'Good God, you wouldn't do that, Sheringham!'

'I don't want to do so, of course. But you really must be frank with me. Now please tell me all about your relations with Stanworth. I may tell you, to save you trouble, that I am already in full possession of all the similar facts with regard to — well, the lady in the case.'

'The devil you are!' Jefferson exclaimed in undisguised astonishment. 'Oh, well, if I've got to tell you, I suppose I must. Though what in the name of goodness it can have to – However!'

He leaned back in his chair and began to fiddle abstractedly with the papers in front of him.

'It was this way. My regiment was in India. Pal of mine and I were both in love with the same girl. No bad blood or anything like that. Good friends all the time. He got her. Wanted to get married at once, but very hard up, of course. We all were. He'd got a lot of debts, too. Damned fool went and drew a check on another man's account. Forged it, if you like. Absurd thing to do; bound to come out. There was a hell of a row, but we managed to keep it confined to a few of us. Chap came and confessed to me; asked what on earth he'd better do. They hadn't found out who'd done it yet, but when they did it would be all up with him. Lose the girl and everything; she was fond enough of him, but straight as a die herself. Couldn't have stood the disgrace. Well, what could I do? Couldn't stand by and see all this happen. Went to the colonel and told him I'd done the blessed thing. Only thing to do.'

'By Jove, you sportsman!' Roger exclaimed involuntarily.

'Sportsman be damned! Wouldn't have done it for him alone. I was thinking of the girl.'

'And what happened?'

'Oh, it was hushed up as much as possible. I had to send in my papers, of course, but the fellow didn't prosecute. Then that hound Stanworth got wind of the story somehow and managed to lay his hands on the check, which had never been destroyed. Perfect godsend to him, of course. Gave me choice of taking on this job with him or letting the whole thing be passed on to the police. No alternative. I had to take on the job.'

'But why on earth did he want you as his secretary? That's what I can't understand.'

'Simple enough. He wanted to push his way in among the sort of people I knew. I was a sort of social sponsor for him. Damned unpleas-ant job, of course, but what could I do? Besides, when I took the job on I didn't know anything about him. Thought he was just a new-rich merchant and I was his only victim in the threatening line. Soon found out, of course; but too late to back out then. That's all. Satisfied?'

'Perfectly. Sorry I had to ask you, but you see how it is. Well, I'm dashed if I can blame you. I'd have done the same thing myself. But I'd like to have the story of it from your own lips.'

'Just told you the story.'

'No, the other one, I mean.'

'What other one?'

'Oh, don't beat about the bush like this. You know perfectly well what I'm driving at. I'll put it in the original form, if you like. Where were you during the night that Stanworth died?'

Jefferson's angry flush returned.

'Now look here, Sheringham, that's too much. I've told you things I never dreamed I'd have to tell anyone, and I'm not going to have you probing any farther into my business. That's final.'

Roger rose to his feet. 'I'm sorry you take it like that, Jefferson,' he said quietly. 'You leave me no alternative.'

'What are you going to do then?'

'Tell the police the whole story.'

'Are you mad, Sheringham?' Jefferson burst out angrily.

'No, but I think you are, not to trust me,' Roger retorted, hardly less so. 'You don't think I want to tell them, do you? It's you who are forcing me to do so.'

'What, through not telling you what – what I was doing that night?'

'Of course.'

There was a short pause, while the two glared at each other.

'Come back in a quarter of an hour,' Jefferson said abruptly. 'I'll think it over. Have to consult her, of course, first.'

Roger nodded acquiescence to this proposal and hurried out of the room. Exultantly he sought Alec.

'I told you so, Alexander,' he cried triumphantly, as soon as he was fairly inside the room. 'Jefferson's on the point of confession!'

'He's not!' Alec exclaimed incredulously.

'He is indeed. And there's a lot more to it than that. I've bluffed him into believing that I know a lot more than I do really, and he's going to tell me all sorts of other things as well. He's let one cat out of the bag already. I can tell you. Mrs Plant is in it, after all!'

'Oh, rot!' Alec replied with decision. 'That's out of the question. I know she isn't.'

'Don't be so absurd, Alexander,' Roger retorted somewhat nettled, 'How can you possibly know?'

'Well, anyhow, I'm sure she isn't,' Alec replied obstinately.

'But my dear chap, friend Jefferson has just gone off to consult her as to whether he shall tell me the whole story or not. I threatened him with the police, you see, if he didn't.'

'I suppose you taxed him outright with the murder, did you?'

'No, Alexander, I didn't,' Roger answered wearily. 'The word murder was never so much as mentioned. I simply put it that I wanted to know what he was doing on the night of Stanworth's death.'

'And he wouldn't tell you?' Alec asked, somewhat surprisedly.

'He certainly would not. But he told me a lot of other things. He was in Stanworth's power all right. I haven't got time to tell you the whole story, but there's motive enough for him to kill Stanworth himself, even without the introduction of Mrs Plant's side of it. Oh, the whole thing's as plain as a pikestaff. I can't understand why you're so sceptical about it all.'

'Perhaps I make a better detective than you do, Roger,' Alec laughed, a trifle constrainedly.

'Perhaps,' Roger said without very much conviction. He glanced at his watch. 'Well, I'd better be getting back. I wonder if you'd believe it if I showed you Jefferson's confession in writing! Would you?'

'I very much doubt it,' Alec smiled.

Jefferson was no longer alone in the morning room when Roger returned to it. To the latter's surprise Lady Stanworth was also there. She was standing with her back to the window and did not look round at his entrance. Roger shut the door carefully behind him and looked inquiringly at Jefferson.

That gentleman did not waste time.

'We've talked the matter over,' he said curtly, 'and decided to tell you what you want to know.'

Roger could hardly repress an exclamation of surprise. Why should Jefferson have imported Lady Stanworth into the matter? Obviously she must be involved, and deeply, too. Could it be that Jefferson had taken her into his confidence with regard to Mrs Plant? How much did she know, if that were the case? Presumably everything. Roger felt that the situation was about to prove not a little awkward.

'I'm glad,' he murmured, half apologetically.

Jefferson was carrying the thing off well. Not only did he appear to be feeling no fear at all, but his manner was not even that of defiance. The attitude he had adopted and which sat perfectly naturally upon him was rather one of dignified condescension.

'But before I answer you, Sheringham,' he said stiffly, 'I should like to say, both on behalf of this lady and myself, that we consider – '

Lady Stanworth turned to him. 'Please!' she said quietly. 'I don't think we need go into that. If Mr Sheringham is incapable of understanding the position into which he has forced us, there can hardly be any need to labour the point.'

'Quite, quite,' Roger murmured still more apologetically, and feeling unaccountably small. Lady Stanworth was perhaps the only person in the world who consistently had that effect upon him.

'Very well,' Jefferson bowed. He turned to Roger. 'You wanted to know where I was on the night that Stanworth shot himself?'

'On the night of Stanworth's death,' Roger corrected, with a slight smile.

'On the night of Stanworth's death then,' Jefferson said impatiently. 'Same thing. As I said before, I fail entirely to see how it can concern you, but we have decided under the circumstances to tell you. After all, the fact will be common knowledge soon enough now. I was with my wife.'

'Your *wife?*' Roger echoed, scarcely able to believe his ears.

'That is what I said,' Jefferson replied coldly. 'Lady Stanworth and I were married secretly nearly six months ago.'

chapter twenty – six

Mr Grierson Tries His Hand

For some moments Roger was incapable of speech. This disclosure was so totally unexpected, so entirely the reverse of anything that he had ever imagined, that at first it literally took his breath away. He could only stand and stare, as if his eyes were about to pop out of his head, at the two entirely unmoved persons who had sprung this overwhelming surprise upon him.

'Is that what you wished to know?' Jefferson asked courteously. 'Or would you wish my wife to confirm it?'

'Oh, no; no need at all,' Roger gasped, doing his best to pull himself together. 'I – I should like to apologise to you for the apparent impertinence of my questions and to – to congratulate you, if you will allow me to do so.'

'Very kind,' Jefferson muttered. Lady Stanworth, or Lady Jefferson as she was now, bowed slightly.

'If you don't want me any more, Harry,' she said to her husband, 'there are one or two things I have to do.'

'Certainly,' Jefferson said, opening the door for her.

She passed out without another glance at Roger.

'Look here, Jefferson,' exclaimed the latter impulsively, as soon as the door was closed again, 'I know you must be thinking me the most appalling bounder, but you must believe that I shouldn't have tackled you in that way if I hadn't got very solid and serious reasons for doing so. As things have turned out, I can't tell you at present what those reasons are; but really it's something of the greatest possible importance.'

'Oh, that's all right, Sheringham,' Jefferson returned with gruff amiability. 'Guessed you must have something up your sleeve. Bit awkward, though. Ladies, and all that, y'know,' he added vaguely.

'Beastly,' Roger said sympathetically. 'As a matter of fact, that's a development that had never occurred to me at all, you and Lady Stanworth being married. If anything, it makes things very much more complicated than before.'

'Bit of a mystery or something on hand, eh?' Jefferson asked with interest.

'Very much so,' Roger replied, gazing thoughtfully out of the window. 'Connected with Stanworth, and – and his activities, you understand,' he added.

'Ah!' Jefferson observed comprehendingly. 'Then I'd better not ask any questions. Don't want to learn anything more about that side of things. Seen too many poor devils going through it already.'

'No, but I tell you what,' Roger said, wheeling suddenly about. 'If you could answer a few more questions for me, I should be more than grateful. Only as a favour, of course, and if you refuse I shall understand perfectly. But you might be able to help me clear up a very tricky state of affairs.'

'If it's anything to do with helping somebody Stanworth got hold of, I'll answer questions all night,' Jefferson replied with vigour. 'Go ahead.'

'Thanks, very much. Well, then, in the first place, will you tell me some details regarding your wife's relations with Stanworth? It doesn't matter if you object, but I should be very glad if you could see your way to do so.'

'But I thought you said you knew that story?'

Roger did not think it necessary to explain that the lady to whom he had been referring was not Lady Jefferson. 'Oh, I know most of it, I think,' he said airily, 'but I should like to hear it all from you, if I could. I know that she was in Stanworth's power, of course,' he added, making a shot in the twilight, 'but that I'm not quite clear as to the precise way.'

Jefferson shrugged his shoulders. 'Oh, well, as you seem to know so much, you'd better have the whole lot straight. Stanworth nosed out something about her father. His brother was in love with her, and Stanworth gave her the option of marrying him or having her father shown up. He could have had the old earl put in the dock, I believe. Naturally she chose the brother, who, by the way, didn't know anything about Stanworth's activities, so I understand. Quite an amiable, rather weak sort of a fellow.'

'And since then, of course, Stanworth had the whip hand over her?'

Jefferson winced. 'Yes,' he said shortly. 'Even after her father died, she wouldn't want the family shown up.'

'I see,' said Roger thoughtfully. So Lady Stanworth had little enough reason to love her brother-in-law. And since Jefferson fell in love with her, her cause would naturally become his. Truly he had motive and to spare for ridding the world of such a man. Yet, although Jefferson and his wife might easily have concocted the story of his whereabouts that night, Roger already felt just as convinced of the former's innocence as he was before of his guilt. The man's manner seemed somehow to preclude altogether the idea of subterfuge. Had he really killed Stanworth, Roger was sure that he would have said so by the time that matters had reached this length, bluntly and simply, just as he had told the story of his own downfall.

But in spite of his convictions, Roger was not such a fool as not to put the obvious questions that occurred to him.

'Why was your marriage secret?' he asked. 'Did Stanworth know about it?'

'No; he wouldn't have allowed it. It would have looked like a combination against him. He wanted us separate, for his own ends.'

'Did you hear the shot that killed him?' Roger said suddenly.

'No. About two o'clock, wasn't it? I'd been asleep two hours.'

'You did sleep with your wife then, in spite of the necessity of preserving secrecy?'

'Her maid knew. Used to go back to my room in the early morning. Beastly hole-and-corner business, but no alternative.'

'And only Stanworth's death could have freed you, so to speak?' Roger mused. 'Very opportune, wasn't it?'

'Very,' Jefferson replied laconically. 'You think I forced him somehow to shoot himself, don't you?'

'Well, I – I – ' Roger stammered, completely taken aback.

Jefferson smiled grimly. 'Knew you must have some comic idea in your head. Just seen what you've been driving at. Well, you can rest assured I didn't. For the simple reason that nobody or no threats on earth could have made him do a thing like that. Why he did it, Heaven only knows. Complete mystery to me. Can't fathom it. Thank God he did, though!'

'You don't think he might have been – murdered?' Roger suggested tentatively.

'Murdered? How could he have been? Out of the question under the circumstances. Besides, he took jolly good care of that. I'd have murdered him myself before this – hundreds of times! – if I hadn't known it would make things worse than before all round.'

'Yes, I've heard about that. Kept the evidence addressed to the interested parties, didn't he? I suppose everyone knew that?'

'You bet they did. He rubbed it in. No, Stanworth never meant to be murdered. But my God, I had a fright when I saw him lying there dead and the safe locked.'

'You were going to try and open it when I interrupted you yesterday morning, of course?'

'Yes, properly caught out then,' Jefferson smiled ruefully. 'But even if I'd found the keys, I didn't know the combination. Lord, what a relief that note of his was. You know about that, I suppose?'

'You got a note by the post before lunch, did you?'

'That's right. Saying he was going to kill himself. Rum business. Can't explain it. Almost too good to be true. I feel another man.'

'And so are a good many other people, I imagine,' Roger said softly. 'And women, too. His activities were fairly widespread, weren't they?'

'Very, I believe. Never knew much about it, though. He kept all that sort of thing to himself.'

'That butler now,' Roger hazarded. 'He looks a pretty tough customer. I suppose Stanworth employed him as a sort of bodyguard?'

'Yes, something like that. But I don't know about "employed".'

'What do you mean?'

'He was no more employed than I was. That is to say, we got a salary and we did our work, but it wasn't a sort of employment either of us could leave.'

Roger whistled softly. 'Oho! So friend Graves was another victim, was he? What's his story?'

'Don't know all the details, but Stanworth could have had that man hanged, I believe,' Jefferson said coolly. 'Instead he preferred to use him as a sort of bodyguard, as you say.'

'I see. Then Graves hadn't much cause to love him either, I take it?'

'If he hadn't known what would happen afterwards, I wouldn't have given Stanworth ten minutes of life in Graves' presence.'

Roger whistled again.

'Well, thanks very much, Jefferson. I think that's all I wanted to know.'

'If you're trying to look for someone who induced Stanworth to shoot himself, you're wasting your time,' Jefferson remarked. 'Couldn't be done.'

'Oh, there's a little more in my quest than that,' Roger smiled, as he let himself out of the room.

He hurried upstairs, glancing at his watch as he did so. The time was nearly five minutes to four. He scurried down the passage to Alec's room.

'Finished packing?' he asked, putting his head round the door. 'Good, well come along to my room while I do mine.'

'Well?' Alec asked sarcastically, when they were once more ensconced in Roger's bedroom. 'Has Jefferson written out his confession?'

Roger paused in the act of laying his suitcase on a chair.

'Alec,' he said solemnly, 'I owe friend Jefferson an apology, though I can't very well tender it. I was hopelessly wrong about him, and you were hopelessly right. He didn't kill Stanworth at all. It's extremely annoying of him considering how neatly I solved this little problem of ours; but there's the fact.'

'Humph!' Alec observed. 'I won't say, "I told you so," because I know how annoying it would be for you. But I don't mind telling you that I'm thinking it hard.'

'Yes, and the most irritating part is that you're fully entitled to do so,' Roger said, throwing his pyjamas into the case. 'That's what I find so irksome.'

'But I suppose you've found somebody else to take his place all right?'

'No, I haven't. Isn't it maddening? But I'll tell you one significant fact I've unearthed. That butler had as much cause as anyone, if not more, to regret the fact that Stanworth was still polluting the earth.'

'Had he? Oh! But look here, how do you know that Jefferson didn't do it?'

Roger explained.

'Not much so far as actual hard-and-fast-evidence goes, I'm afraid,' he concluded, 'but we greater detectives are above evidence. It's psychology that we study, and I feel in every single bone in my body that Jefferson was telling the truth.'

'Lady Stanworth!' Alec commented. 'Good Lord!'

'Some men are brave, aren't they? Still, I daresay she'll make an excellent wife; I believe that's the right thing to say on this sort of occasion. But seriously, Alec, I'm absolutely baffled again. I think I shall have to turn the case over to you.'

'Well, do,' Alec retorted with unexpected energy, 'and I'll tell you who killed Stanworth.'

Roger desisted from his efforts to close the lid of his bulging case in order to look up in surprise.

'You will, eh? Well, who did?'

'Some unknown victim of Stanworth's blackmail, of course. The whole thing stands to reason. We were looking for a mysterious stranger at first, weren't we? And we thought he might be a burglar. Translate the burglar into the blackmailer's victim and there you are. And as he burnt the evidence himself, and we haven't the least idea who was on Stanworth's blackmailing list, we shall never find out who he was. The whole thing seems as clear as daylight to me.'

Roger turned to his refractory case again. 'But why did we give up the burglar idea?' he asked. 'Aren't you rather overlooking that? Chiefly because of the disappearance of those footprints. That must mean either that the murderer came from inside the house or that he had an accomplice there.'

'I don't agree with you. We don't know how or why the footprints disappeared. It might have been pure chance. William might have raked the bed over, somebody might have noticed it and smoothed it out; there are plenty of possible explanations for that.'

With a heave Roger succeeded in clicking the lock with which he was struggling. He straightened his bent back and drew his pipe out of his pocket.

'I've talked enough for a bit,' he announced.

'Oh, rot!' Alec exclaimed incredulously.

'And it's about time I put in a little thinking,' Roger went on, disregarding the interruption. 'You run along down to tea, Alexander; you're ten minutes late as it is.'

'And what are you going to do?'

'I'm going to spend my last twenty minutes here doing some high-speed cogitating in the back garden. Then I shall be ready to chat with you in the train.'

'Yes, I have a kind of idea that you'll be quite ready to do that,' said Alec rudely, as they went out into the passage.

chapter twenty – seven

Mr Sheringham Hits the Mark

Roger did not reappear until the car was at the front door and the other members of the party already making their farewells on the steps. His leave-taking was necessarily a little hurried; but perhaps this was not altogether without design. Roger did not feel at all inclined to linger in the society of Lady Jefferson.

He shook hands warmly enough with her husband, however, and the manner of their parting was sufficient to assure the latter, without the necessity of any words being spoken on the subject, that his confidences would be regarded as inviolate. The taciturn Jefferson became almost effusive in return.

Arrived at the station, Roger personally superintended the purchase of the tickets and deftly shepherded Mrs Plant into a non-smoking carriage explaining that the cigars which he and Alec proposed to smoke would spell disaster to the subtleties of *Parfum Jasmine*. A short but interesting conversation with the guard, followed by the exchange of certain pieces of silver, ensured the locking of the door of their own first-class smoker.

'And so ends an extremely interesting little visit,' Roger observed as soon as the train started, leaning back luxuriously in his corner and putting his feet on the seat. 'Well, I shan't be sorry to get back to London, on the whole, I must say, though the country is all very well in its way. I always think you ought to take the country in small doses to appreciate it properly, don't you?'

'No,' said Alec.

'Or look at it in comfort from the windows of a train,' Roger went on, waving an appreciative hand towards the countryside through which they were passing. 'Fields, woods, streams, barley – '

'That isn't barley. It's wheat.'

' – barley, trees – delightful, my dear Alexander! But how much more delightful seen like this in one charming flash, that leaves a picture printed on the brain only to give way the next instant to another equally charming one, than stuck down in the middle, for instance, of one of those fields of barley – '

'Wheat.'

' – of barley, with the prospect of a ten-mile walk in this blazing sunshine between you and the next long drink. Don't you agree?'

'No.'

'I thought you wouldn't. But reflect. Sunshine, considered from the purely aesthetic point of view, is, I am quite willing to grant you, a thing of – '

'What *are* you talking about?' Alec asked despairingly.

'Sunshine, Alexander,' returned Roger blandly.

'Well, for goodness' sake stop talking about sunshine. What I want to know is, have you got any farther?'

Roger was evidently in one of his maddening moods.

'What with?' he asked blankly.

'The Stanworth affair of course, you idiot!' shouted the exasperated Alec.

'Ah, yes, of course. The Stanworth affair,' Roger replied innocently. 'Did I do that bit well, Alec?' he asked with a sudden change of tone.

'What bit?'

'When I said, "What with?" Did I say it with an air of bland innocence? The best detectives always do, you know. When they reach this stage of the proceedings they always pretend to have forgotten all about the case in hand. Why they do so, I've never been able to imagine; but it's evidently the correct etiquette for the job. By the way, Alec,' he added kindly, 'you did your part very well. The idiot friend always shouts in an irritated and peevish way like that. I really think we make quite a model pair, don't you?'

'Will you stop yapping and tell me whether you've got any farther with Stanworth's murder?' Alec demanded doggedly.

'Oh, *that?*' said Roger with studied carelessness. 'I solved that exactly forty-three minutes ago.'

'*What?*'

'I said that I solved the mystery exactly forty-three minutes ago. And a few odd seconds, of course. It was an interesting little problem in its way, my dear Alexander Watson, but absurdly simple once one had grasped the really vital factor in the case. For some extraordinary reason I appeared to have overlooked it before; hence the delay. But don't put that bit in when you come to write up the case, or I shall never land the next vacancy for a stolen-crown-jewels recoverer to an influential emperor.'

'You've solved it, have you?' Alec growled sceptically. 'I seem to have heard something like that before.'

'Meaning Jefferson? Yes, I admit I backed the wrong horse there. But this is a very different matter. I've really solved it this time.'

'Oh? Well, let's hear it.'

'With the greatest pleasure,' Roger responded heartily. 'Let me see now. Where shall I begin? Well, I think I've told you all the really important things that I managed to elicit from Mrs Plant and Jefferson, haven't I? Except one.' Roger dropped his bantering manner with startling suddenness. 'Alec,' he said seriously, 'that man Stanworth was as choice a scoundrel as I've ever heard of. What I didn't tell you is that he gave Mrs Plant three months in which to find two hundred and fifty pounds for him; and hinted that if she hadn't got it already, a pretty woman like her would have no difficulty in laying her hands on it.'

'Good God!' Alec breathed.

'He even went farther than that and offered to introduce her to a rich man out of whom she would be able to wheedle it, if she played her cards properly. Oh, I tell you, shooting was much too easy a death for friend Stanworth. And the person who did it ought to be acclaimed as a public benefactor, instead of being hanged by a grateful country; as he certainly would be, if all this had got into the hands of the police.'

'You can hardly expect the law to recognise the principle of poetic justice for all that,' Alec objected.

'I don't see why not,' Roger retorted. 'However, we won't go into that at present. Well, to my mind there were two chief difficulties in this Stanworth business. The first one was that at the beginning there didn't seem to be any definite motive for killing him; and afterwards, when we'd found out about him, there were far too many. All those people in the house, Mrs Plant, Jefferson, Lady Stanworth, the butler (who, by the way, appears to be a murderer in a small way already, as I gather from Jefferson; that was the hold which Stanworth had over him) – all of them had every reason to kill him; and the case began to take on the aspect not so much of proving who did it, but, by a process of elimination, of finding out who didn't. In that way I managed eventually to dismiss Mrs Plant, Jefferson, and Lady Stanworth. But besides the people actually under our noses in the house, there were all the others – goodness only knows how many of them! – of whose very existence we knew nothing; all his other victims.'

'Were there many of them, then?'

'I understand that Stanworth's practice was a fairly extensive one,' Roger replied ironically. 'Anyhow, I was able to narrow down the field to a certain extent. Then I began to go over once more the evidence we had collected. The question I kept asking myself was – is there a single item that gives a definite pointer towards any certain person, male or female?'

'Female?' Roger repeated surprisedly.

'Certainly. In spite of everything – the footprint in the flower bed, for example – I was still keeping before me the possibility of a woman being mixed up in it. It didn't seem altogether probable, but I couldn't afford to lose sight of the bare possibility. And it's lucky I did, for it was just that which finally put me on the right track.'

'Good Lord!'

'Yes; I admit I was slow in the uptake, for the fact had been staring me in the face the whole time, and I never spotted it. You see, the key to the whole mystery was that there was a *second* woman in the library that night.'

'How on earth do you know that?' Alec asked in consternation.

'By the hair we found on the settee. I put it away in the envelope, you remember, and promptly forgot all about it, assuming it to have been one of Mrs Plant's. It struck me suddenly in the garden just now that it wasn't anything of the sort; Mrs Plant's hair is very much darker. Of course that opened up an entirely new field for speculation.'

'Good Lord!'

'Yes, it is rather surprising, isn't it?' Roger continued equably. 'That set my brain galloping away like wildfire, I need hardly tell you; and five minutes later the whole thing became absolutely plain to me. I'm a little hazy about some of the details, of course, but the broad lines are clear enough.'

'You mean you guessed who the second woman was?'

'Hardly guessed. I knew at once who she must be.'

'Who?' Alec asked, with unconcealed eagerness.

'Wait a bit. I'm coming to that. Well, then I began to put two and two together. I'd got a pretty shrewd idea already of the personal appearance of the man himself.'

'Oh, it was a man then?'

'Yes, it was a man right enough. There was never any doubt that a man must have done the actual killing. No woman would have been strong enough for the struggle that must have taken place. Stanworth was no weakling, so that gives us the fact that the man must have been a strong, burly sort of person. From the footprint and the length of those strides across the bed he was evidently both tall and largely built; from the clever way in which everything was left he must have been possessed of a fund of cunning; from the manner in which he left that window fastened behind him it was clear that he was thoroughly accustomed to handling lattice windows. Well, what does all that give us? It looked obvious to me.'

Alec was staring intently at the speaker, following every word with eager attention. 'I think I see what you're getting at,' he said slowly.

'I thought you would,' said Roger cheerfully. 'Of course there were other things that clinched it. The disappearance of that footprint, for instance. That *must* have been done by somebody who knew what he was doing. And somebody who heard me say that I was going to fit every male boot in the house into the mark, you remember. Of course it was that which made me so sure at first about Jefferson, because I jumped to the conclusion that it must have been Jefferson whom we saw edging out of the library door. After that I more or less had Jefferson on the brain.'

'I did my best to put you off that track,' said Alec with a slight smile.

'Oh, you did. It wasn't your fault that I clung to him so persistently.'

'I tried hard to stop you putting your foot in it, if you remember.'

'I know. And I daresay it's lucky you did. I might have put things a good deal more plainly to him, with extremely awkward results, if you hadn't dinned it into me so hard.'

'Well,' Alec said slowly, 'what are you going to do about it, now you've presumably got at the truth at last?'

'Do about it? Forget it, of course. I told you my views just now, when I said the man who killed Stanworth ought to be acclaimed as a public benefactor. As that is unfortunately out of the question, the next best thing is to forget as diligently as possible that Stanworth did not after all shoot himself, as everybody else believes.'

'Humph!' said Alec, gazing out of the window. 'I wonder! You're really sure of that?'

'Absolutely,' said Roger with decision. 'Anything else would be ludicrous under the circumstances. We won't discuss that side of it again.'

There was a little pause.

'The – the second woman,' Alec said tentatively. 'How were you able to identify her so positively?'

Roger drew the envelope out of his breast pocket, opened it, and carefully extracted the hair. He laid it across his knee for the moment and contemplated it in silence. Then with a sudden movement he picked it up and threw it through the open window.

'There goes a vital piece of evidence,' he said with a smile. 'Well, for one thing, there was nobody else in the house with just that particular shade of hair, was there?'

'I suppose not,' Alec replied.

There was another silence, rather longer this time.

Then Roger, glancing curiously across at his companion, remarked very airily:

'Just to satisfy my natural curiosity, Alec, why exactly *did* you kill Stanworth?'

chapter twenty – eight

What Really Did Happen

Alec contemplated the tips of his shoes for a moment. Then he looked up suddenly. 'It wasn't exactly murder, you know,' he said abruptly.

'Certainly not,' Roger agreed. 'It was a well-merited execution.'

'No, I don't mean that. I mean, if I hadn't killed Stanworth, he would probably have killed me. It was partly self-defence. I'll tell you the whole story in a minute.'

'Yes, I should like to hear what really happened. That is, if you feel yourself at liberty to tell me, of course. I don't want to force confidences about – well, about the second lady in the case.'

'About Barbara? Oh, there's nothing that reflects on her, and I think you ought to hear the truth. I always meant to tell you the whole thing if you found out that I did it, and of course, if you were intending to take any drastic step, such as telling the police or trying to get Jefferson arrested. That's why I made you promise to tell me before you did anything like that.'

'Quite so,' Roger nodded understandingly. 'A good many things are plain to me now. Why you hung back so much and were so unenthusiastic and threw cold water on everything and pretended to be so dull and refused to believe that a murder had been committed at all, although I'd proved it to you beyond any shadow of doubt.'

'I was trying to keep you off the right track all the time. I really never thought you'd find out.'

'Perhaps I shouldn't have done if the significance of that hair hadn't dawned on me at last. After that everything seemed to come in a series of flashes. Even then I might not have hit on the truth with such certainty if two particular photographs hadn't suddenly developed themselves in my mind.'

'Tell me all your side of it, then I'll tell you mine.'

'Very well. As I said, that hair was the clue to the whole thing. I'd taken it quite idly out of my pocket out there in the garden and was having a look at it, when it suddenly struck me that whose ever it might be it was certainly not one of Mrs Plant's. I stared at it hard enough then, I can tell you, and the second realization occurred to me that, from the colour at any rate, it looked uncommonly like one of Barbara's. Then the first of the pictures flashed across my mind. It was of Graves sorting the post just before lunch yesterday. He had only three letters, and they were all of exactly the same appearance; same shaped envelopes and typewritten addresses. One was for Mrs Plant, one for Jefferson – and one for Barbara. The first two I'd already accounted for, now I seemed to be accounting for the third. Add to all that Barbara's ill-concealed agitation the next morning and the fact that, for no ap-parent cause whatever, she broke off her engagement to you at the same time, and the thing was as plain as daylight – Barbara was also in the library that night and for some reason or other the poor kid had got into Stanworth's clutches.'

'*She* hadn't,' Alec put in. 'It was – '

'All right, Alec; you can tell me all that in the proper place. Let me fin-ish my story first. Well, having got so far, of course I asked myself – What light does this throw on Stanworth's death? Does it give a definite pointer to any person? The answer was obvious. Mr Alexander Grierson! I gasped at first, I can assure you, but when I got rather more used to the idea, daylight simply flooded in. First of all, there was your hanging back all the time; that began to take on a very significant aspect. Then there was your height and your strength, which fitted in very nicely, and I knew that your place in Worcestershire, where you must have spent most of your boyhood, is liberally supplied with lattice windows, so that you might be expected to be up to all the tricks of the trade regarding them. So far, in fact, so good.'

'But what about that footprint? I thought I'd managed that rather neatly. By Jove, I remember the shock you gave me when you discovered that and the way I got out of the library that night. I'd thought that was absolutely untraceable.'

'Yes, that did give me an awkward couple of minutes, until I remembered that you'd run back to get your pipe while I was talking to the chauffeur! And that's where the second of my little pictures comes in. The scene flashed across my mind on that flower bed just after you had stepped on to the path when we were trying to find out who had been in the library and before you smoothed out the fresh footprints you'd made. The old and the new prints were absolutely identical, you see. I suppose I must have noted it subconsciously at the time without realizing its significance.'

'I noticed it all right,' Alec said grimly. 'It gave me a bad turn for the moment.'

'After that all sorts of little things occurred to me,' Roger continued. 'I began to test each of the facts I'd collected, and in each case the explanation was now obvious. Those letters, for instance. I knew they must have been posted between five and eight-thirty that morning; and at eight o'clock behold you coming back from the village and actually saying you'd been down there to post a letter!'

'Couldn't think of any other explanation on the spur of the moment,' Alec grinned ruefully.

'Yes, and curiously enough I questioned the bookmaker motif at the time, didn't I? Then there was your quite genuine anxiety to stop me from assuming complicity on the part of Mrs Plant. I suppose you knew all the time about her and Stanworth, didn't you?'

Alec nodded. 'I was present at the interview between them,' he said briefly.

'The devil you were!' Roger exclaimed in surprise. 'I never gathered that. She didn't say anything about it.'

'She didn't know. I'll tell you all about that. Anything else on your side?'

Roger considered. 'No, I don't think so. I gathered that you had somehow got to know that Stanworth was blackmailing Barbara, and had simply waded in and shot him, as any other decent chap would have done in your place. That's the gist of it.'

'Well,' Alec said slowly, 'there's a little more in it than that. I'd better begin right at the beginning, I think. As you know, Barbara and I had got engaged that afternoon. Well, I suppose you can imagine that a thing like that rather unsettles a chap. Anyhow, the upshot was that when I got to bed that night I found I couldn't sleep. I tried for some time, and then I gave it up as hopeless and looked round the room for a book. There was nothing I particularly wanted to read there, so I thought I'd slip down to the library and get one. Of course I had no idea that everyone wouldn't be in bed, so I didn't trouble to put on a dressing-gown but just went down as I was, in pyjamas. There were no lights on the landing or in the hall, but to my surprise when I got there I found all the lights in the library full on. However, there wasn't anyone inside and the door was open, so I went in and began to look round the shelves. Then I heard unmistakably feminine footsteps approaching and, hardly wishing to be caught like that, I nipped behind those thick curtains in front of the sash window and sat down on the seat to wait till the person, whoever it might be, had gone. I thought it was someone come down like me for a book, and probably also more or less in a state of undress. Not that I really thought much about it at all. I just didn't want to be mixed up in a rather embarrassing situation.'

'Quite natural,' Roger murmured. 'Yes?'

'Through the chink in the curtains I could see that it was Mrs Plant. She was still in evening dress, and I saw at once that she looked rather worried. Very worried, in fact. She began to wander aimlessly about the room, twisting her handkerchief about in her hands and it looked rather as if she'd been crying. Then Stanworth came in.'

'Ah!'

Alec hesitated. 'I don't want to exaggerate or turn on the pathetic tap too much,' he resumed a little awkwardly, 'but I hope to God I never have to see anything again like the scene that followed. Roger, it was almost unbearable! I don't know how I sat it out without dashing through the curtains and getting my hands into Stanworth's throat; but I had the sense to see that anything like that would only make matters very much worse. Have you ever seen a woman in agony? My God, it was absolutely heart-rending. I could never have imagined that a man could be such an indescribable brute.'

He paused, shivering slightly, and Roger watched him sympathetically. He was beginning to realise just how terrible that scene must have been, if it could move the stoical Alec to such a display of emotion.

'You know the main lines of what happened, don't you?' Alec went on, rather more calmly. 'So I needn't go into details. The wretched woman begged and wept, but it had no more effect upon Stanworth than if he had been a stone image. He just went on smiling that infernal, cynical smile and told her not to make such an unnecessary fuss. Then he made that suggestion to her that you told me about, and for the moment I very nearly saw red. As for her, it finished her off completely. She just crumpled up on the chesterfield and didn't say another word. A few minutes later she got up and tottered out of the room. Then I came out of my hiding place.'

'Good man,' Roger murmured.

'Well, of course I knew by this time just how the land lay. I knew what Stanworth was, and I knew where he kept his evidence against these people. I didn't quite know what I was going to do, but it was pretty clear that something had got to be done. Well, he was a bit startled at first, but recovered himself wonderfully and began to be infernally sarcastic and cynical. I told him that I wasn't going to stand the sort of thing I'd just seen; and unless he stopped the whole thing and let me burn all the evidence he'd been talking about, I'd go straight to the police and tell them all about it. That seemed to amuse him quite a lot; and he pointed out that if I did that, everything would come to light which all these people had been paying money to keep concealed, and they'd all be very much worse off than before. That had never occurred to me, and I was rather taken aback for the minute; then I told him that if that was the case I'd unlock the safe myself, even if I had to lay him out to get the key. He simply laughed and tossed his keys on the table. "That's the one for the safe," he said. "I don't quite know how you're going to open it as you happen to be ignorant of the combination, but doubtless you have provided for that contingency." Of course that took me in the wind again, but before I could answer him I heard somebody coming down the stairs.

'"Ah!" he said. "I was quite forgetting. I've got another visitor coming to see me tonight. As you seem to have mixed yourself up in my affairs, the least I can do is to invite you to be present at this interview also. Get behind that curtain again, and I think I can promise you an interesting quarter of an hour."

'Well, I hesitated, while the footsteps began to cross the hall, till he caught me by the arm and sort of snarled, "Get out of sight, you fool. Can't you see you'll make it ten times worse for her by letting her see you?"

'Even then I didn't realise what he meant, but I saw that there was something in what he said, and just managed to get behind the curtain in time. You can imagine what I felt like when the door opened and I saw Barbara come into the room.'

'Ghastly!' Roger exclaimed with feeling.

'Ghastly! That's putting it mildly. Well, I'm not going to tell you the details of what happened then, because there's really no need to and it's only giving people away unnecessarily. All I need say is that Stanworth had got hold of some information about – well, about Mrs Shannon. I don't even know what it was. He ostentatiously pulled a revolver out of his desk, opened the safe, and showed her two or three pieces of paper, holding them so that she could read them without taking them into her hands. Then he told her to sit down on the settee to talk things over, keeping the revolver in front of him on the desk all the time. Well, Barbara sat down, looking very white and frightened, poor kid, but still not knowing in the least what Stanworth was getting at. He didn't keep her in ignorance long. He just leaned back in his chair, informed her calmly that if she didn't fall in with his wishes he'd make the information he's just shown her public property and calmly proceeded to state his terms.

'Lord, Roger, old man, I had some difficulty in holding myself in. What do you think he wanted? He told her absolutely plainly that what he was after was money, and went on to say that he knew quite well that she herself hadn't got enough to satisfy him. Therefore she'd got to marry me within a month, so that she would be able to pay the very moderate sums which he would from time to time require. She could either tell me or not, as she saw fit; it didn't matter to him in the least. If she refused, he was very much afraid she and her mother would have to take the consequences.

'Of course you see what he was getting at. Me! He was practically saying to me that if I didn't marry her and pay his blackmail, he would disgrace and ruin the mother of the girl I loved. Very neat sort of trap, wasn't it? Incidentally, he went on to point out, also for my benefit, that it wasn't the least use trying to do him any sort of bodily harm, because that would only bring things to a head in the way you know, and he never opened the safe without a loaded revolver in his hand, which he wouldn't hesitate for a second to use if it became necessary.

'Well, Barbara behaved like an absolute thoroughbred. In fact, she told him, in so many words, to go to the devil; she wouldn't dream of involving me in the affair, and as for her and her mother, they'd have to take what was coming to them if he chose to behave in such a damnable way, but they'd take it alone. Great Scott, she was wonderful! She practically defied him to do his worst, and said that she was going to break off her engagement to me the very next morning. Then she sailed out of the room with her head in the air, leaving him sitting there. No tears, no entreaties; simply the most overwhelming contempt. Roger, she was just marvellous!'

'I can believe you,' Roger said simply. 'What happened then?'

'I came out again. I think I meant to kill Stanworth then if I got a chance to do so without making a worse mess of things. Remember, I knew already to what lengths he was ready to push the wretched women that he had in his clutches, and though Barbara would certainly never give way to him an inch, I wasn't so sure about Mrs Shannon. Well, there was the safe still open, and there was Stanworth sitting in his chair with the revolver in his hand. He looked at me with a grin as I appeared, and said he hoped I hadn't been too bored. I walked straight up to him without a word (I was beyond talking by then), and I suppose he could see from my face what I had in mind. Anyhow, when I was only a few feet away he whipped up the revolver and fired. Luckily he missed, and I heard the vase shatter behind me. I lunged forward, grabbed his wrist and used all my strength to twist it round till the muzzle was pointing straight at his own forehead. Then I simply tightened my finger over his on the trigger and shot him.

'I didn't stop to think what I was doing, or anything like that; I hardly imagine I was capable of thought at the moment. I just knew that Stanworth had got to be killed, in the same way that one knows that a mad dog or a rat or any other vermin has got to be killed. In fact, once he was dead, I hardly paid any more attention to him at all. He was a filthy thing wiped out, and that's all there was about it. I never felt, nor have felt since, a single moment's compunction. I suppose it's curious in a way.'

'You'd have been a sentimental fool if you had,' Roger said with decision.

'Well, I suppose I'm not a sentimental fool then,' Alec replied with a slight smile; 'for I most certainly haven't. Well, as soon as the man was dead I became as cool as ice. I knew exactly, almost without thinking about it, what had got to be done. First of all, and in case I was interrupted, the evidence in the safe had got to be destroyed, and then I had to make my escape. It didn't take long to burn the documents in the safe. There was one shelf full of them, all done up in envelopes inscribed with various addresses; about sixteen or seventeen altogether, I suppose. I burnt them in the hearth without opening them, and just ran through the contents of the other shelves to make sure that I hadn't missed anything.

'Up till then, mind, it had never occurred to me that the case would ever appear to be anything but murder; and if it was traced back to me, I should simply say that I had shot him in self-defence, after he had first shot at me. I would have gone to the police straight away and told them the whole thing, if it wasn't that that would have given away the facts of blackmail, which it was of course essential to hush up. Then I glanced at the chair in which he was lying, and it struck me that he looked exactly as if he had shot himself, so I began to wonder if I couldn't make the whole thing look like suicide.

'I knew you weren't such a blithering fool as you've been trying to make yourself out to be for the last forty-eight hours – '

Roger interjected, 'Yes?'

'Well, the whole finished effect didn't occur to me at once. I started off by shutting the safe and putting the keys back in his waistcoat pocket; the wrong pocket, as it turned out afterwards. Then I cleared up the bits of vase and shoved them into my pocket for the time being, and examined the revolver in Stanworth's hand. To my joy, I found that I could get at the chamber and extract the first shell without loosening his grip, which I proceeded to do. You were right about my knowledge of lattice windows. I knew that trick with the handle when I was a boy, and patted myself on the back when I realised how I could get out of the room and leave everything locked behind me. Lord, I never thought anyone would spot that!'

'You weren't reckoning for me to be on the trail, my boy,' Roger said with modest pride.

'Well, you certainly made me jump when you discovered it. Let's see now, what did I do next? Oh, yes, the letters. I knew that all these people would be scared to death at the idea of Stanworth having shot himself with the safe still locked, as even if they had the keys nobody could open it without the combination; and I thought that in the agitation of the moment Mrs Plant or somebody might give some vital point away. So I sat down and hammered out letters to the three of them on the typewriter, for I knew by what I'd seen in the safe that both Jefferson and Lady Stanworth were involved in it also. You know what I said in the letters, of course. Well, then, I had a final look round and just by chance thought I'd better glance into the waste-paper basket. The very first thing I saw there was a sheet of paper, only very slightly crumpled, that bore Stanworth's signature. Instantly I thought to myself – why not rig up a statement of suicide just to clinch things? And I typed one out above the signature.

'Of course all this took a devil of a time. In fact, it was about four o'clock by now. I'd been as cool as a cucumber for two hours, but I was getting so tired that I made one or two mistakes after that. I never searched the waste-paper basket, for instance, and so left that other piece of paper with the signature there for you to find; and I forgot to smooth over that footprint on the bed. I did curse myself for that when you found it! Also I ought not to have thrown those bits of vase into the shrubbery between the library and the dining room, I suppose.'

'But how did you get back into the house?' Roger asked.

'Oh, before I locked up the library I went through and opened the dining-room windows. Then I just walked round from the lattice window and in through the dining room, locked the dining-room door, and went up to bed. And that's all.'

'And very nicely timed,' Roger remarked, glancing out of the window. 'We shall be at Victoria in five minutes. Well, thanks very much for telling me like that, Alec. And now let us proceed madly to forget all about it, shall we?'

'There's one thing that's been worrying me rather,' Alec said slowly. 'Do you think I ought to tell Barbara?'

'Good heavens above, no!' Roger shouted, staring at his companion in dismay. 'What on earth would you want to tell her for? She'd only be overcome with shame that you knew anything about her mother's short-comings; and the fact that you'd killed a man more or less on account of her would simply make her wretchedly miserable. Of course you mustn't dream of telling her, you goop!'

'I think you're probably right,' Alec said, gazing out of the window.

The train began to slacken speed, and the long, snaky Victoria platforms appeared in sight. Roger stood up and began to lift his suitcase off the rack.

'I think we might stay up in town this evening and do a dinner and a show, don't you?' he said cheerfully. 'I feel as if I want a little relaxation after my strenuous mental efforts of the last two days.'

Something seemed to be troubling Alec.

'You know,' he said awkwardly, 'somehow I can't help wondering. Are you really sure, Roger, that it wouldn't be best for me to go and tell the police? I mean, it isn't as if they'd have me up for a murder or anything like that; nothing worse than manslaughter, I should imagine. And I dare-say I should get off altogether on the self-defence idea. But are you sure it isn't really the right thing to do?'

Roger gazed down at his companion with disfavour.

'For heaven's sake, Alec, *do* try sometimes not to be so disgustingly conventional!' he said scornfully.

Lightning Source UK Ltd.
Milton Keynes UK
12 December 2010

164293UK00001B/37/P